# Acclaim for Beth Wiseman

## Her Brother's Keeper

"An outsider infiltrates an Amish community to uncover the reason for her brother's sad and confusing death in *Her Brother's Keeper* by Beth Wiseman. Readers will be hooked from the start to find out how this young woman will pull off her charade. An ideal book for someone new to Amish fiction."

—Suzanne Woods Fisher, bestselling author of *Anna's Crossing*

## The Promise

"The story of Mallory in *The Promise* uncovers the harsh reality American women can experience when they follow their hearts into a very different culture. Her story sheds light on how Islamic society is totally different from the Christian marriage covenant between one man and one woman. This novel is based on actual events, and Beth reached out to me during that time. It was heartbreaking to watch those real-life events unfolding. I salute the author's courage, persistence, and final triumph in writing a revealing and inspiring story."

—Nonie Darwish, author of *The Devil We Don't Know*, *Cruel and Usual Punishment*, and *Now They Call Me Infidel*

"*The Promise* is an only too realistic depiction of an American young woman motivated by the best humanitarian impulses and naïve trust facing instead betrayal, kidnapping, and life-threatening danger in Pakistan's lawless Pashtun tribal regions. But the story offers as well a reminder just as realistic that love and sacrifice are never wasted and that the hope of a loving heavenly Father is never absent in the most hopeless of situations."

—Jeanette Windle, author of *Veiled Freedom* (2010 ECPA Christian Book Award/Christy Award finalist), *Freedom's Stand* (2012 ECPA Christian Book Award/Carol Award finalist), and *Congo Dawn* (2013 Golden Scroll Novel of the Year)

## THE HOUSE THAT LOVE BUILT

"This sweet story with a hint of mystery is touching and emotional. Humor sprinkled throughout balances the occasional seriousness. The development of the love story is paced perfectly so that the reader gets a real sense of the characters."

—*Romantic Times*, 4-star review

"[*The House that Love Built*] is a warm, sweet tale of faith renewed and families restored."

—BookPage

## NEED YOU NOW

"Wiseman gets to the heart of marriage and family interests in a way that will resonate with readers, with an intricately written plot featuring elements that seem to be ripped from current headlines. God provides hope for Wiseman's characters even in the most desperate situations."

—*Romantic Times*, 4-star review

"You may think you are familiar with Beth's wonderful story-telling gift but this is something new! This is a story that will stay with you for a long, long time. It's a story of hope when life seems hopeless. It's a story of how God can redeem the seemingly unredeemable. It's a message the Church, the world needs to hear."

—Sheila Walsh, author of *God Loves Broken People*

"Beth Wiseman tackles these difficult subjects with courage and grace. She reminds us that true healing can only come by being vulnerable and honest before our God who loves us more than anything."

—Deborah Bedford, bestselling author of *His Other Wife*, *A Rose by the Door*, and *The Penny* (coauthored with Joyce Meyer)

## THE LAND OF CANAAN NOVELS

"Wiseman's voice is consistently compassionate and her words flow smoothly."
— *Publishers Weekly* review of *Seek Me with All Your Heart*

"Wiseman's third Land of Canaan novel overflows with romance, broken promises, a modern knight in shining armor, and hope at the end of the rainbow."
— *Romantic Times*

"In *Seek Me with All Your Heart*, Beth Wiseman offers readers a heartwarming story filled with complex characters and deep emotion. I instantly loved Emily, and eagerly turned each page, anxious to learn more about her past—and what future the Lord had in store for her."
— Shelley Shepard Gray, bestselling author of the Seasons of Sugarcreek series

"Wiseman has done it again! Beautifully compelling, *Seek Me with All Your Heart* is a heartwarming story of faith, family, and renewal. Her characters and descriptions are captivating, bringing the story to life with the turn of every page."
— Amy Clipston, bestselling author of *A Gift of Grace*

## THE DAUGHTERS OF THE PROMISE NOVELS

"Well-defined characters and story make for an enjoyable read."
— *Romantic Times* review of *Plain Pursuit*

"A touching, heartwarming story. Wiseman does a particularly great job of dealing with shunning, a controversial Amish practice that seems cruel and unnecessary to outsiders . . . If you're a fan of Amish fiction, don't miss *Plain Pursuit!*"
— Kathleen Fuller, author of The Middlefield Family novels

*His Love
Endures Forever*

# Also by Beth Wiseman

# *His Love Endures Forever*

## A LAND OF CANAAN NOVEL

# BETH WISEMAN

THOMAS NELSON
*Since 1798*

Thomas Nelson is a registered trademark of HarperCollins Christian Publishing, Inc.

Thomas Nelson titles may be purchased in bulk for educational, business, fund-raising, or sales promotional use. For information, please e-mail SpecialMarkets@ ThomasNelson.com.

Scripture quotations are taken from the King James Version of the Bible.

Publisher's Note: This novel is a work of fiction. Names, characters, places, and incidents are either products of the author's imagination or used fictitiously. All characters are fictional, and any similarity to people living or dead is purely coincidental.

ISBN: 978-0-7180-8279-6 (repack)

**Library of Congress Cataloging-in-Publication Data**

Wiseman, Beth, 1962–
  His love endures forever : a land of Canaan novel / Beth Wiseman.
    p. cm. — (A land of Canaan novel)
  ISBN 978-1-59554-888-7 (trade paper)
  1. Amish—Fiction. 2. Colorado—Fiction. I. Title.
  PS3623.I83H57 2012
  813'.6—dc23                                                    2012021946

*Printed in the United States of America*

16 17 18 19 20 RRD 6 5 4 3 2 1

To CBW

# Pennsylvania Dutch Glossary

*ab im kopp*—crazy or off in the head

*ach*—oh

*aentis*—aunts

*baremlich*—terrible

*boppli*—baby

*bruder*—brother

*danki*—thank you

*daed*—dad

*dochder*—daughter

*dummkopp*—dunce

*dumm*—dumb

*Englisch*—non-Amish

*Englischers*—non-Amish people

*es dutt mir leed*—I am sorry

*fraa*—wife

*guder mariye*—good morning

*gut*—good

*hatt*—hard

*haus*—house

*kaffi*—coffee

*kapp*—prayer covering or cap

*kinner*—children or grandchildren

*kumm*—come

*lieb*—love

*maedel*—girl

*mamm*—mom

*mammi*—grandmother

*mei*—my

*mudder*—mother

*narrisch*—crazy

*nee*—no

*onkel*—uncle

*Ordnung*—the written and unwritten rules of the Amish; the understood behavior by which the Amish are expected to live, passed down from generation to generation. Most Amish know the rules by heart.

*Pennsylvania Deitsch*—Pennsylvania German, the language most commonly used by the Amish

*rumschpringe*—running-around period when a teenager turns sixteen years old

*schee*—pretty

*sohn*—son

*wedder*—weather

*wie bischt?*—how are you?

*ya*—yes

# One

DANIELLE PERCHED ON THE EDGE OF THE TUB. SHE looked at her watch, then at the pregnancy test in her trembling hand. In two minutes, she'd know if she was going to have a baby.

She bit her bottom lip as she tapped a foot against the white tile floor, her heart beating faster than normal. *Please be a blue minus sign.*

But it was barely a minute later when a positive, pink cross began to appear. She squeezed her eyes closed and tried to will it to blue. *Please, please . . . I can't be pregnant.*

She'd been seeing Matthew for four months, but they'd only been intimate one time. *No one gets pregnant the first time.*

She slowly opened her eyes and swallowed hard at the realization that she and Matthew were going to be parents. After giving it a few minutes to sink in, Danielle tried to focus on the positive. Laying a hand across her stomach, she held her breath and tried to envision the tiny life growing inside of her. It would be a lot to take on since they were both only eighteen, but they were in love. They'd said the words to each other only once, but Danielle was sure he was the right guy for her.

Matthew's parents weren't wild about him dating someone who wasn't Amish, but Danielle knew that Matthew had no plans to be baptized into the Amish faith. He'd made it clear to Danielle that he was just waiting for the right time to leave. *What better time than now?*

She paced the small bathroom, taking deep breaths as she thought about a future with Matthew. It wasn't the first time she'd fantasized about a life with him, but it was the first time her vision included a baby. She'd just assumed that they would eventually get married and have children, but in that order. The Amish were all about having lots of kids, and Danielle planned to be the best mother on the planet, something her own mother hadn't been any good at. She was sure Matthew would be a great father. Even though he planned to leave the Old Order district, Danielle knew that he'd had a good upbringing, something he would pass on to his children.

Looking in the mirror, she pulled her hair to the side and gathered it in a loose braid as she fought the worry that began to creep into her mind. Surely he'd be happy about the baby, even if it hadn't been planned?

*Only one way to find out.*

LATER THAT AFTERNOON, Danielle shifted her weight on the log where they were sitting by the edge of the creek. It was their special place, the spot where Matthew had kissed her for the first time. As the sun began its descent behind the Sangre de Cristo Mountains, Danielle reached for Matthew's hand

and took a deep breath. A rush of adrenaline shot from her toes to her fingertips, and she briefly wondered if he felt it. Or could he see or hear her heart pounding in her chest?

As they sat hand in hand, Danielle held her breath as she watched the water. They were beneath the old oak tree as water trickled atop small rocks on the far side of the creek. She watched two cardinals fly by before she finally blew the air from her lungs.

"Matthew . . ."

He brought her hand to his lips, kissed her fingers, and smiled. *"Ya?"*

She'd practiced how she would tell him about the baby all morning, but as she looked at him, she couldn't recall any of her preplanned speech. All she could think about was whether their child would have Matthew's beautiful eyes, shades of amber and green.

"I'm pregnant." She swallowed hard but kept her gaze fixed on him.

His eyes widened as his jaw dropped. After a few moments, he closed his mouth and stared at the ground.

"I can't believe it either." She reached for his hand and squeezed. "But I love you so much. Together, I think we can do this."

Matthew eased his hand from hers and stood up. He pulled his straw hat off, rubbed his forehead, then paced along the bank as late-afternoon rays from the sun glistened atop the blue-green water. Danielle kept her seat and pulled her pink sweater snug around her. It was a chilly May afternoon in the shadow of the mountains. She glanced at her watch. Four o'clock. It was going to take Matthew a few minutes to realize what this meant for the future.

"Matthew?" Danielle stood up and put her hand on his arm. "I know we weren't expecting all this so soon, and—"

"So *soon?*" Matthew took a step backward as a muscle clenched along his jaw. He blinked his eyes a few times beneath cropped brown bangs. "I wasn't expecting this at *all.*"

Danielle fought the wave of dizziness that came on all of a sudden. Surely Matthew just needed a few more minutes to sort out his feelings. She bit her bottom lip as a faint thread of panic formed a lump in her throat.

He walked closer and hung his head for a moment, fidgeting with his hat in his hands. When he finally looked up at her, Danielle tried to force her confused emotions into order. *Please, Matthew . . . don't say what I think you're going to.*

"Danielle . . ."

She reached up and cupped his cheek in her palm. "I know we're young, but we can be wonderful parents." She paused, clinging to hope that Matthew would drop to one knee. Or at the very least, she hoped the tense lines across his forehead would relax and some color would return to his face.

"I don't want to do this." He pulled away and stepped back again as fear twisted around Danielle's heart. "I—I'm not ready for a family. You know that I've been waiting for the right time to tell *mei mamm* and *daed* that I'm leaving here."

Danielle's mind was a crazy mixture of hope and fear. She swallowed and found her voice. "I know it's not the perfect situation, but you've already said your parents can't shun you because you aren't baptized yet, so maybe this is the perfect—"

"Danielle." Matthew latched on to her arms with both hands. "You're not hearing me. I don't want to get married, and I don't want a family. I want to go to college. I've been telling you that. How I'm going to get a job, then save so I can go to school."

"You can still do all those things. I know how much you want to go to college. I want you to have everything you—"

"Danielle, stop." Matthew held up both palms and avoided her eyes. "I don't love you."

He might as well have closed his hands around her throat and killed her. She couldn't control the trembling that began to take over. "But you said you did," she managed to squeak out after a few moments. "You said you loved me."

"Well, at the time, we were . . ." Matthew looked at the ground, shook his head, and kicked the ground with the tip of his shoe. When he looked back up at her, he eyed her with a critical squint—almost as if she'd been the only one in his parents' barn that day. "I thought *Englisch* girls used birth control, took pills or something."

Danielle's mouth fell open. "I told you I wasn't on birth control, and you didn't seem to care." She touched her stomach with both hands. "It's not like I planned this."

Matthew started to pace again, shaking his head. "*Ach*, this is a mess."

Danielle's stomach twisted. She would have never agreed to be with him in such an intimate way if she'd known he didn't love her. She tried to recall if she'd pushed him into saying the words. She didn't think so, but did it really matter now anyway? *He doesn't love me.* Her own upbringing had been a disaster, and she was determined to be a good mother and to raise her child in a normal home, one filled with love.

She swallowed back the tears building and imagined telling Martha. If Matthew couldn't cope with it, how would

Martha? The older woman had taken Danielle in a year ago, before they'd been joined by Arnold, Martha's new husband. She'd been more of a mother to Danielle than she'd ever had, but this news was going to be upsetting to them both.

Matthew finally stopped pacing and faced her. "Maybe you should give the baby up for adoption?" He looped his thumbs beneath his suspenders and stood taller.

Danielle's bottom lip began to tremble. "No. I'm not giving my baby away." She shook her head as she stuffed her hands in the pockets of her sweater. "No way."

Matthew put on his hat, tapped it into place, then stared down at her with eyes that no longer twinkled of amber and green, but instead were stony as jade. "You're on your own if you do this. I've been trying to get out of here forever. There're a lot of things I want to do."

Danielle wanted to cry, beg, tell him that this was a great excuse to leave the community, but she'd heard him loud and clear. *He doesn't just want to leave the community . . . He wants to leave me.* She slowly backed away, holding her sweater tightly around her as the tears came.

"Please don't cry. I'm sorry, Danielle." He took two steps toward her. "I—I'm just not ready to be a father. Or a husband." He raised his eyebrows. "I don't think I'd be *gut* at either one. You deserve better than—"

"Shut up, Matthew! Just shut up!" She ran to where her car was parked several yards away from Matthew's horse and buggy. As she hurried into the seat, she could hear Matthew yelling something in *Pennsylvania Deitsch.* She couldn't understand his dialect.

Not that she needed to. She'd heard enough.

LEVI SLOWED HIS horse, Chester, to a stop in front of Sarah's house. Sarah's father was sitting in a chair on the front porch, the way he had been the last two times Levi brought Sarah home from a Sunday singing.

"I think he's worried you might try to kiss me good night." Sarah tipped her chin down, grinning.

Levi was glad it was dark. He could feel the warmth in his cheeks even though his cold breath formed a cloud in front of him. Levi wanted to tell her that didn't make much sense. He could have kissed her all the way home, not just when he was dropping her off. But he didn't say anything. He stepped down from the buggy and walked around to Sarah. She eased the heavy brown blanket from around her, then Levi helped her down. She was almost as tall as he was.

"I had a *gut* time." Sarah smiled, her teeth chattering. "*Danki* for taking me."

"*Ya*, it was fun."

Sarah leaned closer, near enough that Levi could have kissed her. "See you next Sunday?"

Levi looked over her shoulder and saw that her *daed* was still on the porch, so he just smiled as he stared into her dreamy brown eyes. "*Ya*."

Sarah was beautiful; a perfect white smile, delicate features, and in the *Englisch* world, she probably could have been on the covers of those fancy magazines. Every guy in Canaan wanted to court her. Levi still wasn't sure why she'd chosen him.

"You're so sweet and shy, Levi. It's one of the things I love about you." Sarah kissed him on the cheek, then quickly turned and ran across the yard toward her house.

Levi moved fast too, hurrying back into the buggy since

Sarah's father was now standing and holding a lantern out in front of him at arm's length. It was completely dark, but a full moon lit Sarah's front yard enough to make him wonder if John Troyer saw his daughter's bold move. He clicked his tongue and moved the horse toward the main road, glad that his house wasn't far. He pulled the blanket Sarah had used onto his lap and adjusted the small battery-operated heater on the floor of the buggy.

Once his shivering was under control, he thought about what Sarah had said. *"It's one of the things I love about you."*

Was that Sarah's way of saying she loved him or just a casual comment? He'd known Sarah since her family moved from Indiana to Canaan about six months ago, but it wasn't until recently that Sarah seemed to take an interest in him. Before that, Sarah had been spending time with Jake King, another newcomer to their small community. The talk around the community was that Jake might even propose. But a few weeks ago, Levi noticed that Sarah was going to the singings alone, and one night she asked Levi to take her home, then continued to do so. He hoped Sarah wasn't expecting him to propose anytime soon. He cared about Sarah, but they weren't anywhere near that kind of promise to each other. Plus, Levi wasn't even baptized yet. Marriage seemed far off in his mind, even though he was twenty-two and his mother constantly pushed him about the issue. Two of his siblings, Jacob and Emily, had both married when they were younger than Levi.

Thankful to be home, and looking forward to the warmth of his house, he pulled into his driveway, parked the buggy, then led Chester to the barn, lighting his path with a flashlight he kept in the buggy. It was then that he heard crying. He pointed the light to the crumpled-up shape in the corner.

"Danielle?" Levi hurried to her and squatted down. He pushed back long strands of blond hair from her face and saw tears rolling down her cheeks. "What are you doing here?" He sat down on the cold dirt beside her. "What's wrong, Ladybug?"

Levi had been calling Danielle by that nickname for almost as long as he'd known her, close to a year now. She'd plucked one of the red and black insects from Levi's hair last spring and told him that ladybugs were lucky, something she wasn't. Levi had told her that life wasn't based on luck, but on faith and God's plan. Danielle had gently placed the bug in her palm, smiled, and said, "I don't know about that, but I want to be lucky like a ladybug." And somehow the nickname just stuck.

"I wasn't ready to go home. I just needed—" Sobbing, she buried her face in her hands. "My life is a wreck. I've made a mess of everything, and Martha and Arnold are going to be so upset with me, and Matthew doesn't love me, and . . ." She started crying so hard that Levi could barely understand her. After a few moments, she lifted her face to his and locked eyes with him. "And . . . and . . . I'm pregnant."

Levi hung his head and sighed before he looked back at her. "*Ach, mei maedel.* Are you sure?" Danielle was his best friend, the only person he felt completely comfortable with. It had been like that since they'd met. She was a high-spirited *Englisch* girl who said whatever was on her mind, and she'd lived life in a way that Levi didn't understand, but from the beginning, they'd fit together like bread and butter.

"I'm sure."

Levi's temples throbbed, and he wanted to leave right then

to find Matthew. He'd never met the man, but he felt the need to punch him in the gut just the same. Matthew lived in a small district near Alamosa, about ten miles away, but Levi'd make the trip to straighten him out . . .

He took a deep breath, reminding himself that it was not their way to be aggressive. But how did Matthew let this happen?

Danielle sniffled and studied his face. "It takes two, Levi. This isn't all Matthew's fault."

Levi gritted his teeth together for a few moments. "Well, he should have . . . I don't know . . . done something different." He paused, shining the flashlight toward the barn window. "Where's your car? You didn't walk here, did you?" His teeth chattered as he spoke.

Danielle nodded in the direction of the light. "It's out there, parked on the other side of the barn. I didn't want your parents to know that I was out here."

"You should have waited inside. It's not that late, and you know *Mamm* stays up until I get home."

Frowning, she sighed. "Your mom doesn't like me. You know that."

"She likes you." He let the lie slip from his lips. Vera Detweiler hadn't liked Danielle since the first time she noticed her spending time with Levi after worship service. Martha was friends with the Amish community, attended the Amish church service every other week, and often brought Danielle with her. His mother saw Danielle as a threat—an *Englisch* girl set on stealing away her baby boy, which couldn't have been further from the truth. If his mother only knew how much time he and Danielle had really spent together, she'd have been doubly worried.

Danielle smiled a bit, but sniffled again. "Thanks for saying that, but we both know it's not true."

Levi gave her a rueful smile. He'd hoped his mom would have relaxed once she found out that Danielle was seeing someone, and now that Levi was seeing Sarah. But no, his mother was still worried. *"You are too close to that girl. She's wild, and she'll lure you into her world,"* Mamm had said. More than once.

Levi pushed back the rim of his hat, and in an effort to avoid another lie, he changed the subject back to her pregnancy. "What are you going to do?"

"I don't know." She swiped at her eyes. "Remember when I got stung by that huge bumblebee when we were picking blueberries?"

Levi nodded. *"Ya*, your hand swelled up pretty bad."

"But you went to your house and got something to put on it, and the swelling went down right away." Danielle almost smiled.

He shrugged. "It was just an herb mixture *Mamm* keeps around the *haus*. It wasn't that big of a deal."

"I could name lots of other times, but the point is . . . you always know what to do about things." She let out a heavy sigh.

Levi scratched his chin, knowing he couldn't fix this for her.

"I'm going to be the best mother in the world," she said. "That's what I'm going to do."

Levi knew that Danielle hadn't seen her own mother in over a year. And that was a good thing since the last time she'd been around, Danielle landed in the hospital; a faint scar on her cheek was a reminder of her mother's cruel blow. That's when the older *Englisch* woman, Martha, had taken her in. Levi figured it was the best thing that had happened to Danielle. Even though Danielle and Martha didn't see eye-to-eye much of the time, it was clear that they loved each other.

"I know you'll be a great *mudder*. What do you think Martha and Arnold will say?"

"I don't think Arnold will say much. He's kinda quiet." She smiled for a moment, swiping at her eyes. "Like you." She bit her bottom lip, pausing before she went on. "But I suspect Martha will have *plenty* to say."

"Maybe not. She loves babies. She keeps Katie Ann's *boppli* all the time."

Levi looked at her and wished they could go back in time. Back to before she fell in love with Matthew. Before she gave him everything and ended up with nothing but a babe in her womb and a new set of challenges ahead of her.

Danielle leaned her head against the barn wall, then turned to him with teary eyes.

"Levi?"

"*Ya?*"

"Do you really think I'll be a good mother?"

He smiled. "*Ya.* I do." He glanced at her stomach. "How long 'til . . . ?"

"I think sometime around Christmas."

They were quiet for a few moments, then Levi asked, "So, what exactly did Matthew say?"

"That he wants to go to school, that he's leaving his community, and that a wife and baby aren't in his plans."

Levi stiffened. "Did you tell him that God has other plans for his life?" After the words were out, he held his breath. Months ago, Levi learned the hard way that if they were going to be friends, he couldn't force the Lord on her. But he'd often wondered if God put Danielle in his path so that he could minister to her, even though it wasn't the Amish way to do so with the *Englisch*.

"Levi, I don't want to be with someone who doesn't want to be with me. I need Matthew to want me, whatever God has planned." She started to cry again. "You don't think being a bad mother is hereditary, do you? You don't think I'll be like my mom, do you?"

Levi shook his head. "*Nee*, I don't. I told you. You'll be a great *mudder*."

Danielle shifted her weight, twisting to face him. As she leaned forward with teary eyes, the movement brought her lips within inches of his. It wasn't the first time he'd wanted to kiss her. But he never did. She was his best friend, and he didn't want anything to mess that up. Plus, her being *Englisch* complicated things. But sometimes it was a struggle, especially now when he wanted so much to comfort her.

"You think I'm a bad person, don't you? Because I slept with Matthew." Danielle leaned back against the barn wall again as she crossed her legs underneath her. Her teeth were chattering, like his. "Tell me the truth, Levi."

He frowned. Everything about her screamed goodness. If only she could find her way to a relationship with God, she'd find the direction she so desperately sought. "You know I don't think you're bad." He playfully rolled his eyes.

"But you're disappointed in me," she was quick to say.

"Danielle, it's not my place to judge. Only God—"

"Yeah, I know."

But she didn't. She was just cutting him off at the mention

of God, like she'd done so many times before. She sat up taller and sniffled.

"I gotta go." She stood up, and so did Levi.

"You gonna be okay? Are you going to talk to Martha and Arnold tonight?"

She shook her head. "No. Martha has her schedule. She eats at seven, bathes at seven thirty, and she and Arnold watch TV until nine." She looked at her watch. "I can't see what time it is, but I know it's after nine, and they're probably in bed."

Levi smiled. He'd heard about Martha's strict schedule from Danielle plenty of times. "If I miss my scheduled bath time, well, I'm just out of luck," Danielle had told him before. Martha lived in a large house with two and a half bathrooms, but it was old and had a small, noisy water heater that required time to heat up between the scheduled bath times. There was no bathing allowed after nine o'clock because that was when Martha and Arnold went to bed. It was one of Martha's many rules.

Danielle wrapped her arms around Levi's waist, and he pulled her close, resting his cheek on the top of her head. "You'll be okay, *mei maedel.*"

Among his people, it wasn't unheard of to be married and pregnant at eighteen. The average family had six or eight children, so they started early. But he knew it was considered young in the *Englisch* world, and the fact that Danielle had no husband . . . It would be hard for her. And the baby.

He walked her to the car and waited until she pulled out of the driveway before he headed toward the house, dropping his flashlight back in the buggy on the way. Enough light shone through the living room window to illuminate his way up the porch steps. He pulled open the screen, then eased the wooden door open, not surprised to find his mother curled up on the couch reading a book, a lantern on the end table. She closed the book when Levi shut the door behind him.

"Does that girl really think we don't know she's in the barn?" *Mamm* spit the words out as if Danielle had committed a crime. She placed her book on the coffee table in front of her. "Why doesn't she just come inside like a normal person?"

Levi dropped his shoes by the front door in the pile with everyone else's, hung his black coat and hat on the rack, and warmed his hands by the fire. "She knows you don't like her."

*Mamm* scowled before shaking her head briefly. "That's not true."

Levi sat down on the couch, leaned his head back, and closed his eyes.

"How's your asthma?"

"It's okay." It had been better for the past couple of years, since they moved from Ohio to Colorado. But *Mamm* still asked about it once a week. Vera Detweiler was a wonderful mother. A bit meddlesome at times, but she loved her *kinner*. Pushing his sister Emily to go out with David Stoltzfus—and then seeing them get married—had only made her more convinced she *should* meddle. He didn't think she was going to change her mind about Danielle, and if anything, *Mamm* was about to like her even less. He hoped Danielle was okay tonight. His heart hurt for her.

"Well, you don't need to be sitting out in the barn, in the cold air, with that girl. That's not *gut* for your asthma." His mother folded her hands in her lap.

15

Levi grinned. "*Ach*, I see . . . but it's fine for me to be out in the cold air carting Sarah around?"

"Don't sass, Levi."

He rubbed his eyes, too tired to argue with his mother. Where Danielle was concerned, he wasn't going to win.

## Two

DANIELLE MADE UP HER BED AND THEN PULLED her blue work dress from the closet. Once she had it on, she twisted her hair into a bun.

She'd worked at The Mountain View Restaurant in Monte Vista for exactly one year today, and her friend Sue said they'd celebrate after their shift ended at two o'clock. Danielle wasn't sure a year logged at The Mountain View was worthy of *celebration*, exactly, but she planned to use the time to share her news with Sue. *Maybe she can help me figure out my next steps.* Danielle had barely done the home pregnancy test when she'd rushed off to Alamosa to see Matthew, confident that together, they'd figure it out. *So much for that . . .*

Just thinking about his reaction caused quick tears to rise. How could any father not want to be a part of his child's life? She sat down on the bed, and a few tears slid down her cheek as she thought about the possibilities. Maybe Matthew would still want to be involved in the baby's life. He didn't love *her*, but maybe he'd love their child. They hadn't really gotten that far in their conversation before she felt the need to bolt.

17

She pulled on her socks and white tennis shoes as she thought about her own mother. Despite the beatings and everything, she loved her mom. But Danielle was glad Vivian hadn't been back to Canaan. The woman probably didn't want to face Martha. "You ever touch this girl again, you'll be dealing with me," Martha had said to her mother. Never had she felt such a measure of protection and fierce love.

Martha was a pain in the neck, for sure. Rules, rules, and more rules. And then there was her quirky character. But Danielle knew that Martha and Arnold loved her, and Danielle knew that she was safe with them, something she'd never felt before. Funny thing was, Danielle still missed her mother, which probably meant that Danielle was messed up in the head. Who'd miss someone who drank too much and beat the snot out of their kid?

She reached down and touched her stomach, closing her eyes. She wasn't sure there was a God, but every now and then she'd offer up a little prayer on the off chance that there was. *Please don't let anything bad happen today.*

Danielle shook her head. The idea of a God who'd allow all the bad stuff in the world just didn't compute in her mind. If He was God, why didn't He just fix everything and have everyone live in perfect harmony? Why all the suffering? *Why me, pregnant by a guy who doesn't love me?*

She took a deep breath, wiped her eyes, and dabbed on lip gloss before she headed downstairs. Entering the kitchen, she smelled burned toast and it made her smile. Every morning, the same odor greeted her. It was familiar. It was home.

"Good morning and happy Monday." Arnold looked up at Danielle from the kitchen table, smiling broadly, his kind gray eyes twinkling. Then he went back to buttering a piece of dark toast. Danielle was sure Arnold was the kindest man on the planet. And the fact that he adored Martha made her like him all the more.

Danielle sat down at the table, and Martha slid an omelet from the skillet onto her plate. It wouldn't have been Danielle's first choice for breakfast, simply because there was no telling what was in Martha's omelets, but it was food. Awhile back, they'd had omelets and Martha had used leftover squash as filler. This morning Danielle picked at the egg until something bright red oozed out. She tried to recall what Martha made for dinner last night. The woman wasn't much of a cook, except for a great chicken lasagna she made at least once a week.

"Beets?" Danielle squeaked out, trying not to sound too negative. She pushed the pinkish mush around on her plate and hoped she didn't vomit right there at the table. Food in general didn't sound good, but this made her want to hurl.

"Just try it." Martha put her hands on her hips and frowned. "You are the pickiest eater."

Danielle turned to Arnold and lifted her shoulders and her eyebrows, hoping he'd jump on her side. He just smiled.

Martha sat down at the table with her own omelet, and they all bowed their heads in prayer. Danielle went through the motions, knowing what would happen if she didn't. The first time Danielle had said she'd rather not pray, Martha had refused to serve her any food.

Danielle bit into her piece of toast, watching as Arnold dutifully ate his omelet, then she shifted her eyes to Martha, who was already dressed in a red and white pantsuit that had to be from the '70s. Then of course there was the pink butterfly clip, always holding her brown and gray hair on top of her head.

When Martha spit her first bite of omelet into her napkin, Danielle started to laugh, which felt good after all the crying she'd been doing.

"Arnold, good grief. How could you eat that?" Martha quickly snatched up everyone's plate and put them on the counter.

"It wasn't bad, dear. Not at all." Arnold reached for another piece of toast as he winked at Danielle.

"Well, if ever there was a need for a dog, it would be this morning." Martha put her hands on her hips and stared at the plates still full of food. "Look at this mess."

Danielle didn't think even a dog would eat it. She buttered herself a piece of toast, thinking that was all she could stomach anyway.

"Maybe we *should* get a dog," Arnold said before taking a bite of toast.

"What for?" Martha scraped the omelets into the trash.

Arnold finished chewing and took a sip of milk before he spoke. "Because they make nice pets." He grinned.

Martha turned around and leaned against the counter. "I was just kidding. Last thing we need is another mouth to feed."

Danielle's bite of toast caught in her throat. She'd thought about telling Martha and Arnold about her pregnancy, but maybe now wasn't the best time. She pressed her lips together and lowered her head. Not that there'd be a good time. Martha wouldn't throw her out, but maybe adding a baby to their little family was too much to ask for. She'd saved some money, but not nearly enough to get a place of her own. And she didn't think she could survive on her wages from the restaurant, especially not with a baby. To say nothing of how she'd figure out paying a babysitter . . . She felt the tears coming on again.

Martha strode over to her, her face drawn. "Honey, what's the matter?" She touched Danielle on the arm, and Danielle wanted nothing more than to rise and sink into Martha's arms. To tell her everything. She needed someone to be happy about this, to welcome the news. Even Levi'd been disappointed in her. Despite his efforts to comfort her, she could tell. And she was fearful that Martha would feel the same.

"Danielle?" Martha said, her frown deepening.

"Nothing. I'm just tired. And *late*." She pushed back her chair and moved toward the door. "I work until two, but I'm going to spend some time with Sue after work, so I'll see you after that."

Martha called out to her, but she kept going, pretending she hadn't heard.

MARTHA FINISHED CLEANING the kitchen, then sat down at the table with Arnold. "Danielle was starting to cry. Did you see that?"

"Yes, I did." Her husband frowned as he rubbed his chin. "You never can tell with these teenagers. It could be anything at their age."

"Well, at least you raised one and lived to tell about it. I still feel like I'm in new territory, even after a year." Martha drummed her fingers on the table. "It wasn't much of a breakfast. Why don't we go eat at The Mountain View for lunch, and we can check to make sure she's okay?"

"That sounds like a good idea." Arnold leaned over and

kissed Martha on the cheek, which still warmed her heart just like it did when they were first married. "And you haven't raised any teenagers until *now*. Danielle loves you and you love her—after that, you just find your way through, day by day."

Martha grunted. "She's ornery and a slob. Have you seen her room? It stinks in there." She grimaced until she saw Arnold grin, then she couldn't help but smile along with him. "Yes, I love her. Like she's my own."

Arnold passed her a section of the paper. "The girl needs a good dose of God in her life. What happened to your deal that she attend church with one of us?"

Martha unfolded the paper. "Hmph. She always has some excuse. Sick or something."

Before Martha married Arnold, she'd been attending the Amish church in town, and she'd told him that wouldn't change. She loved her Amish friends, and even though she didn't always understand the service—partly in German and *Pennsylvania Deitsch*—her Amish friend Katie Ann would translate for her later during the big meal after church. That was the best part of going to the Amish worship, the meal afterward. She was blessed to know her Amish friends and to be accepted in their world.

Arnold was born and raised Catholic, and he wanted to keep it that way. So Danielle had two choices when it came to worship services. Not that it mattered where the girl went to church if she wasn't talking to God, listening to Him, and trusting His will. Martha constantly prayed for Danielle, that she'd find her way to the Lord.

"Is she still seeing the Amish boy in Alamosa?" Arnold scratched his head. "Matthew, right?"

"Yeah. Not often. He works a lot, and Danielle said his parents aren't too thrilled about him seeing someone who isn't Amish." She stretched her aching back and sat taller. "The Amish are scared their kids will leave the Old Order and run off with one of us sinful *Englischers.*"

Arnold chuckled and a smile stayed on his face.

Martha folded her arms across her chest and stared him down. "What? Why are you looking at me like that?"

Arnold pointed a finger in her direction. "Let's turn it around. What if Danielle chose to marry into the Amish faith? How would you feel about that?"

She threw her hands up in the air. "Since Danielle barely believes in God, I don't see *that* happening." She paused as she tapped a finger to her chin. "You'd think Levi could reach her, given how close they are. That she'd listen to him about matters of faith."

"His mother probably does her best to keep them from being alone," Arnold said. "Hard to get into matters of the Almighty if you don't have much time."

"Oh, they've spent plenty of time together. But I'm sure Vera doesn't know about most of it." Martha rolled her eyes. "You'd think Vera would ease up since the two have proven that they're just friends. I've even had to have words with Vera about her attitude toward Danielle." She raised her chin as she reached a hand behind her head to tighten her butterfly clip.

They were quiet for a few moments, then Arnold asked, "Why is it, given all the other young men around her, that Danielle has taken up with an Amish boy in Alamosa? And her best friend is also a young Amish man. She doesn't really have any close Amish girlfriends, so why do you think these two particular fellows hold a place close to her heart?"

Martha sighed. "I think she feels safe with those boys."

They were quiet for a few moments as Arnold leaned back in his chair. "I know her relationship with her mother was bad, but what about her father?"

"He died about seven years ago. Car wreck, Danielle said. Apparently that's when her mother started to drink heavily. She doesn't talk about it a lot, but she's mentioned that there were lots of men in and out of her mother's life for a while too." Martha paused. "You know, she's never said very much about her father, just that he wasn't around much. Worked a lot."

Arnold stood up and pushed his chair in. "I'm going into town to find us a dog."

Martha stiffened and calmly placed her palms on the table. "Do what?"

"You heard me, my dear. I'm going to get a dog."

She frowned. "I'll start cooking better. I promise."

Arnold laughed. "Not for scraps, but because I think a dog is good for any family."

Martha thought about her parrot that died a couple of years ago. Her Elvis had been like a person. He'd talked, for starters. Smart as a whip, that bird. She'd never owned a dog, but she was pretty sure you couldn't teach one to talk.


LEVI FOLLOWED HIS father to a picnic table outside the Barkers' house after they installed a solar panel for the *Englisch* family. Mrs. Barker had invited them in for lunch, but *Daed* had thanked her and said they'd brought their own. The smell of Mrs. Barker's baked chicken wafted out her open windows, and Levi was sure it was better than their own ham sandwiches. After lunch, they'd clean up their tools and head to their next stop. Levi knew this was the best opportunity to talk to his father about what had been bothering him.

"*Daed*, do you . . ." He paused and took a deep breath. "Do you think God talks to us through our dreams?"

His father finished chewing a bite of his sandwich. "*Ya*. I think so." He dabbed his mouth with a napkin, looking across the table at Levi. "Why do you ask?"

Levi shrugged, unsure how much of the dream he wanted to share with his father. It had been so real, but confusing. He'd woken up in a cold sweat this morning, certain that God had spoken to him directly. But as the morning went on, he'd talked himself out of it. God would never ask him to do something like what he dreamed. "Just wondering."

"There're lots of times in the Bible when the Lord speaks to people in their dreams." *Daed* unwrapped a piece of apple pie that *Mamm* had put in each of their lunch pails.

Levi nodded, recalling some of those dreams. The angel telling Joseph to take Mary as his wife, and when he told him to take Mary and Jesus to Egypt to escape the evil king. God also used a dream to help Joseph, and then there was Pilate's wife . . . Levi reflected on those dreams for a while as he thought about his own.

After they'd both finished their pie, Levi stuffed his trash into his black lunch pail. When his father stood up, so did Levi, and they both walked back to the area where they'd left their tools.

Levi would do anything that God asked him to do. But

there was no way it could have been God talking to him last night. Or had Levi misunderstood the Lord's instructions?

After they had everything loaded into the buggy, they left for their next stop. About fifteen minutes into the trip, his father turned left onto a country road Levi had never been on. There was a stream on the left, and for a while Levi couldn't pull his eyes away from the slow current. But when he finally did, he recalled his dream in vivid detail.

He'd walked along a river's edge, the blue water sparkling brighter than any river he'd ever seen and rushing atop boulders that protruded here and there amidst the rapids. The leaves on the trees were a brilliant shade of emerald as tiny drops of fresh dew twinkled and hung on the leaves in the wake of a new morning. He'd strolled along casually as if he'd been there a thousand times before, even though he couldn't recall such a place. He'd felt lighter than normal as he walked barefoot along a path that he somehow knew had recently been cleared just for him.

A silver canoe came up the river with one passenger paddling against the current. The man looked about Levi's age and wore blue jeans and a short-sleeve white shirt. On his head, a red baseball cap sat atop a head full of wavy brown hair. He'd waved the paddle in Levi's direction, smiling, then said, "A wife is bound to her husband as long as he lives."

Levi had waved back and continued along the bank. He remembered thinking about Sarah during the dream and how he wasn't ready to get married. Moments later, his father stood along the worn path. He shook Levi's hand, almost as if they were strangers. "Remember, love is patient and kind." Then he'd smiled and eased around Levi.

Next, a man stepped out of the woods in front of Levi. A man Levi had never seen before. He had light brown eyes flecked with gold, a long gray beard, and he was dressed in a black suit like the *Englisch* wear. Gold-rimmed spectacles hung low on his nose, and when he smiled at Levi, one corner of his mouth lifted higher than the other. His voice was soft, and Levi had to strain to listen.

"For this cause shall a man leave his father and mother and shall be joined unto his wife, and they two shall be one flesh," the man had said. Then, as his father had done, the man eased around Levi and walked away, singing. Levi recognized the tune. "For God So Loved Us."

Even now, as he recalled the dream, it was amazing to him that he could remember it all in such detail. It wasn't until the end of the dream that he came to a complete stop in the middle of the path, a peacefulness washing over him, and Levi knew he was in the presence of the Holy Spirit and surrounded by God.

And he heard only two words. Powerful words unlike anything he'd ever heard.

*Marry Danielle.*

Levi shook his head, hoping to clear the dream from his mind. He took a deep breath and stared out the window of the buggy. There was no way that God would be telling him to marry Danielle. Forgetting the part about them only being friends—and her being pregnant—something else had been drilled into his head since he was a child.

*Do not be unequally yoked with unbelievers.*

Back in Ohio, they'd had few *Englisch* friends because of this. His mother had explained it to him in a way he could understand when he was a young boy. She'd said, "We're not here to judge whether or not someone outside of our faith is a Christian. They can tell us they are, but we don't know it to be true or not. We can only be sure about the baptized members of our community. We *know* that we are equally yoked spiritually with our own kind."

Things were different here in Canaan. The town was small with almost as many Amish as there were *Englisch*, and over time Levi's people had learned to trust folks outside of their own, even socialize with them and allow them to attend worship in some cases. Martha and Danielle were examples of that, although Danielle hadn't been to one of their services in a while.

Levi wasn't even sure if God approved of his friendship with Danielle since they were in such different places spiritually. He just couldn't believe that the Lord would ask him to marry her.

But as they drove on, the dream began to replay again in his mind.

# Three

DANIELLE CARRIED A LARGE TRAY STACKED WITH burgers around the corner and saw Sue seating Martha and Arnold. They both waved and Danielle nodded. After she delivered the food to her customers, she went back to Martha and Arnold's table.

"Aw, Arnold, I'm surprised you could tear yourself away from one of Martha's noon meals." Danielle grinned at him before turning to Martha and widening her smile.

"Very funny, missy." Martha tried to frown, but the corners of her mouth lifted into a smile. "We had to come into town anyway because Arnold wants to get a *dog*." Martha rolled her eyes. "Of all things."

"I thought you didn't want another mouth to feed." Danielle touched her stomach but quickly folded her arms across her chest. Martha had a lot of money, but you'd never know it. Everything in her house looked like it was from another era, including her clothes.

Martha shrugged. "How much can one dog eat?" She paused, twitching her mouth back and forth. "I bet dogs aren't nearly as smart as parrots."

"Dogs are very smart," Arnold said as he eyed his open menu. He looked over the top of it. "How does someone get to be your age, Martha, never having owned man's best friend?"

"Possibly because I'm a *woman*." Martha opened her menu. "But if you want a dog, dear, then we shall have one."

Danielle hid a smile as she pulled out her pen and order pad, trying to picture Martha with a dog. To her knowledge, Martha had only owned one pet in her life, a parrot named Elvis that she'd adored. Danielle had heard the stories about Elvis's elaborate funeral a couple of years ago, complete with a custom-made casket.

Danielle stared at the two of them, pretending to look at the menus, when they all knew they'd order the same thing, as always. Her stomach churned as she thought about how and when she would tell them that she was pregnant. Would they regret taking her in? Be disappointed in her like Levi was?

But Levi was Amish, more sheltered. Danielle knew he was saving himself for marriage. Danielle had been too. She'd watched a steady stream of men come and go in her mother's life, and she'd decided years ago that she would wait for someone special. Someone like Matthew . . . *I should have waited.*

She shoved the thought from her mind. "I'm guessing you're having the same thing as always?"

Martha smiled as she closed her menu. "I'm in the mood for a burger."

*Of course you are.* Danielle grinned as she wrote the order down. "Dry with pickles and extra cheese. Cheddar."

"And make sure the burger is—"

"Cooked until it's dead," Danielle finished for her. "I know. Arnold?"

"I'll have the same."

"Comin' right up," she said, taking their menus and rushing to the kitchen. Dry, overcooked burgers sounded gross to Danielle, *but whatever.*

After Martha and Arnold ate, Danielle delivered their check. Martha sat up straight and cleared her throat.

"So, Danielle, what's wrong with you? Why were you crying this morning?"

Danielle froze. "Uh, what?" This wasn't the time or place to tell Martha and Arnold about the baby.

Martha stared at her for a long moment, and Danielle worried Martha would see right through her and figure it out somehow. Danielle held her breath.

"We just want you to know that you can talk to us about anything," Arnold said in a soft, soothing voice.

"Right." Martha's voice wasn't nearly as gentle and comforting as Arnold's, but her soft brown eyes searched Danielle's face.

"I . . . uh, I . . ." Danielle wanted to tell them so badly she could hardly stand it, but fear gripped her around the throat. She swallowed hard.

"Honey, what is it?" Martha's eyes began to water when Danielle's did.

"Nothing."

Martha and Arnold locked eyes, then Martha turned back to Danielle. "Well, it's clearly not *nothing*, but we're here if you need us. Okay?"

Danielle nodded. It was all she could do right now. "I have to get back to work." She sniffled, forcing a smile. "I'll see you later, okay?"

"That sounds good," Arnold said right about the same time Martha opened her mouth to speak.

Danielle gave a quick wave before she headed back to the kitchen to pick up her next order. On the way, she decided not to tell Sue about the baby yet either. She wanted to visit Matthew one more time. Maybe he was just in shock the other day. Maybe the news had soaked in and he'd changed his mind about things.

She'd much rather tell Martha, Arnold, and Sue, "I'm pregnant, but Matthew and I are getting married. We're going to be a family." It sounded way better than, "I'm pregnant and on my own. Matthew said he doesn't love me . . ."

She blinked back tears, determined to get through the next couple hours. Then she'd drive to Matthew's house and ask for a few minutes of his time. Matthew and his father were rebuilding the fence around their property this week, so she wouldn't have to go up to the house and be face-to-face with Matthew's mother. Anna Marie Lapp cared for Danielle about as much as Levi's mother, Vera, did.

But if Matthew changed his mind and decided to marry her, then maybe even Mrs. Lapp would come to accept her. *But do I really want to be married to someone who doesn't love me?*

She delivered a tray of food, then glanced at her watch, anxious to give it one more try with Matthew. Sue might be a bit upset that Danielle was canceling their plans, but this was something she had to do.

LEVI AND HIS father finished their next job earlier than expected and stopped in Monte Vista to purchase supplies for the jobs they had scheduled—two painting jobs this week and one more solar panel installation. Unlike in Ohio, Levi's father had chosen to only farm a small section of acreage here to grow hay. There just wasn't much frost-free weather, only about three months, and their business didn't leave much time for farming anyway. Levi missed the farming. He felt close to God when he was nurturing the land, a living, breathing part of creation. His mother had a small garden with fresh vegetables, but that was about it.

Sometimes when the work piled up, Levi wished his brother, Jacob, was available to help, but he ran their country store next to the main house, selling mostly freight and warehouse-damaged groceries. It used to be popular mostly for their Amish friends, but *Mamm* started adding crafts and cookbooks, which drew in more of the *Englisch* now. Most of the Amish had to work outside the home, not unlike in other states. It was getting harder and harder to survive on farming alone. His Uncle Eli and his new wife, Katie Ann, ran a shop not far away that sold furniture and handmade items, and Abbey's Bakery was always busy.

Even though Levi sometimes missed the way things were in Middlefield, moving to Canaan had been a good choice for them. Land was cheaper, there was more room to spread out, and Levi had to admit that his asthma was better. And Emily had blossomed here.

After *Daed* pulled the buggy to a stop in front of the hardware store in town, Levi hitched the horse to the post. When they'd first moved to Canaan, there wasn't anywhere to tether the horses, but his father—along with several other Amish men—had highly encouraged the local businesses to install hitching posts if they wanted the Amish to do business with them.

Levi followed his father into the store, keeping his head down. He wasn't fond of crowds, and the hardware store was unusually crowded for a Monday afternoon. Levi and his family had moved to Canaan a few years ago, but the district had been there for eight or nine years. *You would think by now that the* Englisch *would stop staring.*

*Daed* stopped on the aisle with trays full of nails, then pulled a handwritten list from his pocket and handed it to Levi. "Stock up on what I have listed. I'm going to go check prices on a few other things we need."

After his father left, Levi scanned the list, then searched for the things they needed. He'd filled two bags with penny nails when he heard shuffling footsteps to his left. He kept his head down, looking for finishing nails, but when the man stopped right next to him, Levi looked up.

His heart started beating out of his chest. The man's brown eyes were flecked with gold and his beard was long and gray. He was dressed in a black suit like the *Englisch* wear with gold-rimmed spectacles hanging from his nose. Levi swallowed hard, even as the man smiled.

"Finding everything you need?" The man's voice was deep but gentle. He didn't look like someone who worked at the hardware store. The employees all wore gray shirts and black pants, and had name tags.

"*Ya*. I am." Levi forced himself to look back at the list, even though he felt a bit weak in the knees. But the man didn't move, and when Levi looked back at him, the man was still smiling, one side of his mouth curled up more than the other.

"So hard to choose, isn't it? There're so many different options."

Levi just stared at him and nodded.

"I see you have a list." The man pointed to the piece of paper in Levi's hand, but Levi couldn't take his eyes off the *Englisch* fellow. He just nodded again as the man continued. "Always good to have a plan." He chuckled. "Although plans change."

Levi forced a smile before he looked back at his father's list of items, but his vision blurred and he couldn't make out the things *Daed* had written. He held the paper at arm's length and still couldn't read it. He saw movement out of the corner of his eye and heard feet shuffling down the aisle. Then singing.

"For God so loved us, He sent the Savior; For God so loved us, and loves me too . . ."

Levi jerked his head up and toward the man, but he must have picked up his pace . . . because he was gone.

DANIELLE WAS DISAPPOINTED when she didn't see Matthew working on the fence with his father. She'd driven all around the property with no sign of either of them, so reluctantly she pulled in the driveway and walked to the door. Matthew's family owned a brand-new home in Alamosa, about a twenty-minute drive from Canaan. It wasn't a big home, but Danielle could still smell the new wood and stain as she stepped on the stone blocks leading to the doorway.

She took a deep breath, hoping Mrs. Lapp wasn't the one to answer the door. Matthew was an only child, which was unusual for the Amish, but Matthew had told her once that his parents had trouble conceiving. Danielle thought briefly about the irony.

As she'd feared, Mrs. Lapp opened the door. Instead of the traditional prayer covering, the woman looked as if she'd haphazardly thrown a white scarf over her head to cover her grayish-brown hair bound in a bun. She was dressed in a knee-length brown dress with a black apron, as expected. But her eyes were swollen, and there was no doubt in Danielle's mind that she'd come at a bad time.

"Hello, Mrs. Lapp. Is Matthew here?"

"No. He's not." Mrs. Lapp raised her chin and stared at Danielle. Usually, the woman at least tried to pretend that she liked Danielle. She'd never been rude before. "I'm surprised that you don't know where he is."

"What?" She paused, her heart thudding painfully in her chest. "No, ma'am. I haven't talked to him since yesterday."

Mrs. Lapp sniffled as she reached into her pocket. She pulled out a folded piece of paper and pushed it toward Danielle. "You know nothing about this?"

Her accusatory voice caused Danielle to hesitate, but after a moment, she took the piece of paper and unfolded it. She read the short note, written in English and *Pennsylvania Deitsch*.

*Mamm* and *Daed*,

*Es dutt mir leed.* I think you both know in your heart that I cannot stay here. I am going to Cousin John's *haus* in Indiana by bus. I saved for the ticket—don't worry about me. I will telephone when I arrive. Forgive me, but I don't want to be Amish.

*Lieb* you always, your son, Matthew

Danielle reread the note. The Amish only went to school through the eighth grade, and she didn't understand their native dialect, but the note was clear. He'd run away from her too. She handed it back to Mrs. Lapp as she blinked back her own tears. "I'm sorry," she managed to say before a tear rolled down her cheek. She quickly wiped it away.

"I can see by your reaction that this is a surprise to you too, no?"

Danielle nodded as she choked back more tears. "I'm sorry," she repeated.

Mrs. Lapp pulled a tissue from her pocket and dabbed at her own eyes. "We've thought maybe Matthew wasn't happy here, but we never thought he would leave like this. So sudden. And just leaving a note." Her voice rose, a mixture of hurt and anger. "It's like he is running away." She clenched her fist for a moment, then took a deep breath. "John is our cousin who is no longer Amish. I wonder how long Matthew has been planning this." She stared at Danielle for a moment. "And I wonder why he didn't tell you about it."

"I don't know," Danielle lied.

They were both quiet for a while, and Danielle wondered if Mrs. Lapp might invite her in. Perhaps they could console each other. Maybe Danielle would tell the woman that she was going to be a grandmother.

Then Mrs. Lapp withdrew, quietly closing the door in her face.

And Danielle ran to her car.

MARTHA PACED BACK and forth in the den, glancing at her watch. Danielle had said she was going to spend some time with Sue after they both got off work, but it was getting close to dark, and Danielle wasn't answering her cell phone. Martha had tried to call several times, and each time, the call went straight to voice mail. Martha stuffed her worry aside and went outside to check on Arnold and the newest member of their little family.

She opened the door and stepped onto the porch, shaking her head, but smiling. She watched as Arnold laughed and threw a bone for Dude. What kind of a name was that for a dog anyway? Martha thought about her friend Katie Ann who'd named her cat Mrs. Dash because she dashed around the barn all the time. Being Amish, Katie Ann didn't know that Mrs. Dash was the name of a spice. At least Arnold hadn't named his dog after a spice. *Like Old Bay, Cavender, or Morton,* she thought, mentally running through her seasonings.

"Good grief. You couldn't get a yappy little dog, huh? Had to get the biggest dog they had?"

At the animal shelter, they'd said Dude was "part hound and who knows what else." All Martha knew was that he was big. Black and tan—and probably a hundred pounds—he was going to eat more than leftover omelets. But seeing Arnold's joy was worth all the dog food and leftovers the animal was sure to eat. The dog watched her for a long moment and then bolted up the steps toward her.

"Dude!" Arnold cried.

Martha backed up a few feet and slammed against the outer wall of the house as Dude crossed the porch and jumped up, throwing his front paws on her shoulders. Thankfully, he only ran his long wet tongue the length of her face one time before Arnold succeeded in calling him back. The dog immediately turned and bounded down the steps, as if his duty of greeting her was now done and he was free to pay attention to his new owner.

Martha pushed back strands of her hair that had fallen out of her clip, straightened her blouse, and marched down the steps, prepared to tell Arnold that he was going to have to train that dog. But when she reached the bottom, she just put her hands on her hips and shook her head.

"Isn't he wonderful, my dear?" Arnold tossed the bone, and Dude galloped across the yard, that long tongue of his hanging out of his mouth.

"Yes. He is wonderful." Martha eased herself down to a seat on the porch steps, knowing that if she'd take off a few pounds—like thirty—it sure would help her old knees.

Arnold glanced her way. "What troubles you, my dear? You look worried."

Martha sighed. "I'm worried about Danielle."

"She doesn't always call when she's late," Arnold said, a little out of breath as he tossed the bone again.

"I know." She paused. "But it's the combination of her being upset about something *and* being late that worries me."

Martha looked at her watch and decided not to get too concerned until dinnertime. Danielle didn't like to miss a meal, even if she wasn't always thrilled with the menu.

When dinnertime had come and gone, Martha decided to go look for her, and Arnold offered to drive. Such a good man; he knew she didn't like to drive at night. She thanked God at least once a day for bringing Arnold into her life.

They drove around Monte Vista and past a couple of spots that Danielle had been known to frequent with her friend

Sue. And they went by Sue's house. When Sue answered the door and said that Danielle had canceled their plans to hang out after work, Martha's worry meter jumped a few notches. She figured Danielle must be at Matthew's, but he lived in Alamosa. Martha had never met the kid, and she didn't know exactly where he lived. Maybe Levi knew.

They pulled into the Detweilers' driveway, and Martha told Arnold he could wait in the car while she talked to Levi. She hurried to the door, her teeth chattering. She'd be glad when June arrived. Some of their days were bearable this time of year, but after the sun went down, the temperatures dipped into the thirties. She thought back to the bitter cold winter they'd just had and was doubly thankful that summer swiftly approached.

"Martha, come in out of this *wedder*." Vera opened the wooden door, then pushed the screen wide. "It's after the supper hour. What brings you out this time of night?"

"Arnold's in the car. I can't stay. I just wondered if Levi was here. I'm looking for Danielle and thought he might know where she is."

Vera folded her hands in front of her and pressed her lips together. Same expression she always got at the mention of Danielle, which made Martha want to smack her. Martha dug her nails into the palms of her hands and waited her out.

"Come in, Martha, and I'll go get Levi."

Martha stepped inside, welcoming the warmth of the fire. A few minutes later, Levi walked into the den. He didn't usually have much to say, but he sure was a looker, that boy—with his sandy blond hair and adorable smile. A tall kid with a solid build. Martha wasn't surprised that he'd snagged the cutest little Amish girl in their district, that Sarah Troyer.

"Hi, Levi. Danielle seemed upset this morning, and she's late getting home today. I haven't heard from her. I've called her cell phone, and it only rings once, like it's off. Anything going on with her that I should know about?" Martha squinted one eye and stared up at him.

"No, ma'am. I—I don't know where she is." Levi pulled his eyes from Martha's almost instantly and scratched the left side of his face.

Martha took a step closer. "Levi. Is something going on with Danielle?"

They all turned when loud footsteps came pounding down the stairs. Vera met her nine-year-old daughter at the bottom.

"Betsy, what have I told you about jumping down the stairs like that?" Vera latched on to Betsy's hand and guided her into the room. "Say hello to Mrs. Becker."

"Hello, Mrs. Becker."

Betsy made Martha nervous as a cat in a room full of rocking chairs. The little girl was a genius nine-year-old who didn't know how to sort out her own thoughts before she spoke. Once she'd told Martha—in front of a group of Amish ladies—that Martha's teeth would be whiter if she wouldn't drink as much tea and brushed with straight peroxide. Vera had reprimanded the child for being rude, but it didn't ease the embarrassment.

It wasn't rocket science, but Martha did cut down on the tea, brushed with straight peroxide now, and was proud of her much-improved smile. She ran her tongue across her teeth. "Hi, Betsy." She waited for Betsy to share whatever was on her mind, and Martha prayed it wouldn't have anything to do with her.

"Did you know that there are no words in your *Englisch* language that rhyme with *month, orange, silver,* and *purple*?"

Martha breathed a sigh of relief. "No, I didn't know that, Betsy."

"It's true."

Martha tried to smile before she turned back to Levi. "I'm worried about Danielle. She was crying this morning. And I've already called her friend Sue, trying to get hold of her since they had plans after work. But Sue said Danielle canceled, and I don't know where that boyfriend of hers lives."

"I doubt she's there," Levi said quickly, drawing all eyes to him. "I mean—it's late, *ya*? She wouldn't go there this late, is what I meant."

Martha eyed him for a long moment. She knew when people were telling the truth. Levi might not be lying, but he seemed to know *something*. "Okay. Well, if you hear from her for any reason, will you tell her to call us?"

"*Ya.*"

Martha left, deciding she and Arnold were spinning their wheels. Maybe Danielle was already at home by now. So they headed that way.

LEVI WAITED UNTIL Martha and Arnold had time to get back on the road before he pulled his coat and hat from the rack by the door.

"Where are you going?" his mother's voice snapped. "You're not going to go look for that girl, are you?"

"That *girl* is Danielle, *Mamm*. And you know we are *gut* friends. I think I might know where she is."

"You just told Martha that you didn't know where she is." His mother scowled, then kept going before Levi could answer.

"This night air is not *gut* for your asthma, and it's too cold to travel in the buggy."

"I'll be fine, *Mamm*. I won't be out late."

His father was already upstairs for the night, but he knew his father would have agreed with his mother. They didn't travel at night unless they had to.

Levi kissed his mother on the cheek. "I'll be back soon." He wasn't a child.

But Danielle was still a girl, and she was scared.

# *Four*

LEVI HITCHED THE BUGGY UP OUTSIDE OF THE small *Englisch* church on the far side of town. The turn-of-the-century structure housed a small congregation of Christians on Sunday mornings, and no matter what religion you practiced, the church was a sight to see with its brightly painted stained glass windows on all sides. It had one of those historic plaques out front, and the door was never locked. Levi figured it wouldn't hold more than thirty or forty people.

It was called Sangre de Cristo Chapel, which meant "blood of Christ" in Spanish, and the Sangre de Cristo Mountains climbed behind the church. There was a sign that hung lopsided on the outside of the door that read: "All are welcome here in the house of the Lord."

Levi had already seen Danielle's car outside. He eased the tall wooden door open and walked into the dimly lit church with only six rows of pews on either side. Danielle was sitting in the front row. She glanced over her shoulder.

"What are you doing here, Levi?"

He kept walking, then slid into the seat beside her. "What

are *you* doing here?" He'd always found it ironic that Danielle came here when she was upset, since she didn't like to talk about God. But every time he did find Danielle here, it gave him hope. Last time he'd found her here after she'd hit a bird while driving her car. "You should have seen the bird's mate," she'd told him as she cried. "He just stood there over the lifeless little body. When a car came by, the living bird would fly up, but then go right back down to his partner after the car passed. I killed his mate. I'm a murderer."

Levi had done his best to comfort her then, and he hoped his words and presence would be enough to comfort her now.

"I'm testing God," she finally said, sniffling as she stared straight ahead. Levi knew it was pointless to argue with her when she was like this, but he spoke up anyway.

"You can't test God."

As he expected, her head quickly spun to the right. "If He is real, then He needs to help me. He needs to bring Matthew back, make him realize that us being a family is the best thing . . . for all of us."

Levi took a deep breath. "Did Matthew go somewhere?"

She faced forward again. "He ran away. From me. From the baby." Then, before Levi could comment, she turned to him again and started to cry. "I'm not a bad person. I'm really not. If there was a God, He'd help me. But all this bad stuff keeps happening to me. My father died, and I loved him so much." She lowered her head. "My mother was crazy before he died, and then got a hundred times worse after. And now . . ." She buried her head in her hands.

Levi wasn't sure what to say.

"I thought Matthew loved me, or I would have never . . ."

She kept her head buried in her hands. Levi wanted to reach an arm around her, but he sat still and just listened. "Now I'm an eighteen-year-old with a baby on the way, with no boyfriend or husband. I'm alone." She cried harder.

"You know Martha and Arnold love you, Danielle. Why don't you just tell them?"

She shook her head. "It's going to be such a burden for them. And Martha is going to yell at me."

"You don't know that. And . . . a child isn't a burden. A child is a blessing."

They were quiet for a few moments, both staring past the small pulpit to where Jesus hung on a simple wooden cross at the front of the church. Levi's heart was beating faster than ever.

"Have you told anyone that you're pregnant?" he asked.

She shook her head, and Levi worried he might pass out. He opened his mouth, then shut it again. He did that two more times before the words finally found their way out.

"Marry *me*, Danielle." He couldn't even look at her, knowing she would think it was crazy. But Levi had thought about the dream and the man in the store all day. God was calling him to marry Danielle. He knew it. It hurt him to know that he would be leaving his people, not baptized into the faith. But he couldn't take an *Englisch fraa* and then be baptized Amish. The bishop would never allow it. It was the sacrifice God was asking of him.

Danielle slowly turned to face him, and a smile spread across her face. *She must be considering it,* he thought. Until she burst out laughing.

"Levi! Are you out of your mind?"

"I thought you'd say that," he said as relief flooded over

him. He'd done what God called him to do. He certainly couldn't force her to marry him.

"What would make you ask me that? I mean, I love you and all . . . but you know what I mean." Danielle playfully slapped him on the arm, but he was still recovering from her words. *She loves me?* It was nice to hear, since he loved her too. But he loved his sister, his mother, his father, brother, and so on. There were all kinds of love, and his and Danielle's wasn't the marrying kind.

"I don't want you to have to raise the *boppli*, I mean baby, all on your own. I just thought . . ." He shrugged. "I don't know."

She lifted her head and gazed into his eyes. "You're sweet, Levi. Some girl will be very lucky to have you, but you won't be able to be my best friend anymore." She paused, frowning. "And that will be hard. Maybe Sarah Troyer?"

Levi shook his head. "*Nee.* I don't think so." He frowned. He liked Sarah well enough, but he couldn't picture them like that. "So . . . if you would have married Matthew, then we wouldn't have been friends anymore?"

"I would like to think we could have stayed friends, but I guess it would have changed between us some." She turned to face him. "Don't you think?"

"I guess so."

They were quiet for a while, and Levi stifled a yawn. "How long do you plan on sitting here?"

"I told you. I'm testing God to see if He'll fix things. If He's real, then He can fix everything."

"Danielle . . ." He let out a heavy sigh. There was no way for him to educate Danielle about the Lord in one night. It would take a lifetime of learning, or at the least more time than Danielle was willing to devote.

They both turned around when they heard the door close behind them. A man came down the aisle carrying a broom and a dustpan.

"Sorry to disturb you, folks," he said as he waved. "Just doing a little cleanup."

Levi waved back, and he and Danielle watched the man start pulling cobwebs out of the corners of the front of the church—big clusters of dust that Levi didn't remember seeing earlier. But the light was dim, and he hadn't been studying the condition of the old church.

"God fixes everything in His time," Levi finally whispered. "He always has a plan." He knew Danielle would fire back with something, and his mother's words about being unequally yoked flew back into his mind. How could he have possibly thought God was calling him to marry her?

To Levi's surprise, Danielle didn't say anything. Her eyes were fixed on the man clearing the cobwebs from the corner. "Do you know him?" she asked, keeping her eyes straight ahead.

Levi squinted to see better in the poorly lit area. "*Nee*, I don't think so. Do you?"

She spoke softly. "I—I'm not sure." After a brief pause, she added, "Maybe. I don't know." She shrugged before she leaned her head against his shoulder and wrapped her hand around his arm. The man turned and came back down the aisle toward them, his eyes aglow in the dim lighting. It was then that Levi realized he recognized the man.

Except last time Levi saw the fellow, he was holding a

paddle in his hand, not a broomstick. The man winked at Levi on his way out of the church.

DANIELLE CLUNG TO Levi like a life vest after having the strangest feeling she'd ever had in her life. It was the craziest idea, marrying Levi.

Or was it?

"Levi?"

"*Ya?*"

"What if . . . what if we *did* get married?"

She eased away from him and looked up just in time to see his eyes close for a moment as he swallowed hard. Gasping, she asked, "Oh no. Did you already change your mind?"

"Uh, no . . . no, I guess not. I mean no." He shook his head, rubbed his chin, then stared into her eyes. "What made *you* change your mind?"

"I don't know." She lowered her head. "Never mind, Levi. I can't marry you." She looked up at him, unable to deny that she loved him, but she loved him enough not to ruin his life. "You're my best friend, and I know we love each other. But not in that way. And you would have to leave the Amish faith. I know how important that is to you."

Levi didn't say anything.

She was pretty sure he was relieved. Levi was such a good person. He'd only offered because he felt like it was the right thing to do, so that the baby would have a father.

Levi twisted in his seat to face her. He scratched his forehead. "Then why were you reconsidering?"

She opened her mouth to respond, then closed it. *No, it's*

*crazy* . . . "Why'd you ask me in the first place?" She turned to him and searched his gorgeous brown eyes, noticing his slightly wind-bronzed face stretched over high cheekbones. She wondered if he knew how handsome he was.

Levi took a long time to answer. "I think I am supposed to marry you."

"*Supposed* to?" Danielle grunted. "Gee, Levi. Thanks. What every girl wants to hear."

"*Nee*, well, maybe that wasn't the right word." He gazed into her eyes. "Please. Tell me why you were reconsidering it."

"I, uh . . . I thought I heard . . . something." Danielle couldn't explain it. It was a voice in her head she didn't recognize, but yet familiar at the same time.

"What?" Levi's expression tightened. "Tell me."

"I thought I heard someone say that I should marry you. Maybe I'm losing it. Maybe the man cleaning the cobwebs was just mumbling or something." She shrugged. "I don't know."

Levi dropped to one knee in front of her and reached for her hand. "Danielle, I think God is speaking to us. I had a dream that I should marry you, and now you have the same feeling. The Lord is speaking to us. Marry me, Danielle."

Danielle blinked back tears as she cupped Levi's cheek in her hand. "You are a good person, Levi. Way better than me. And I love you." A tear rolled down her cheek. "But there is no way that I'll marry you."

Once again, Danielle couldn't tell if it was pain or relief that clouded Levi's expression. Levi was so religious that if he felt like God was calling him to marry her, then he'd try to persuade her for sure. It was her job to keep things in perspective, to protect them both, no matter what weird feeling she'd had come over her.

"Danielle," Levi sighed, "I really think—"

"No, Levi." Danielle put a finger to his lips. "You will marry a nice Amish girl. Someone even better than Sarah, if she's not the right girl for you. And have lots of little Amish children. You've done what you thought was right, asking me to marry you." She shook her head. "And I almost went for it because you are such a wonderful person. But I can't do that to you."

Levi didn't say anything, which confirmed for Danielle that he was relieved. He got up and sat down beside her again. "Martha is worried about you," he said.

"Uh-oh. I should have called her, I guess. Did she send you looking for me?"

"*Nee*, but she came by our *haus* wanting to know if I knew where you were."

"I guess I better go home." She rose and hugged herself, feeling a chill in the air without his big body beside her. "Levi, it's freezing this time of night. You shouldn't have come."

"That's what *friends* do." Levi shrugged as one corner of his mouth curled down.

"Oh, don't act like your feelings are hurt. I know you're glad to be officially off the hook." She forced a smile as she playfully pushed a finger against his muscular chest, wishing things were different. She'd loved Matthew in a different way than she loved Levi. Mostly because she'd just never considered a relationship with Levi. He didn't want to leave the Amish district the way Matthew had always wanted to. Danielle hadn't ever felt guilty about her relationship with Matthew, that she was pulling him away from his people. If anything, she'd thought she was supporting him as he sought his way out.

"C'mon," she said, offering him a hand. "You better go. It's just going to get colder."

Levi stood up and gave her a long, tender hug. He towered over her by almost a foot. Sarah Troyer—or whoever Levi chose as a wife—would be a lucky girl. Levi was handsome, caring, and someday he'd make a great husband and father. For someone . . .

LEVI PULLED AWAY from Danielle, dressed in her blue jeans and long-sleeved white shirt, and helped her put on her navy jacket. He recalled the way Danielle used to dress— before Martha made her clean up her act. It used to make Levi uncomfortable when Danielle showed her midriff in the warmer months, or when she'd worn something overly revealing. They'd still become friends, but Levi was glad that Danielle opted for more conservative clothing over time. But right now, he couldn't keep from staring at her belly. It seemed so odd that a new life was growing inside of her. They started walking down the aisle of the church toward the back. Levi silently prayed. He thanked God that Danielle was safe and asked the Lord to guide her as she entered this new time in her life. He prayed for the *boppli* too.

He pulled his coat tighter around him and pushed his hat down firmly on his head as Danielle opened the door and they entered the cold.

"I feel bad that I'm getting into a car with a heater, and you'll be driving home in the buggy." Danielle's breath clouded in front of her, and Levi wished he was getting into the car with her.

"I'm used to it," he said as he waited for her to fish her keys from her pocket. There was four years difference in their ages, but at that moment, Danielle had never looked younger to him. She was going to have hard times ahead, but Levi knew that Martha and Arnold would be there for her and the baby. For the hundredth time, he wondered what kind of man Matthew Lapp could be to run out on her.

They'd only taken a few steps from the church when Levi stopped and slowly turned around.

"Levi? What are you doing?" Danielle tugged on the arm of his coat, but Levi kept his eyes on the tiny church as the dim light filtered through the stained glass windows. He felt an overwhelming urge that God was encouraging him to ask again. He resisted, clearer than ever about what he'd be giving up—the Amish life he'd always wanted. But the feeling was not going away; it was only getting stronger. And that meant one thing. *God.*

As they stood at the steps of the Sangre de Cristo Chapel, Levi turned to Danielle. "I'm going to marry you. And I think we should get married in this church."

"Levi, we've been through all this, and—"

"We should get married in three weeks." He spoke with as much authority as he could muster up amidst his own heavy reservations.

"No! I'm not marrying you. I can't be Amish, Levi."

"I know that. We'll live *Englisch* and be a family." He grabbed her shoulders. "Please, Danielle. I really believe God wants us to get married. I know you feel it too."

Danielle's jaw dropped for a moment, and then she clamped it shut. "No. I don't. I don't know what I felt. I—I'm just confused. Matthew just ran off and left me. I'm not even over that."

He straightened and her face softened, as if she were aware she might be hurting him. "Look. You're my best friend, Levi. And what you're trying to do is admirable. But I will not let you ruin your life like this."

"Who says it'll ruin my life?"

"I do!" Danielle slid past him and ran to her car.

Levi let her go, watching as she drove away, but then felt compelled to walk back into the church. He sat in the first pew and started to pray. Levi had been so sure of what God wanted from him.

But then why hadn't He made it as clear to Danielle?

DANIELLE STARTED APOLOGIZING the minute she walked into the den where Martha and Arnold were sitting, but stopped abruptly.

"Wow! That's a big dog!" She walked to the enormous tan and black animal lying at Arnold's feet. She squatted and scratched his ears. "What's your name?"

Martha took off her reading glasses and closed the book she was reading. "That's Dude, and where've you been?"

Danielle looked up at Arnold. "He's so great, Arnold. And so big." She giggled when Dude stood up and knocked her from her squatting position onto her behind. Then the dog tried to crawl into her lap. "Easy there, big guy." She nuzzled up to him and let him lick her face. She turned to Martha. "I'm sorry. I should have called."

"Sue said you canceled your plans, and we've been worried. I don't pay for a cell phone for you just so you can keep it turned off." Martha crossed her legs as she folded her arms across her chest.

"I know. I'm sorry. Matthew and I broke up, and I wanted to go to his house to talk to him one more time."

Martha lowered her hands into her lap, her expression softening. "I'm sorry, honey. Is that why you've been so upset?"

Danielle nodded. "Yeah, I just needed some time, and I needed to know if it was really over between us before I said anything. And it is."

"So you talked to him, but there's no chance of a reconciliation?" Martha raised an eyebrow.

"He wasn't there, but, uh, no. There's no chance of us getting back together. He . . ." Danielle paused, swallowed hard. "He actually left town to go to his cousin's house in Indiana. He's leaving the Amish faith."

"Oh boy. I bet his folks are beside themselves. And here all this time, they probably thought all they had to worry about was you stealing their son away." Martha shook her head. "I'm sorry you're hurt, honey, but God must have another plan for you."

"I guess." Danielle knew it was the best response; otherwise Martha would try to push a conversation about God. Again.

"I always thought that if you were going to date an Amish boy, that Levi Detweiler would be quite the catch." Martha cackled, slapping a hand to her leg. "Ol' Vera would have a heart attack if she ever heard me say that."

Arnold scratched Dude behind the ears. "Why are you attracted to these Amish fellows anyway?"

Danielle shrugged. "I didn't go out looking for an Amish guy to date." It was just a weird coincidence. "But Levi did . . ." She stopped, her heart beating hard. She'd almost told Martha that Levi asked her to marry him, but Danielle was still sorting out her own feelings, not ready to deal with Martha's reaction to that news.

*Shouldn't I be mourning the loss of my relationship with Matthew?* But with each passing second, Matthew seemed further removed, and not just geographically.

"What's that about Levi?" Martha asked as she reached for the remote and turned the television down.

"Uh, Levi found me tonight."

"Where? I thought we looked for you in all your usual places."

Danielle avoided Martha's eyes as she stood up and moved to the couch. Martha always sat in her old tan recliner, and they'd bought Arnold one of his own shortly after they were married. Danielle sat on the old red and gold couch across from them. "Don't make a big deal about this, but sometimes I go to that little church in town, the one with the stained glass windows."

Martha smiled a little as she lifted her chin. "Do ya now?"

"I asked you to not make a big deal over it. It's just that it's quiet, and I like to go there to think." Danielle's heart was pounding as she wondered if she should just tell Martha and Arnold everything. Now. But thoughts of Levi dominated. His sweet face, his strong arms around her . . . his offer to marry her. Was he crazy? Levi was the most religious person she knew, and she couldn't imagine him leaving the Amish for a life with her. Even though she'd temporarily lost her mind and almost agreed to his proposal.

She leaned her head back against the couch when Martha seemed to tune in to the television program with Arnold. Closing her eyes, she tried to picture herself with Levi . . . the two of them, a family, raising a baby. More than once, she'd wanted Levi to kiss her, but she'd known that would change the way things were between them. But now she found herself envisioning his lips on hers. What would it be like to kiss her best friend?

# *Five*

Thursday, Sarah walked into the Detweilers' dry goods store to pick up a few things on her mother's list. And to see if maybe she could catch a glimpse of Levi. The dry goods store was on the same property as the Detweilers' home, and since it was almost four o'clock, she knew that Levi and his father would be pulling in from work soon, in time to clean up before the supper hour at five. Even if she didn't get to see Levi, this would be a good time to chat with Levi's older brother, Jacob, about something she'd seen.

"*Wie bischt*, Sarah?" Jacob said from behind the counter as she walked in.

"I'm *gut. Danki*, Jacob."

Jacob was only a year older than Levi, but if Levi hadn't told Sarah that, she'd have thought him much older. He already had a receding hairline. Maybe his wife of two years, Beth Ann, was aging him. Beth Ann was on the whiny side. Sarah was glad Levi's hair wasn't receding so quickly.

"If you're lookin' for Levi, he ain't home yet."

Sarah felt her cheeks warm as she waved a playful hand at

Jacob. "*Nee, nee*. I'm just here to pick up a few things for *mei mamm*." She reached into the pocket of her black apron and pulled out the list.

"Need help finding anything, let me know." Jacob stacked some papers on the counter as he gave her a wise smile.

"*Ya, danki*. I'm sure I'll find everything." She returned the smile and headed down the first aisle. Five minutes later, she was back at the counter carrying the six items in a small basket. She put them on the counter.

"That was fast."

Jacob started scanning the items with a gadget Sarah had seen in stores that had electricity, then she looked up and saw lights overhead.

"Jacob Detweiler . . ." She put her hands on her hips, grinning. "You're running electricity in here." She pointed to the cash register, then up at the lights.

He chuckled. "Solar panels. *Daed* and Levi installed them a couple of weeks ago. *Daed* was even thinking about putting some at the main house, but *Mamm* threw a fit. Said she was happy with things the way they are."

"Solar panels in the *haus* is too *Englisch* for me, but I can see where it would be a big help here at the store." She lifted a brow. "What does the bishop have to say about it?"

Jacob shrugged. "The bishop figures we're only taking advantage of all the sunshine the good Lord gives us here." He put her items in a bag.

Sarah peeked out the window. No sign of Levi yet, but she had other business here anyway. "I ran into the *Englisch* girl, Danielle, the other day. First time I've seen her in a while." Sarah pulled a twenty-dollar bill from her apron pocket and put it on the counter. "She used to attend our worship service sometimes with Martha, but she hasn't attended in weeks." She paused. "Anyway, I was at the pharmacy picking up a prescription for *mei* sister when I saw her down the aisle." Sarah knew what she was doing was wrong. Gossiping. But she knew how close Levi and Danielle were, and it worried her. She also knew her mother's generation would never ask what she was about to ask Jacob, but she wanted Jacob—and particularly Levi—to know what kind of girl Danielle was. "Do you know . . . is she with child?"

Jacob's cheeks reddened above his brown beard as he avoided her eyes. "Uh, I wouldn't think so, since she ain't married."

"Isn't she dating an Amish fellow in Alamosa?"

"*Ya*, Matthew Lapp. Don't know him. I've just heard Levi mention his name."

Sarah shook her head. "I was just surprised to see her buying one of those testing kits, you know, that tell you if, you know . . . you're in the family way."

Jacobs face reddened even more. "I wouldn't know about those things." He handed her three dollars and some change back.

"*Danki*. See you at worship on Sunday?"

"*Ya*."

Sarah smiled, picked up her bag, and headed out the door. Still no sign of Levi. But that was okay. Jacob would tell him what kind of girl Danielle was, and that made the trip worth it.

LEVI WALKED OVER to the store after he got the horse settled in the barn for the night. "Need help closing up?" He walked to where Jacob was totaling receipts behind the counter.

"*Nee*. Just about done." Jacob didn't look up. "You missed your girlfriend. She just left."

"My girlfriend?" His immediate thought was Danielle, but only because she'd been on his mind since Monday night. He'd wanted to go by and see how she was doing, but he and his father had barely made it home in time for supper the past couple of nights. "Sarah?"

"How many you got?" Jacob looked up and grinned.

"She's not really my girlfriend. We've been to a few singings, but . . ." He shrugged. "I don't know."

"She sure is *schee*."

He nodded, although he hadn't thought much about Sarah the past few days. He'd been busy with thoughts of Danielle and the baby; trying to forget about his dream, the man in the hardware store, and the fellow at the church. He couldn't help but worry that he was ignoring signs from God to marry Danielle, but he was relieved not to be going into the *Englisch* world. He'd even talked to the bishop about setting his baptism soon. Then he wouldn't be tempted by such silly notions.

"I'll see Sarah on Sunday," he mumbled.

"You don't sound too excited about that." Jacob walked around the counter toward the door. Levi followed him out, then stepped aside while Jacob locked up.

"It's not that. I'm just tired." Levi and Jacob walked to the barn where Jacob's horse had been stabled for the day, the cold wind slapping them in the face.

"Sarah said she ran into Danielle at the pharmacy in town," Jacob said as he led his horse out of the barn.

Levi's heart jumped at the mention of Danielle, which it

didn't used to do. "*Ya*, they know each other from worship service, I guess."

They were quiet as Jacob attached the harnesses and readied the buggy. Then Jacob stepped into his buggy, closed the door, and leaned out the window. "It wonders me if they *like* each other."

"Why would you say that?" Levi stuffed his hands in the pockets of his black coat, rocking back and forth on his heels to try to stay warm.

Jacob shrugged, then clicked his tongue to set the horse in motion. "*Ach*, never mind. Women are odd ducks. Now, I gotta go and get home to mine." He grinned, then hollered as he pulled away, "Tell *Mamm* I sure could use one of her lemon pies. You know, Beth Ann don't like lemons so I never get one."

"I'll tell her." Levi turned toward the house, wondering if Jacob was holding something back.


FRIDAY MORNING, DANIELLE hurled until her ribs hurt. It had been like that the past two mornings. And afternoons. And nights. If this was what pregnancy was like, she was going to hate it.

She was still hugging the toilet in the upstairs bathroom when Martha banged on the door. "Danielle, are you okay in there?"

She still hadn't gotten up the courage to tell Martha or Arnold, but they were going to figure it out if she kept getting sick. She'd even left work yesterday halfway through her shift. "I'm okay."

"Still sick to your stomach? Want me to make you some soup? Or is there anything I can get for you?"

For all their joking around with each other, and Martha's peculiar ways, Danielle knew how lucky she was to have the woman in her life. "Yeah, still kinda sick, but I'll be out in a minute."

"All right. But you let me know if you need something. Opening a can of soup doesn't require any real cooking, so don't be afraid." She chuckled, and Danielle heard footsteps descending the stairs.

She finally pulled herself off the floor, splashed water on her face, and blotted herself dry. Staring in the mirror, she touched her stomach. It was hard to believe that something so incredibly tiny was already causing this much havoc, just two months into her pregnancy, according to her calculations. She pulled her hair from what was left of her ponytail, ran a comb through it, then pulled it back again. After brushing her teeth, she left the bathroom and headed back to her room.

As she dressed for work, she thought about Matthew. And Levi. When she thought about Matthew, tears threatened to spill. But thinking about Levi brought a smile to her face. She still couldn't believe he'd asked her to marry him. Even if he had proposed out of some weird obligation to answer God's "call." *Maybe that's how God works. You have to give up something you love as a sacrifice to Him. Then He will give you a good life.*

As she tied her tennis shoes, she tried to recall any sacrifices she'd made in her life. The only thing she could think of was that she hadn't hit her mother back after all the times she'd struck her. Danielle had sure wanted to. But she'd just taken it, knowing Mom would feel bad later. *I wonder what Mom's doing right now . . . Does she miss me?*

But was not hitting her mother back really the kind of sacrifice God was looking for? She tried to think of anything she'd given up for the good of another person, anything similar to the sacrifice Levi had been willing to make. When nothing came to mind, she decided she should ask Levi. He'd know if God required sacrifices to be in His good graces.

What exactly did God want from her? She realized that even though she'd tried to stop thinking about a God she wasn't sure existed, thoughts of Him had been more prevalent in her mind lately. She touched her stomach and wondered if the baby she carried was the reason.

Maybe today she'd tell Sue she was pregnant. She'd been wanting to, but the restaurant had been super busy, and then she'd left early yesterday. She dreaded it, really, and practiced how she'd say it in her mind. *Yeah, remember how I told you that me and Matthew were so in love? Well, yeah, so . . . uh, we made a baby. And then he got so freaked out he ran away.*

Danielle sighed. No matter how many times she tried to come up with the right way to say it, it only ended up sounding totally embarrassing.

AFTER A LONG day and two trips to the bathroom to vomit, Danielle was thankful her shift was over. It was hard to keep her mind off a queasy stomach when she was delivering heaping plates of food—or worse, the dried remains—all day at a restaurant.

"Hey, let's talk," she told Sue when they gathered up their purses in the back. "Here, or we can go somewhere else."

Sue pushed her black-framed glasses up on her nose and frowned. "What's wrong?"

"Nothing." Danielle shrugged as they made their way into the main dining room. "Just thought we'd catch up."

"I can't today. My mom's car broke down, and I told her I'd hurry home from work so she could use mine."

"I'll make it quick. There's something I gotta tell you." Danielle waited until they'd left the building before she said anything more. *Keep it simple,* she told herself. *Just tell her.* "Sue, I'm pregnant."

Sue stopped, her eyes grew wide, and with chattering teeth she said, "I'll text my mom and tell her I'll be a little late."

Silently, they walked to the coffee shop down the street. Sue wrapped her arm through hers, seemingly trying to figure out what to say. "So, what did Matthew say when you told him?" Sue asked when they reached the door.

"I'll tell you everything when we get inside. It's chilly out here."

And then she did. All of it, from beginning to end. Only leaving out Levi and his crazy proposal.

"That's terrible, Danielle." Sue covered her face with her hands, rubbed her eyes for a moment, then looked back at her. "What are you going to do?"

"Raise the baby on my own. What else can I do?" She shoved aside another thought about Levi.

Sue looked down, circling the rim of her coffee cup. "Well . . . there are options."

Danielle stiffened. "Like what?"

"Adoption . . . or abortion." Sue looked her in the eye.

"I'm not giving my baby away." Danielle swallowed back the lump in her throat. "And I'm certainly not killing him or her."

"Okay . . ." Sue bit her lip for a few moments. "But take it from me, Miss In Vitro herself, it's hard not having a father. While it worked out great for my mom—a baby and no messy marriage stuff—I always felt cheated. I *missed* having a dad. Don't you think . . . Danielle, don't you think it's a bit selfish not to even *consider* adoption?"

Danielle blinked back tears.

Sue reached over and touched her hand. "I'm not trying to upset you, but I want you to think carefully about what you're doing. This will change your whole life. As well as your baby's." She eased her hand back and took a sip of her mocha. "What did Martha and Arnold say?"

"I haven't told them."

"Well, Martha's loaded, so money won't be an issue." Sue shook her head. "My mom would kill me if I got pregnant. How ironic is that? But there's no way we could afford it. I'm already helping out with the household expenses." She narrowed her eyebrows. "Why didn't you use birth control?"

Danielle rubbed her forehead. "I don't know. We were just in the moment, and . . ."

"Just one time?"

"Yeah. Can you believe it?" Danielle took a sip from her mug but quickly put it down. Something about the smell and the taste was making her nauseous. She was still thinking about Sue's comment about being selfish, but Danielle knew in her heart that she could never give up her baby for adoption. And she couldn't even think about any other options. She wanted to succeed where she felt like her own mother had failed, to love a child with all her heart. She dabbed at her eyes.

"I'm sorry, Danielle." Sue took a deep breath. "This is about you, not me. I've just been so angry at my mom. When I was little, I kept waiting for her to marry someone so I could say I had a father. But instead, the guys came in and out of the house like there was a revolving door." She held up a palm toward Danielle. "And I'm not saying you'd do that. I'm just saying that I always wished I had a father."

"Well, I can't force Matthew to be with me." She paused, wondering if she should go on. "But Levi asked me to marry him."

"*What?*" Sue sat straight up and blinked her eyes a few times. "I thought you guys were just good friends." Shock gave way to a smile. "He sure is hot, though. What did you say?"

"I said no, of course. He's my best friend. We're not like that."

Sue shook her head. "What is it about you and Amish guys?"

Danielle shrugged, hearing the same question from Arnold again. "I don't know."

"Well, I wouldn't let that Levi Detweiler get away, Amish or not." Sue laughed.

"What's so funny?"

"I'm trying to picture you in all that Amish garb."

Danielle thought for a few moments, then smiled. "I don't see it either. But I couldn't be Amish anyway. They're super religious. And I'm not. He'd have to leave the community, and that just wouldn't be right."

Sue leaned back in her chair and circled the rim of her mug with her finger. "Why did Levi ask you to marry him when he's dating that Sarah girl? Does he know you're pregnant?"

Danielle cringed at the sound of that. "Yes, he knows. That's why he asked. To make an honorable woman out of me, I guess."

Sue tapped a finger to her chin. "How far along are you?"

"I know where you're going with this. I'm not going to marry Levi and have everyone think the baby is his. He'd be humiliated by his family and Amish friends. I'm not doing that."

"Do you love him?"

"Yes. Of course," Danielle said easily. "But not the way I loved Matthew. It's different with Levi. I can tell him anything. We're playful with each other. He's honest, kind, a hard worker, and I just . . . love him for the person he is. We're *friends.*"

"Oh, I see." Sue's sarcastic tone was evident. "But Matthew runs off and leaves his parents a note, doesn't say a word to you, and leaves you alone and pregnant. That's the kind of person you *love*-love? Wait! Don't answer." Sue held up a finger. "If Matthew and Levi were both drowning, and you could only save one of them, who would it be?"

She paused, thinking of them both struggling in the water, and her reaching for one . . . "That's a dumb question, and I'm not answering it."

Sue leaned back, arms crossed in self-satisfaction. "If you were that in love with Matthew, then you would have picked him right away. But you didn't."

"That doesn't mean anything."

But even as she said it, Danielle knew that it meant everything.

Because as soon as Sue posed the question, Danielle knew who she'd save.

*Levi.*

# Six

DANIELLE HURRIED DOWN THE STAIRS SUNDAY morning, hoping she wasn't too late. "Wait! I'm going with you."

Martha was crossing the den toward the front door when Danielle hit the bottom stair and moved toward her. Martha turned around.

"Well, well. It's been weeks since you've gone to church with me."

Danielle stopped abruptly and grabbed her chest. "*What* did you do to your hair?"

Martha put a hand on the back of her hair underneath the butterfly clip and gave a little push. "I know. It didn't exactly turn out the color I was hoping for."

Danielle covered her mouth with her hand for a moment, then eyed Martha's new dye job some more. "It's purple."

"It's a dark *burgundy*. Now let's go. The Lord will be glad you're back in church." Martha turned back around and opened the front door. She always dressed in a knee-length, dark-colored dress to attend worship with her Amish friends, and she insisted Danielle dress conservatively as well.

Danielle followed Martha out the door wearing clothes that had been previously approved, a navy skirt that hit below the knee and a white blouse. Danielle knew the outfit looked like a private school uniform, especially with the short white socks and white tennis shoes she was wearing. But it made Martha happy, and Danielle knew she hadn't been living up to her end of the bargain that they'd made last year to go to church every week. Martha didn't have to know that Danielle had an ulterior motive today. She followed Martha to the car.

"Don't you want to wear a hat or something?"

"God doesn't care about the color of my hair." She turned and glared at Danielle.

Danielle smiled. It wasn't God that Danielle hoped to see today at church.

LEVI HOPED THE men sitting next to him couldn't hear his stomach rumbling. He'd overslept this morning and barely had time to eat a biscuit before they'd left for the Stoltzfuses' house. Lillian and Samuel were hosting worship, and as was customary, the men sat facing the women, with the bishop and elders in the middle. With only about fifty folks in attendance representing their small district, he'd been surprised to see Danielle walk in with Martha.

In the beginning, Martha's presence at worship had caused worry for some of the older members of their community, but over time they'd all grown to trust and love her. She was a strange woman, but loving and kind. Levi strained his neck to see around his cousin Eli, to see Danielle. She smiled when they locked eyes, and for reasons Levi couldn't explain, he felt like he was seeing Danielle for the first time. She looked beautiful, her hair pulled to the side in a loose braid, her modest blouse and skirt, with just a hint of lip gloss. His mind began to whirl about the conversations they'd had recently. If he'd thought for one minute that Danielle might convert and become Amish, maybe he would have tried to be more than just friends with her, right from the beginning.

He'd prayed for days that he hadn't somehow let God down, but he knew that he'd done what he felt God had called him to do. He'd asked Danielle to marry him, and she'd said no. He couldn't force her. The thought of his relief shamed him, but he'd always planned to raise his *kinner* according to the *Ordnung* and their Amish beliefs. Danielle was gathering in fellowship with those who had a strong faith . . . but he wasn't at all sure that she was ready to accept his God as her own.

Most of the service was in German and *Pennsylvania Deitsch*, but after the meal, Martha always asked questions, so maybe some of it was rubbing off on Danielle. Or maybe it was the baby, and all that was changing for her now, that had her seeking. Either way, he found himself particularly glad to see her today.

Sarah was sitting one row behind Danielle between her own mother and Levi's mother. They'd already spoken this morning, and Sarah had voiced her disappointment that no one was hosting a Sunday singing this evening. Levi wasn't all that disheartened. He and his father had had a hard week of work, and getting to bed early sounded good to him. Or maybe he and Danielle could have a little time together . . . He locked eyes with her again, and she smiled. He'd heard his mother talk about women who were expecting, how they glowed. Maybe that's what it was with Danielle today. She'd never looked more beautiful.

When worship was over, the women busied themselves setting the food out, and most of the men gathered outside on Lillian and Samuel's porch. Since their arrival two years ago, Lillian and Samuel had worked hard to turn their old farmhouse into a fine home, and their progress inspired him. Levi had his eye on a house down the road from where his own family lived. It needed a lot of repair, but Levi could see in his mind's eye what it could look like with hard work. He had mentioned to Jacob the house on ten acres, and although Jacob had been interested in taking on the project, his wife-to-be was not. So Jacob had ended up building a new house for him and Beth Ann, something much smaller than they could have had if they'd restored the other house. Levi hoped the house would still be available when he chose to get married.

*Married.* His eyes slid to Danielle as she passed by a window.

After listening to Samuel share a few jokes with the men, Levi moseyed back into the house, moving toward the tables set up in the living room, attempting to stay out of the women's way. But Danielle walked up to him, biting her lip the way she often did when something serious was on her mind.

"Hi, Ladybug."

"Hey." She took a deep breath. "After we eat, can we take a ride in your buggy and go somewhere to talk?"

"*Ya.* What's wrong?" Levi scratched his chin, his stomach churning from a combination of hunger and wondering what she wanted to talk about.

"Nothing, really. I just need to talk to you."

Levi tried to read her expression, but it was blank. "Okay."

"Great. Let me know when you're ready to leave later." She seemed to force a smile, then went back to helping in the kitchen. Not a minute later, Sarah was in front of him.

"I'm surprised to see your friend Danielle here today. She hasn't attended one of our worship services in weeks." Sarah folded her hands in front of her and smiled.

"*Ya*, I know." Levi was surprised too, but his mind was more on the food he hoped would be served soon.

Sarah touched him on the arm. "I know there isn't a singing tonight, but maybe . . ." She flashed her beautiful smile at him. "Maybe we can go for a ride later."

"I—I can't today." Levi put a hand on his hip as he shifted his weight. He felt like he was cheating on Sarah, but that wasn't quite right. Sarah wasn't officially his girlfriend, and Danielle was just his friend. Guilt started to wrap around him just the same, which was confusing. But he knew Sarah would see Danielle leave with him later. "I have to take Danielle somewhere."

"Oh. Where?" Sarah's smile was back, but it wasn't the same cheery expression from a few moments ago.

"Uh . . ." He hadn't been prepared for that question. "I'm not sure. She wants to talk." Levi tried to smile, but Sarah's icy eyes bored into him, so he quickly stilled his expression. Then his mother walked up, and he hoped she'd save him from an awkward moment.

"And what do you two have your heads together about?" *Mamm* grinned from ear to ear as she gently nudged Levi. "Planning another outing together?"

Levi held his breath. *So much for saving me from an awkward moment.*

"No. Levi was just telling me that he has to take Danielle somewhere." Sarah tucked her chin as she folded her hands in front of her.

*Mamm's* eyes locked with Levi's. "Where in the world do you need to take Danielle? She rode here with Martha." His mother's clipped words spewed out as if spending time with Danielle was a sin greater than most.

"*Mamm*, it's not important. Just to talk. We're friends." Then Levi turned to Sarah. "Can we get together for the next singing?"

Sarah's face lit up. "*Ya*. I'd like that." Then a friend of Sarah's motioned to her, and she excused herself. But his mother's feet were rooted to the ground in front of him as she glared at Levi.

Levi shook his head. "Don't say it, *Mamm*."

His mother glanced around before she whispered, "I just hate to see you ruin any opportunity with Sarah. She's such a nice girl." *Mamm* smiled. "And she sure is smitten with you." She waved her arm across the room toward Danielle, still whispering. "And from what I hear, Danielle has a boyfriend in Alamosa. One of our people." She gave a quick shake of her head and frowned.

"Her boyfriend, Matthew Lapp, left town. He left a note for his folks that he didn't want to be Amish, and he didn't even tell Danielle good-bye. That's probably why she needs to talk. She's upset."

"I'm sorry to hear that." His mother pressed her lips together and stared into his eyes.

"Are you, *Mamm*?" Levi clenched his fists at his side. "Because I'd like to get my hands on that Matthew. He is a coward, running away like this, and—"

"Levi. Stop it," she hissed, drawing him to one side. "We don't act like that, with such aggression. And I'm sure Danielle can handle her own problems."

"Well, I'm her friend. So if she needs to talk, then I'll take her somewhere to talk." Levi walked across the room to where his father and some of the other men were taking their seats at one of the tables . . . before he said something to his mother that he would regret.

DANIELLE COULD BARELY stomach a few crackers during the meal after church. But by the time she and Levi reached a quiet place to talk, Danielle knew her upset stomach was more than morning sickness. It was Levi.

He pulled off the road into a small park not too far from town, with a jungle gym, swings, and a few picnic tables. There were just enough trees to give it a cozy feel without obscuring the view of the mountains.

"You look nice in that outfit," he said, grinning as they got out of the buggy.

"*Danki*, dear sir."

Levi chuckled. "Quit trying to speak *Deitsch*."

He tethered the horse to a tree in the park as Danielle sat down on one of the picnic tables nearby, resting her feet on the wooden bench. There wasn't a cloud in the sky, and with the sun beaming down and no breeze, it felt warmer than it had in weeks.

Danielle leaned forward and put her elbows on her knees, then cupped her chin in her hands. She honed in on the swing set, and she could see herself pushing her son or daughter someday. And there would be laughter. Lots of laughing. She smiled.

Levi came and sat down beside her. "So, what did you want to talk about?"

"Can't we just hang out together for a while?" She drummed her fingers against her temples.

Levi put his elbows on his knees too, dangling his hands as he stared at his feet. "*Ya*, we can. But you said you wanted to talk. Might as well tell me now."

Danielle's heart was beating hard. "Do you remember when I first met you?"

"*Ya*. I was taking something to Martha from *mei mamm*. Jam, I think." They were quiet for a few moments. "Why?"

She shrugged. "I just wondered if you remembered." She paused, then twisted to face him. "Do you remember the first time we hung out together?"

"*Ya*, I do." He looked up at her. "You came to worship with Martha, and I could tell you weren't happy about it. After church we all played volleyball, then I asked you if you wanted to go for a walk."

Danielle grinned. "I think your mother about fell over."

Levi smiled too, but then narrowed his eyes. "What's on your mind, Ladybug?"

"Why do you think we got to be such good friends?"

"Who knows why God puts people in our lives?" Levi looked into her eyes. "If anyone needed a friend, it was you. I thought if I befriended you, then other members of our community would accept you too. I think you scared everyone when you first arrived." He shrugged but grinned. "You dressed . . ." He raised one eyebrow. "Uh . . . very *Englisch*."

She nudged him playfully. "Yes, I know that I probably dressed a little tacky for your people." She glanced down at her conservative outfit. "My, how things change."

"I like when you dress like you do for worship." Levi blushed before pulling his eyes away from hers.

Danielle felt her own cheeks warming as she twisted the hem of her skirt between her fingers and tapped one foot nervously.

"Danielle, why don't you just get to the point?" Levi pushed back the rim of his hat and gazed at her. "You can tell me anything."

"I would save you if you were drowning!" she blurted out, her eyes filling with tears. She quickly lowered her head.

Levi leaned down, then gently lifted her chin. "What are you talking about?"

She stared into his kind eyes, then slowly leaned forward and kissed him on the lips. Not the cheek, like she'd done a couple of times in the past. She lingered there, near his lips, needing to know if he was feeling more than just friendship too.

When she finally backed away, Levi blinked a few times. "Wow." His eyes were round. "What was that for?"

Danielle cupped his cheek in her hand. "Do you still want to marry me, Levi?"

Levi leaned back a little and sat taller. "I thought you said you didn't want to." His jaw tensed, and Danielle wondered if he'd changed his mind.

"I've decided I do want to marry you. If you still want to marry me."

Levi stood up, paced in front of the table, then reached into his pocket for his inhaler. Danielle knew that stress often caused him to wheeze. She waited for him to inhale twice. He finally turned around to face her. "I—I'm just surprised."

Danielle walked to where he was standing and looked up at him. "If you've changed your mind, it's okay. I'll still love you." She grinned. "As my best friend." But inside she was hoping with all her heart that Levi would want to raise a family with her. "I would have never asked, if you hadn't asked me first. But if you're in love with Sarah and don't think we could ever really be a couple, then I understand. Really." She knew her voice rose at least an octave by the end, and she was trying hard not to cry, not to guilt him into it.

She waited for his answer.

LEVI SWALLOWED HARD. He'd thought he'd done what God asked and that he was free of what had become a burden, but as Danielle stared at him through teary eyes, he knew he was going to make it his mission to be the best husband and father that he could. But at the same time, his heart hurt, knowing he would be leaving the Amish faith.

"*Ya*, Danielle. I do want to marry you, and I'll raise the *boppli* as my own." He didn't move as he waited for her reaction. She just stared at him. "What's wrong?"

She swiped at her eyes. "Nothing. I'm just . . ." She started to cry as she mumbled. "I'll be Amish if you want me to."

Levi struggled to keep his own emotions intact. "Danielle, we'll make this work." He lifted her chin and stared into her eyes. Even though he wanted what she offered, more than anything in his life, a still, small voice in Levi's head said that Danielle wasn't ready for that. He just shook his head. "I can't ask you to do that."

"Could you even be happy, living outside of your community?" Danielle sniffled.

Levi thought about the house down the street from his parents. "I know of a place not far from my folks' *haus* that's for sale. Even though we wouldn't be Amish, we'd still be in the area. It needs a lot of work, but maybe together we could make it into something special for our family."

"I don't have much money saved, Levi. You should probably know that." Danielle sighed.

"I've been saving money. I have enough for a down payment, and we'd just do like so many other young people here. We'll get a mortgage." Levi's heart was racing, but there were a couple of things he had to know. "Danielle . . ."

"Yeah?"

"Do you love me?" His heart beat faster.

"I think I've always loved you." She smiled.

"I know that. But do you think you can love me the way a *fraa* should love her husband?"

She was quiet for a few moments. "Haven't you heard that couples who are best friends first always have the best shot at having a successful marriage?"

That was not the answer Levi was looking for, but how could he fault her for her honesty? He felt exactly the same way, and would pray that their love and friendship would grow into a relationship of increasing depth, a true marriage blessed by God. But there was one other thing he needed from Danielle.

"I need you to try to have a relationship with God. It's important to me."

Danielle sighed again. "I *am* trying. I went to church today, didn't I?"

Levi smiled, knowing he had his work cut out for him. "Then let's get married."

And this time, Levi initiated the kiss. He tried to push all the worries to the background. Awkward feelings were interspersed with peace and hope . . . a concrete knowledge that he was doing the right thing, doing what God was calling him to do.

He pulled back and cradled her cheek in his hand.

*Please, Lord, tell me this is right . . .*

# *Seven*

VERA DETWEILER KNEW THAT THE RAGE SHE FELT was not something God approved of, but it was there just the same. Levi had lost his mind, and it was her job as his mother to talk him out of ruining his life.

"Calm down, Vera," her husband said when her voice grew louder.

"I will not calm down, Elam!" She pointed a finger at Levi. "This is *narrisch*, and our *sohn* is *ab im kopp*." She swallowed back tears. "You will ruin your life by marrying Danielle and leaving our community."

"It's my life to ruin," Levi said with enough sarcasm to make Vera want to take him over her knee like she'd done when he was a small boy. He walked closer to her. "I feel called to marry her, *Mamm*. I told you that. Maybe the Lord is using to me to help Danielle to have a relationship with Him."

Vera threw her hands up and glared at Elam. "Can't you talk some sense into our boy?"

Elam shook his head. "Vera, this news is displeasing to me

too, but Levi is a grown man. A man who has not been baptized. He has to be the one to make this choice."

Vera had never felt more alone, or more disappointed in Elam. Her worst fear was coming true, and this was all her husband had to say? One of their children was leaving them to live amongst the *Englisch*. Vera had known Danielle was trouble the minute she'd laid eyes on the girl. She covered her face with her hands and cried.

"*Mamm*, please don't cry." Levi neared her.

"Levi, why the rush?" she asked as she lowered her hands. "If you really think this is what you want, then why don't you become engaged and wait a few months? You might change your mind, and at least you won't already be married to that girl."

"That girl is going to be *mei fraa, Mamm*. And I'm going to buy the property down the road, the farmhouse on the ten acres. We will be nearby."

Vera tensed. "You will not be nearby in spirit." Losing the battle, she held on to one last hope. "Why not have Danielle study the *Ordnung*? Lillian did that before she converted and married Samuel. Maybe after a year or two, Danielle would be ready to be baptized into our faith." She touched Levi on the arm. "Have you considered this, *sohn*?"

Levi shifted his weight from one foot to the other, scratched his forehead, and was about to speak when Vera spoke first.

"Please tell me the girl believes in God. Please tell me she is a Christian. I see her at worship service, but not very often lately. Martha has shared with me that Danielle has a long way to go with her relationship with the Lord. Has she crossed that distance?" She cupped her son's face. "She does believe in our Lord, doesn't she?"

"Yes, *Mamm*."

It was a small consolation, but it was better than hearing that Danielle had no faith at all. She closed her eyes and tried to picture Danielle as her daughter-in-law, but the image wouldn't come. Had Levi not paid attention when Vera and Elam advised all the *kinner* to avoid being unequally yoked? This was an example of what could happen. She wondered how Martha felt about this news. Vera and Martha had grown fairly close over the past couple of years. At one point, Vera had even thought Martha might convert to their faith. Martha knew much about the *Ordnung*, was loved by those in their community, and everyone overlooked her peculiar ways.

But if one thing had ever threatened Vera's relationship with Martha, it had been the initial attraction between Danielle and Levi. It had worried her from the beginning. She'd thought that when Danielle starting seeing an Amish boy in another community that the girl would become another Amish family's problem.

"What about poor Sarah?" Vera finally asked. "I thought you might have feelings for her."

"*Mamm*, even if I wasn't marrying Danielle, I don't think I would have married Sarah."

Vera brought a hand to her chest. "You don't *think*? How do you know? Sarah is much more suited to you." She shook her head. "This is a *baremlich* situation."

"*Mamm*, even though Danielle is going to be *mei fraa*, I will still love the Lord no matter where I am. I will still practice the ways of the *Ordnung*, and—"

"No, Levi. You won't." Vera started to cry again, and finally Elam spoke up.

"Your *mudder* is right about that, Levi." Elam had been standing near the fireplace, but he walked to the middle of the room toward Levi. "You will be living outside of our boundaries and not following the *Ordnung*. You'll be using electricity, listening to music, watching television, and probably even driving a car. Even if you continue to worship with us like some of our *Englisch* friends, things will still change. We can't stop you from marrying Danielle, but don't fool yourself into thinking that you will still be living our ways. You will not."

"It doesn't mean my relationship with God is changing." Levi stared at the floor, and Vera's heart hurt for her son. Of all her *kinner*, she would have never expected that Levi would be the one to leave the faith. He'd always talked about raising his family based on the *Ordnung*. What could possibly have changed? This had to be hard for him. And Danielle had surely pushed Levi into this ridiculous marriage.

"I just don't understand," Vera said softly. "I thought you always wanted to raise your *kinner* Amish, to instill in them the values and beliefs your *daed* and I taught you."

"I did, *Mamm*." Levi turned away from both his parents, pulled out his inhaler, and breathed in quickly. Then he turned back around. "I know you don't understand, but as I said, I feel that God is calling me to marry Danielle. How can I ignore this?"

Vera sighed. "*Sohn*, if it is a true calling, should it hurt so much?"

"God doesn't always ask us to do things that don't cause pain, and we can never know His plan. You and *Daed* taught us this."

Vera took a deep breath as her husband gave a slight nod. "I have to go check on Betsy." She dabbed at her eyes and shook her head. "I can't talk about this anymore."

She turned and headed upstairs. First thing tomorrow, she would go talk to Martha. She needed to know if Martha was happy about this or if she had an ally.

LEVI WAITED UNTIL his mother was upstairs before he spoke to his father. "*Daed*, how do I know if I'm making a mistake?" He lowered himself onto the couch and leaned his head back. His father sat down beside him.

"Your *mudder* was so worked up, I didn't want to say much. But, Levi, this is a serious matter. You are walking away from a life that we believe in, one we don't think the *Englisch* understand." He paused, shaking his head. "Things have changed so much since I was a boy. Back then, outsiders would have never been allowed to be so involved in our lives, and they surely wouldn't have attended our worship services unless for a special occasion. I'm not saying that Martha and Danielle aren't *gut* people. I'm saying they aren't like us. This is the danger that comes from mingling with those outside of our own kind. There is a reason that the *Ordnung* says to avoid those who are unequally yoked. Your situation is an example of this. We've brought this heartache upon ourselves."

"*Daed*, I'll still pray, still love God, and live by what I've been taught. Does everything have to change?" Levi swallowed back a lump in his throat.

His father thought for a few moments. "Everything won't change. But much will. It's unavoidable when you enter into a life in the *Englisch* world. And—I must say, *sohn* . . . I, too, am having a *hatt* time understanding why you're doing this. I thought you and Danielle were just *gut* friends. When did this become a romance?"

Levi longed to tell his father the entire truth. *Daed* was a wise man, but instead he just said, "Not long ago."

"Then give it some time. Make sure that it blossoms into the kind of real love that lasts a lifetime."

Levi was quiet for a few moments, wishing he had that luxury. He and Danielle hadn't decided when to tell everyone that she was pregnant, and he didn't want to say anything until after they'd discussed it. "God is calling me to marry Danielle, *Daed*. I know it."

His father ran a hand through his gray beard. "Just be sure. Marriage is a lifelong commitment."

DANIELLE WAITED UNTIL after supper on Friday night before she finally told Martha and Arnold that she was pregnant. It had been almost two weeks since she'd found out. Through her tears, she also told them how Matthew had run out on his parents—and her. She hadn't seen Levi all week, but he'd left a note in her mailbox that he'd be by tomorrow. Unlike a lot of people in the Amish community, Levi chose not to have a cell phone. He said that the bishop allowed it, but only if it was used for work. Danielle knew that lots of Amish bent that rule, but not Levi. She hoped he hadn't changed his mind.

Martha rubbed her upper lip with her finger as she sat in her recliner listening to Danielle's news. Danielle hoped Martha wouldn't mention options, the way Sue had. In Danielle's mind, there were no other choices. But Martha's face was somber, and for once, the woman seemed to be at a loss for words. Danielle glanced at Arnold, hoping he'd be able to calm Martha down when she blew. Arnold's expression was similar to Martha's. Danielle held her breath and waited.

"So . . . ," Martha finally said. "When is this baby due to arrive?"

"I haven't been to the doctor, but I'm guessing around Christmas." Danielle blotted her eyes with a tissue, sniffling.

"Hmm . . ." Martha looked at Arnold for a moment, then back at Danielle. "I guess we have lots to do then, don't we? We'll need to fix up the extra room upstairs." She crossed one leg over the other. "Don't cry now. We're not going to throw you out or anything." She smiled. "Our little family is about as untraditional as you can get. Me and Arnold married late in life, our runaway semi-adopted daughter, a big ol' hound named Dude, and now . . ." Her smile grew. "A baby."

Danielle started crying out of relief, and because Martha referred to her as a daughter, but also because she had more to say.

"Honey . . ." Martha lifted herself from the recliner, walked to the couch, and sat down beside Danielle. She put an arm around her and pulled her close, something Danielle could never remember her own mother doing. "It might not be the ideal situation, but a baby is a blessing."

Danielle recalled Levi saying the same thing. "There's more," Danielle whispered as she eased out of Martha's arms. "I'm going to marry Levi. He asked me, and we love each other." She sat taller, as if that would make her more convincing.

Martha's eyes grew round. "Do *what*?"

Danielle glanced at Arnold in his recliner. His eyes were also wide, and he had leaned forward in the chair.

"Levi asked me to marry him. He said he feels called by God to do this. At first I said no, but then he convinced me that it's the right choice. And I know we're best friends, but we love each other too, and we want to be a family, and . . ." Danielle took a breath, knowing she was rambling but wanting to have everything out in the open. "We're going to live in that old house down the street from where his parents live. We're going to fix it up, and—"

"Stop." Martha stood up, walked to the fireplace, and placed both hands on the mantel. After a few long moments, she turned around and faced Danielle. "You cannot ask Levi to do this."

Danielle's heart almost broke. She'd thought Martha might be happy, the one person who would share her joy about being a mother. "I didn't ask him." She squeaked the words out. "Not at first anyway. He asked me."

"Vera has told me that out of all her children, Levi is the most devout to the faith. And now you're telling me that he is going to leave everything he loves to marry you, a young woman who is pregnant with someone else's baby?"

Danielle started to sob.

"Honey, I'm not trying to hurt you, just stating a fact. Why would Levi do this?" Martha shook her head. "And why would you let him? It's a noble gesture, but it's a huge sacrifice. Do you realize how much?"

"Then I won't marry him!" Danielle jumped off the couch and faced Martha.

Arnold stood up and walked between the two women.

"Ladies, let's calm down. I have something to say about all this. Everyone sit down."

He spoke with such authority, Danielle and Martha did as instructed; Martha returned to her recliner, and Danielle went back to the couch. Arnold stayed standing, glancing back and forth between them, his eyes ultimately landing on Danielle.

"Do you love Levi, Danielle?"

She nodded.

"And he asked you to marry him?"

Danielle nodded again. "I even offered to become Amish, but Levi said no."

Arnold smiled at Martha. "Snookums, you're just going to have to let these young people make their own decisions. Remember, we're not in control . . . any more than Danielle and Levi are."

Martha folded her arms across her chest, scowling like a small child. "Yes, dear."

Arnold sat down beside Danielle on the couch. He lifted her chin, then kissed her on the cheek. "A baby is a blessing from the Lord, so however it happened, God has chosen this path for your life. But you still have free will, Danielle. Make good decisions."

Danielle hugged him, and by the time she eased away, Martha was on the other side of the couch, her arms outstretched. Danielle slowly fell into the woman's arms and cried as Martha stroked her hair.

"Aw, Danielle. I love you, honey. If this is really what you and Levi want, I'll help you however I can."

Danielle cried harder. She'd always known that Martha

loved her, but it was the first time she'd said it. "I love you too," she whispered.

Still stroking Danielle's hair, Martha sighed. "But ol' Vera is gonna come unhinged. You know that, right?"

LEVI WAS AT his cousin Eli's house first thing Saturday morning.

If anyone knew about complicated family stuff, it would be Eli. His first wife had died, and he'd raised six children by himself; then he married Katie Ann and now raised her son as his own.

"*Guder mariye*, Levi." Eli pushed the front door open, and the house smelled of freshly cooked bacon and homemade biscuits. Levi stepped over the threshold.

"*Guder mariye.* I'm sorry to come by so early, I just wanted to know if I could talk to you for a few minutes."

Eli grabbed his hat from the rack. "*Ya.* I was just heading out to the barn to load a dresser I finished and haul it to the store. Katie Ann already left with Jonas to go open the store before the Saturday rush." He smiled, motioning with his hand for Levi to follow him. "I could use a hand loading it."

Levi followed, closing the door behind him. Eli and Katie Ann had opened a shop at the front of their property not long after they'd gotten married a year ago. They'd named it Blessings and Such, and it had become popular with the *Englisch.* Eli's daughter Frieda helped Katie Ann run the shop. Eli stayed busy building furniture and tending the land.

After they loaded the dresser onto the small flatbed trailer

Eli had hooked up behind the buggy, he asked Levi what was on his mind.

Levi leaned against the fence separating the front yard from the rest of Eli's property. "I'm getting married."

Eli grinned. "Sarah Troyer?"

Levi knew this was going to be a common response. "Uh, *nee*. I'm marrying Danielle Kent."

His cousin's smile faded.

"The *Englisch* girl?" Eli pulled off his hat, scratched his forehead. "I thought I'd heard you were courting Sarah Troyer."

Levi looked at the ground as he kicked at the dirt with one foot. "I've taken her to a few singings." He looked back up at Eli. "But that's really all."

Eli walked to where Levi was standing and leaned against the fence beside him. Together they watched the sun rising above the Sangre de Cristo Mountains. Then Eli turned to face Levi. "Why are you marrying Danielle? Are you leaving the faith?"

Levi swallowed hard and nodded. "*Ya*."

They were quiet for a few moments.

Eli turned toward the gradual glow rising behind the mountain range. "Your parents must be mighty upset, no?" He kept looking forward.

"*Ya*."

Eli twisted to face Levi. "Is the girl with child?"

Levi was surprised he asked, but answered truthfully. "*Ya*, she is."

Eli faced forward again. "Will she consider our ways, study the *Ordnung*, and join our district?"

"*Nee*. Her faith is . . . is not as strong as it could be." Guilt fell over him for being ashamed of his future wife, but it didn't change the facts. "I feel called to marry her, Eli. I think it's the right thing to do."

Eli turned to face him, his eyebrows narrowed. "It is the right thing to do. It takes two to make a baby, *mei* boy. You are responsible for this *boppli* and your *fraa*. But this is not how God intended us to do things." He smiled briefly. "Marriage first. Then *bopplis*." His smile faded. "You must now make a home for your family—there is no choice in it. However, it saddens me that this will pull you from your faith. Are you sure Danielle won't consider converting? Maybe she needs a mentor, someone to teach her the *Ordnung*?"

Levi thought about how Danielle offered to do that very thing. But he knew in his heart that she wasn't ready to make a commitment like that. "It's not my child, Eli." He paused. "Danielle got pregnant by an Amish man in Alamosa."

Eli's eyes widened. "Then let that man do the right thing. He can choose to live Amish or *Englisch*." His voice grew louder.

"He told Danielle he didn't want a family or a baby." Levi looked at the ground again, feeling his cousin's eyes still on him. "He ran off. Left his parents a note that he didn't want to be Amish, and didn't even tell Danielle good-bye."

Eli shook his head. "Not much of a man."

"*Nee*. He's not."

"But why does this job of marrying Danielle and raising her child fall on you?"

Levi looked up, put his hands on his hips. "It just does. I know that I'm being called by God to do this. At first Danielle refused to marry me, but she's reconsidered, and . . ." Levi lowered his arms and hung his head, quiet for a long moment.

"I'm sure that this is my path to walk. But it doesn't mean I'm not afraid that I might be making a mistake."

"Then don't go through with it. At least wait until you're certain."

Levi swallowed hard and then shook his head. Fear and worry blocked the voice of God, and Levi knew he'd allowed himself to be consumed with both emotions lately.

Eli stroked his beard. "Why are you telling me all this?"

"You've been married twice. I thought that you might . . ."

"Understand? More than most?" He shook his head and cocked one bushy brow. "*Nee*, you are in uncharted territory, *mei* cousin. Even for me. Maybe you should talk to the bishop. You already told your folks?"

"*Ya, Mamm's* pretty upset." Levi paused. "I—I had wondered . . ."

"Spit it out. What is it?"

"I need to know if you love Katie Ann's *sohn* as much as your other *kinner*?" Levi drew in a breath. "I mean, since Jonas isn't yours."

Eli was quiet for a long while before he pointed to the front porch. "Let's sit."

Levi followed him to the rockers. They each sat down, and Eli looped his thumbs beneath his suspenders.

"Levi, listen to me closely, *sohn*." He paused, taking a deep breath. "Answering your question . . . *ya*, I *lieb* Jonas as much as *mei* other *kinner*. And if you wed Danielle, you will love the *boppli* as your very own. But this is not the issue. Leaving the faith is. If you have come to quiz my mind about loving a child, well . . . children are a blessing from God, however they might fall into our lives." He shook his head. "But leaving to live in the *Englisch* world is something I'm not sure you have thought through."

"But I'm not baptized. I have the right to choose." Even though Levi said the words with confidence, his heart hurt as each one left his lips.

"*Ya*, you do. It is your choice. But I would not be a *gut* friend and cousin to you if I did not warn you about this big decision." He faced Levi. "Do you love Danielle enough to give up all of this?" Eli waved a hand across the prairie in front of him, the house behind him. "A life within our community?"

Levi swallowed hard again as he recalled Danielle's tears, the kisses they'd shared. "I love her," he said softly. "I'm closer to her than I am to anyone."

"But do you love her in the marriage way? Are you committed to living in the *Englisch* world with her, raising her child as your own, and taking care of your family?"

Levi sighed, then stood up. "I have to go. I just wanted to know if you loved Jonas as much as your other children." He couldn't stand to hear any more negative thoughts about what he was getting ready to do. It was hard enough. He thanked his cousin, then made his way to his buggy.

Maybe it just wasn't in God's plan for him to be Amish.

# Eight

MARTHA WASN'T SURPRISED TO SEE THE MATRIARCH of the Detweiler household standing on the doorstep early Saturday morning. With dreaded anticipation of Vera's visit, Martha had gotten up early, dressed, and applied her makeup. She'd barely secured her butterfly clip when she heard three crisp knocks on the door. She was glad Arnold and Danielle had offered to do the grocery shopping, a task Martha didn't cherish.

"Come in, Vera," Martha said as she pulled the door wide.

Vera marched through the door with her jaw thrust forward and her lips pinched together. Her black apron was unusually wrinkled atop a dark purple dress, and strands of brown hair hung from beneath her prayer covering.

Martha closed the door and motioned for Vera to sit down on the couch, but Vera held her stiff position in the middle of the room.

"Please tell me that you are not happy about this situation with Levi and Danielle."

Martha folded into her recliner. "Good grief, Vera. Can

you please just sit down? Let's try and discuss this as the friends we are."

Vera huffed a bit, but finally took a seat, folding her hands in her lap as she sat on the edge of the couch. "I don't know what Danielle did to convince Levi to marry her, but—"

"No, no, no." Martha straightened in her chair and pointed a finger at Vera. "If you want to talk about this in a civil manner, Vera, then we will. But you will not come into my home and talk any smack about Danielle." It seemed fitting to toss one of Danielle's own words in Vera's direction. "Now, shall we start again?"

Vera took a deep breath. "Martha, they're not in *lieb*. They're friends. That doesn't make a marriage. You know that."

Martha knew Vera was right, but only partly. And she tried to keep in mind that Vera was hurting. "I know those two kids haven't been romantically involved, Vera. But they do love each other. And I think we've both always known that." Martha leaned back in her chair and crossed her legs. "You're upset because Levi is choosing not to be baptized and remain Amish."

Vera threw up her arms. "Of course I am. Levi has always wanted to abide by the *Ordnung* and raise his *kinner* in our faith, and I don't know what Danielle said to—" She stopped abruptly. "What are we going to do? Surely you're not happy about this either. Levi barely makes enough money to provide for himself, and Danielle is so young." She shook her head. "It wonders me why they're doing this. I thought Levi would end up marrying Sarah Troyer."

Martha rocked slightly in the chair. "Honestly, Vera, I'm not particularly happy about it. They're rushing into it."

"*Ya!* They are!" The hint of a smile touched Vera's lips.

"I wish they would wait." Martha shrugged. "But I do think some of the best marriages start out when two people are best friends first. I know that's not what you want to hear, but that's my thinking about all this. But the bottom line is that they're grown-ups. It's really up to them."

"Danielle is only eighteen, and I know you're not her mother, Martha, but you're the closest thing she has. She's still a baby."

Martha laughed. "Oh, give me a break, Vera. Your people are always getting married at eighteen, and sometimes even younger. So don't try to use that argument." Martha uncrossed her legs and leaned forward. "You can't control Levi. If he chooses to do this, then you can't stop him. I questioned Danielle about all of this and asked her if she realized what a sacrifice it was for Levi." Martha paused. "Did you know that Danielle offered to convert?"

"No. Levi didn't mention that. I asked him why they didn't wait a year or two and give Danielle time to learn the *Ordnung*. Remember how Lillian studied before she was baptized and married Samuel? I just wish they'd give it more time."

Martha twisted her mouth from one side to the other, shaking her head. "I guess they're in a hurry because of the baby."

"*What* baby?" Vera jumped off the couch as she grabbed her chest.

*Oops.* "Uh-oh. I guess I just assumed they mentioned that." Martha squeezed her eyes closed for a few seconds, then stood up and walked toward Vera. "Breathe, Vera. You're going to hyperventilate."

Once Vera did take a breath, she almost choked. Then she flopped back down on the couch. "A baby? I can't believe Levi wouldn't be more responsible than this. Didn't we teach him anything? How could he do this? And I thought they were only friends." She gasped. "And what about poor Sarah? Levi's been carting her to Sunday singings, and all the while he's been playing hanky-panky with Danielle."

"Oh boy." Martha covered her eyes with her hand. This was surely going to bring on one of her headaches later. She eased her hand away and took a deep breath. "Uh, Vera . . . the baby isn't exactly Levi's."

Vera's mouth pulled into a sour grin as her eyebrows lifted. "What do you mean, *exactly*? Either it is or it isn't."

Martha sat back down and shifted uneasily in her chair. "Danielle was dating a guy in Alamosa." She pointed a finger at Vera. "One of *your* people. He got her pregnant and then ran off. He decided he doesn't want to be Amish *or* a father."

Vera just sat with her mouth open, so Martha went on.

"Vera, there is a baby coming into the world, a blessing, and even though this isn't what we expected for the kids, it's—"

"How dare you." Vera stood up and walked toward Martha. "Don't act like Danielle is your daughter. She's a runaway who broke into your home and you took her in. I have been raising Levi for twenty-two years." She swiped at her eyes, but that didn't soften the anger in her voice. "He is my *sohn*, and everything we have hoped and dreamed for him is slipping away because of an *Englisch* girl who got herself pregnant. Levi only wants to save his friend. And you are willing to let him!" She threw her hands in the air again.

Martha stood up, wishing Vera would just keep her seat. This up-and-down business was killing her back. "You know, Vera, I'm going to let you get away with most of that because I know how upset you are. But I love Danielle as if she were my own. She's had a hard life. You know her history. Perhaps . . . perhaps this is the new start she needs. Can you for one moment try to picture the two of them together, raising a child? They'll be right down the street. They'll probably still go to the Amish worship service, and you can't shun Levi because he hasn't been baptized."

Vera stared at Martha for a long while. "You think you know everything about our ways because we have opened our hearts to you. But you don't know nearly as much as you think. And if Levi marries Danielle, he is no longer my *sohn*."

Martha put both hands on her hips and glared at Vera. "For a group of people who claim that only God can judge, you sure are full of it this morning, Vera. You'd disown your own son because he didn't do what you want?"

Vera took a deep breath. "*Nee*. I would disown my son because he walked away from the Lord, whether he realizes it or not, by being with this girl. She doesn't have a strong faith, and he is unequally yoked with her."

"I dislike that term, Vera. Unequally yoked. We are all the same in the Lord's eyes."

Vera turned around and walked to the door.

"Oh, Vera, don't go. Let's talk this through."

But Vera slammed the door behind her.

Martha opened the door and yelled the first thing that came to her mind. "You're not acting very Amish, Vera!"

DANIELLE'S STOMACH GROWLED as she and Arnold unloaded groceries. Arnold had tried to do the task on his own, but Danielle assured him she was quite able to help.

But that was Arnold, always chivalrous. She smiled to herself. *Like Levi.*

They were making their last trip inside when Levi pulled up in his buggy. Arnold went on ahead, and Danielle waited for Levi to hitch his horse to the fence post.

"You're just in time for lunch."

Levi took the bag of groceries she was holding and followed her toward the house. "Did you tell Arnold and Martha—about us?"

Danielle turned around, and Levi's face was pale as he slowed his steps. "Yes. They're okay." She faced him on the porch before they went inside. "What about your parents?" She cringed, knowing Vera probably freaked out.

Levi took a deep breath. "It could have gone better." He offered up a shy smile that seemed forced to Danielle.

"We don't have to do this, Levi." Martha's words echoed in Danielle's head. *"It's a noble gesture, but it's a huge sacrifice. Do you realize how much?"* She bit her lip, thinking they'd covered everything related to their choice, but she wanted Levi to be sure.

"I want to marry you, Danielle. I've thought about those kisses all day." When he smiled, it seemed genuine.

"Me too." Danielle could feel her cheeks warming, but she wasn't sure how to tell him that the kisses felt awkward. She'd barely slept the night before. She'd tried, over and over, to picture them married, and as much as she wanted to, she couldn't. Every time she pictured them sleeping side by side in the same bed—doing anything more than sleeping—it seemed unnatural. She and Levi loved each other, but would that ever grow into the kind of love she'd always dreamed of? She wondered if Levi felt the same way. Before all this happened, she could talk to him about anything. Now things between them seemed . . . strange. She pulled the door open and went inside, Levi following.

"Oh boy," Martha said as she and Arnold unpacked and put away the groceries. "I had a visit from your mother this morning, Levi." She turned to face them both, holding a can of soup in each hand. "And I'm afraid the cat is out of the bag. I didn't know Vera didn't know about the baby." She shook her head as her eyebrows lifted in apology. "Gonna be a rough time for you, Levi."

"Yes, ma'am," Levi said with a sigh. He put the bag of groceries on the kitchen table, his own brows drawn inward. "She'll be okay." He smiled at Danielle, and the way he said it reassured her. Maybe they really were doing the right thing. She thought about what Sue said, and about how much she'd resented not having a father. She didn't want her own child to grow up missing a dad.

Martha turned around again, facing them both. "I'm going to support both of you, but I can't live with myself unless I ask this." She raised her chin and stared hard at Levi. "Son, are you sure this is what you want to do?"

"*Ya*. I'm sure." Levi didn't hesitate. He looked at Danielle. "Are we still on for next Saturday in that little church you visit?"

"I'd like that." Danielle smiled as she fought the worry building in her heart.

Arnold washed his hands, then extended a hand to Levi. "I wish you all the best." Then he walked to Danielle and kissed her on the cheek. "And you too, dear." He winked. "But now I need a sandwich."

Martha chuckled. "That's my Arnold." She pulled out a

chair at the kitchen table. "Sit down, dear. I'll make you your lunch." She pointed to Levi. "You sit too."

After they all ate a ham and cheese sandwich and chips, Levi asked Danielle if she'd like to go see the house he was planning to buy for them. Danielle knew what house he was talking about, but she'd never been inside. The place had been for sale for a long time.

As they pulled up in Danielle's car, she swallowed hard. You could barely see the porch for all the high weeds, and the house was white . . . at one time, barely visible from a few splotches of paint left along the clapboard siding. It seemed bigger to Danielle the closer they got.

"It needs a lot of work, but it's all I can afford." Levi led the way up to the front porch. "I can make it something nice, though."

"How many acres?"

"Ten." Levi tested the porch steps before he motioned for Danielle to follow. "I'll have to get a mortgage, but I have enough to put down. And with the money I make working with *Daed* . . ." Levi stopped, and Danielle realized what he was thinking.

"Surely you'll still be able to work with your father? That won't change, will it?" She tugged on his shirt until he turned around. When he did, he looked lost, like a little boy in man form. "Levi, I'm not doing this if you are going to lose your relationships with your family. I can't let you do this if that's how it's going to be."

Levi's expression hardened as he stared into her eyes. "Danielle, I'm marrying you. I'm going to be a *gut* father to the *boppli*. This is what God is calling me to do."

"I don't want to be a burden." She hung her head, but he quickly lifted her chin and smiled.

"Nothing about marrying you is a burden. Now, let's check out our house. I've been in here plenty of times. The door is never locked."

Danielle followed Levi inside, her eyes growing round as she looked around the living room. Bringing her hands to her chest, she wondered how they would ever live here. Martha's house was outdated, but it was luxurious compared to this. Even Danielle and her mother had never lived anywhere like this. The place looked like it should be condemned. One window in the living room had a missing pane, which immediately made Danielle wonder what animals might have already taken up residence in the house. A layer of thick dirt coated the wood floors; it was hard to tell what condition they were in. In the far corner, there was a rocking chair lying on its side, missing one arm. The walls were white, the paint chipping.

"It's in rough shape, I know. But I've always dreamed of fixing this place up." Levi smiled as he eyed the living room like he'd won the lottery. Danielle clutched her stomach. "It's got three bedrooms. Come see." Levi motioned for her to follow him. She tiptoed down a hallway and watched him kick at the bottom of a door before forcing it open.

"This is the master bedroom."

Danielle forced a smile, noticing it was in the same condition as the rest of the house. "It's big." She walked around, looking for a closet . . . but then a bigger issue caused her stomach to lurch. "Levi?"

He walked closer to her. "I know it's a wreck, but we can get it clean enough to live in while we fix it up. This is okay, isn't it? I'll work hard to make it nice. We can do this together."

Bless his heart. He sounded so hopeful. "There's no electricity," she finally said, her voice squeaking toward the end.

"I know. It's pretty old. I don't know of any Amish family who ever lived here since the district is so new, but whoever lived here didn't have electricity."

She asked the burning question. "We'll have electricity, right?"

Levi scratched his forehead, frowning. "I can't really afford that. And I've never had electricity anyway. Can you live without it? At least for a while?" Levi smiled. "As soon as I can afford it, I'll have *Daed* help me install some solar panels. That would be cheaper than having it all wired for electricity, and it's allowed by the bishop." His smile faded. "Not that it really matters, huh?"

Danielle was quiet as she tried to envision her new married life. *No television? Blow-dryer? Radio?* How was she going to charge her cell phone? She brought a hand to her chest. "How long?"

Levi took off his hat and scratched his head. "I don't know. I guess I didn't give it that much thought. I always figured I'd marry an Amish girl . . ." He shrugged. "If it's that important to you, I'll try to borrow more money from the bank."

She shook her head. "No. I don't want you doing that. I can live without it." She poked him playfully on the arm. "For a while."

"Let me show you the rest of the house."

Levi walked her down the hallway and showed her the other two bedrooms, and there was one bathroom at the end of the hallway. Good-sized bedrooms, but both were also in need of an overhaul. She picked the larger of the two rooms to be the baby's room.

"The kitchen is a *gut* size." Levi walked around, eyeing the old gas range. There wasn't a refrigerator. "Looks like the stove will be okay for now."

It looked a hundred years old to Danielle, like the rest of the house, and unlike any stove she'd ever seen. She eased back into the living room, glad there was a big fireplace. She'd practically frozen last winter, her first year in Canaan. Despite all her money, Martha was frugal when it came to air-conditioning and heat, and Martha's small fireplace didn't heat the upstairs very well.

Levi faced her, hands on his hips. "Don't look so worried. I'll have it livable by the time we get married."

It sounded strange to hear him say the word *married*, but she just nodded, unable to fathom how this old house could possibly be fit for human habitation in a week.

Or how she was going to survive in a home without electricity.

# Nine

VERA'S STOMACH CHURNED ALL THROUGH THE quilting party on Tuesday, knowing she needed to talk to Sarah. When Sarah finally thanked Lillian for hosting the party and began saying her good-byes, Vera seized the opportunity to speak with her privately.

"I'll help you carry your things," Vera said as she quickly reached for the casserole dish that Sarah was trying to balance on one hip while positioning her quilting basket on the other. "Betsy, I'll be right back." She pointed a finger at her young daughter, hoping Betsy would behave until she returned.

Vera was running out of time to put a stop to this ridiculous wedding her son had planned for Saturday. *Just four days away!*

"*Danki*, Vera." Sarah smiled as Vera handed her the dish when they arrived at her buggy. Sarah didn't have a clue what was going on. Vera hated to be the one to break the news to her, but she needed Sarah's help. Telling the tale as quickly as she could, she watched Sarah's eyes well up with tears.

"I'm sorry, dear. But I need to know the name of the

boy in Alamosa. I need to visit his family. This is not Levi's responsibility."

Sarah sniffled. "His name is Matthew Lapp." She paused, shaking her head. "But why would Levi marry Danielle unless he loved her? He must love her." A tear rolled down Sarah's cheek.

"*Nee, nee.*" Vera took a deep breath. "He thinks he's had a calling from God to marry Danielle, but I believe this is the devil's work . . . calling him away from his faith. Matthew Lapp's family needs to know the truth. Maybe there's hope that Matthew will come forth and marry Danielle."

"I don't understand." Sarah dabbed at her eyes, then looked up at Vera. "I guess that's why he never invited me to do anything else."

"Levi is just very confused, and we've got to get that boy right before he messes up his life and walks away from the Lord." She leaned closer to Sarah. "For now, let's not mention this to anyone. Hopefully I can talk to the Lapp family, and maybe they can make Matthew come to his senses and take responsibility for this child." Vera raised an eyebrow. "And, Sarah . . . I implore you to do what you can to stop Levi from making the biggest mistake of his life."

AN HOUR LATER—and against her husband's wishes—Vera climbed into the backseat of Wayne's car. Their *Englisch* friend provided rides back and forth from Canaan to Alamosa for not much more than the cost of gasoline. Vera handed him a basket of blueberry muffins, the way she always did when he drove her somewhere.

"Wayne, I'm sorry to trouble you, but when we get into Alamosa, I'm going to need to ask around until I find the Lapp family." Vera eased back against the seat.

"No need," Wayne said as he reached for a muffin. "It's a small Amish district, and I drive the Lapp family sometimes. The wife's name is Anna Marie. Husband is John. And they have one son." He took a bite of the muffin, crumbs spilling into his lap.

"Matthew? Is that the son's name?"

Wayne finished chewing. "I believe so, although I've never met him."

Vera cringed, knowing how painful all this must be for Anna Marie Lapp, especially since Matthew was her only son. She wasn't looking forward to the visit, but it was her only hope to stop the wedding.

Twenty minutes later, Wayne pulled off a gravel road and into a driveway several miles outside of Alamosa. He stopped in front of a newly constructed white home. "This is it."

"I won't be long." Vera opened the car door and stepped out.

The Lapp home was a bit fancy for Vera's taste on the outside. There weren't any flower beds or shrubs yet, but the wind chimes and hummingbird feeders hanging around the porch were much too ornate with bright colors and chrome enclosures. The two rocking chairs on the porch were white, but there was a small, glass-topped table in between them that also felt quite lavish. Vera grimaced as she walked up the steps to the front door. Too many luxuries weren't good for any family. It sent a bad message to their young people—that it was okay to partake of the ways of the *Englisch. And their girls* . . . She gave her head a quick shake and squelched the thought.

After two knocks, a woman opened the door, and Vera's dread doubled over the task at hand. Anna Marie Lapp was dressed almost exactly the same as Vera—in a dark brown dress, black apron, and white prayer covering. But the woman had dark circles underneath sad eyes, a pinkish nose, and a tissue in one hand.

"Can I help you?" she asked from the other side of a screened door. Her partial smile couldn't hide the sadness in her voice.

"I'm Vera Detweiler from Canaan. It wonders me if I might talk with you for a few minutes?"

Anna Marie nodded, and Vera stepped backward so Anna Marie could open the screen door. "Come in. I'm Anna Marie Lapp."

Vera crossed the threshold into the living room, the smell of fresh paint hanging in the air. Anna Marie closed the door behind her. A dark blue couch and two matching recliners circled a heavily etched oak coffee table with a vase full of artificial flowers. Vera couldn't fault her for that. Weather conditions in the San Luis Valley made it difficult to grow just about anything unless you were familiar with the climate changes. A fancy oak hutch was against the wall, filled mostly with books, but there was one picture on the shelf of a boy. He was dressed in Amish clothes and looked to be around Levi's age. *Matthew?* Even though pictures weren't allowed, Vera knew that sometimes youth in their *rumschpringe* would pose for pictures. But for Anna Marie to display such a picture was inappropriate. She thought briefly if she would bend such a rule if Levi ran away.

"I was just making some coffee. If you'll join me in the

kitchen, I'll pour us both a cup." Anna Marie forced another smile and stuffed the tissue in the pocket of her apron.

"*Danki.*" Vera followed her into the kitchen. The counter-tops were a faint shade of yellow with decorative glass knobs on the cabinets, and the refrigerator and stove were shiny white—propane, like hers, Vera assumed. She quickly scanned the room to see if there was any electricity. There wasn't.

Anna Marie poured two cups of coffee and motioned for Vera to take a seat in one of the four high-back chairs sur-rounding a small table in the middle of the room. "What brings you to Alamosa, Vera?"

Vera accepted her coffee and sat down. She circled the rim of her coffee cup with her finger. "It's about your son, Matthew."

Anna Marie brought a hand to her chest as her eyes began to tear. "Please tell me that nothing has happened to him. He's supposed to be at our cousin John's *haus* in Indiana."

"*Nee, nee.* Nothing has happened," Vera said, shaking her head. She took a deep breath, knowing the blow she was about to deliver was selfish. But didn't Anna Marie deserve to know that she had a grandchild on the way? "Matthew used to spend time with an *Englisch* girl. Danielle, right?"

Anna Marie weighed the comment with a critical squint. "*Ya.* We always worried that he would venture into the *Englisch* world to live with her." She lowered her head for a moment, then looked back up. "But he ended up leaving her too and running off to Indiana to live with our cousins who no longer live Amish."

"I know how upsetting it can be to have one of your own leave the faith." Vera took a deep breath.

"Do you?" Anna Marie's voice had such hope in it, clueless

that Vera's mission was not to befriend her or offer her consolation. "Has this happened to one of your *kinner*?" She paused. "And are you a friend of Danielle's?"

Instinctively, Vera shook her head and avoided the first part of the question. Vera knew that she needed to handle this situation carefully; otherwise, she could end up as equally destroyed as Anna Marie. "I know Danielle, but I wouldn't call us friends."

Anna Marie narrowed her eyebrows. "What is the purpose of your visit, Vera?" She took a quick sip of coffee. "I'm glad to make your acquaintance, but you must have traveled here to speak with me for a reason, no?"

"*Ya*." Vera took a deep breath, then she looked up at Anna Marie, whose curious hazel eyes met hers. "I'm afraid I have some shocking news." She forced herself to go on. "*Mei sohn* is going to wed Danielle this Saturday coming."

"*Ach*, Vera. I'm so sorry." Anna Marie reached over and briefly touched Vera's hand. "There is nothing more painful than to lose one of our own to the outside world. Will he still be nearby? Matthew is such a long way from us, and . . ." She pulled the tissue from her pocket and blew her nose. "I'm sorry. *Mei* husband—John—and I are just so upset."

"Maybe there is a way that you can convince Matthew to come back home?" Vera said hopefully.

"Our boy made his choice. He wasn't baptized yet, so he was able to do that. But we are confused about why he felt the need to run so far from us. Our hearts are broken." She sniffled. "He's our only child. We were unable to have more."

Vera reached over and put her hand over hers. "He is running from something else, Anna Marie." She paused for a long while, keeping her eyes locked with the woman's. "Danielle is pregnant, and the baby is Matthew's."

Anna Marie jerked her hand out from under Vera's. "*Nee.* It isn't true."

Vera nodded, but gave Anna Marie time to let the news soak in before she spoke. "And *mei sohn* Levi is marrying her because Matthew . . ." She paused. "Well, he left her. And Danielle and Levi are friends. Levi is trying to do an honorable thing, but I thought that maybe if you talked to Matthew that—"

"*Ach*, I see." Anna Marie stiffened. "You are here to save your own *sohn*."

Vera stared back at Anna Marie long and hard. "Can you blame me?"

Dawning realization shone across Anna Marie's face, even as she continued to weep. "I'm going to be a *mammi*?"

Vera nodded.

"And Matthew knows about the *boppli*?" She dabbed at her eyes with the tissue.

Vera nodded again.

"How could he do this? How could *mei* boy shirk his responsibility like this? Danielle could have been baptized, and we would have accepted her and the *boppli* into our lives."

Vera thought for a moment. "Maybe he is just afraid, worried his family will be shamed since they are with child and not married. Would he listen to you?"

Anna Marie shook her head. "I don't know. But I will write him a long letter about this matter."

There was no time for that type of correspondence. "Maybe you should call him, tell him that another man is about to marry Danielle on Saturday and that he plans to raise the child as his own. Maybe that will bring him home to do the right thing."

She nodded, recognizing the urgency. "I will travel to our *Englisch* friends up the road and use their phone."

Vera was surprised that Anna Marie didn't have a cell phone since her home seemed more modern than most. Or at the least a nearby phone shanty. She stood up. "I'm sorry to bring you this news. But I hope you can understand why I came."

Anna Marie stood up too and sniffled. "I do. *Danki.* How do I contact you?"

Vera reached into her apron pocket and pulled out a piece of paper. "Here is our phone number. The phone is in the barn, but there is an answering machine if I miss your call."

Anna Marie took the piece of paper, then followed Vera out of the kitchen to the front door. "I will call you this evening. I must spend much time in prayer, then I will call Matthew."

Vera nodded. "God's peace to you."

"And to you."

Anna Marie closed the door, and Vera made her way down the porch steps and back to the car where Wayne was patiently waiting. She would pray that Anna Marie could get through to Matthew . . . or that Sarah could reach Levi.

*Please . . . either one, Lord.*

SARAH WAS HOLED up in her room—fuming. She'd had her choice of every eligible suitor in their district. Even though there were only seven young men within her age group, she knew she could have any of them. But she'd chosen Levi . . .

*How is Vera faring with Matthew's mother?* She paced back and forth.

Sitting down on her bed, she brought her knees to her chest and wrapped her arms around her legs, shivering—partly from the chill in her room and partly because she was so mad she could spit.

Sarah had never liked Danielle Kent, even before Sarah found out that Levi was going to marry her. *What a waste of a good Amish man.* Danielle dressed provocatively and tossed her hair in a proud manner. It was no wonder she'd gotten herself pregnant. But to drag Levi into her mess was just inexcusable. She puffed out a breath of frustration, then let go of her legs and swung them over the side of the bed, thankful that Lizzie was downstairs. Sarah was too old to be sharing a bedroom with the twelve-year-old, but since Sarah and Lizzie were the only girls out of the seven children, she didn't have much of a choice.

Sarah slid her black leather shoes back and forth against the wooden floor, thinking.

Vera's words echoed in her mind. *"Do what you can to stop Levi from making the biggest mistake of his life."*

Sarah could feel her bottom lip twitching as her mind whirled with thoughts that God wouldn't approve of. Or would He? Surely God wouldn't want Levi ruining his life in this way. She couldn't believe that she wasn't just losing Levi, but she was losing him to an *Englisch* girl who was pregnant with someone else's child. There had to be some way to make Levi change his mind, to get him to call off this wedding. And she didn't have much time to figure it out.

*Think, Sarah, think.* She tapped her finger to her chin. Sarah knew that it was wrong to be vain, but just the same, she knew that she was prettier than Danielle. What was it about Danielle that would make Levi want to marry her, especially under these circumstances? Maybe he found her exciting because she was *Englisch*?

Sarah had been in her *rumschpringe* for three years, but she'd never taken full advantage of the freedoms that the running-around period allowed for. She'd seen a few movies, but she'd never worn blue jeans or other *Englisch* clothes, nor snuck out of the house, nor done some of the other things that her friends had done. *Am I boring? Compared to Danielle?* But after some thought, she realized that being more *Englisch* wasn't the answer. She needed to somehow lure Levi back into the Amish world, make him never want to leave. Not even for a pregnant *Englisch* girl he was trying to save from single motherhood.

She thrust backward on her bed, slinging her arms to her sides, as she wondered what Danielle did to entice Levi into her world. And to *marry* her. Maybe she should have thrown herself more at Levi, as Danielle surely had. But Levi was so shy, she hadn't even been able to get him to kiss her. She had to find some way to make Levi see Danielle for the person she really was. Although, if being pregnant by another man and unmarried wasn't enough for him to see . . . Sarah wasn't sure what would be. She was sitting back up on the bed when the door to her room eased open.

"*Mamm* says come downstairs. We're having devotion." Lizzie put her hand on her hip like the bossy twelve-year-old she was. "Now."

Sarah waved a hand at Lizzie. "Get out of here. I'll be there in a minute."

"It's my room too."

Sarah closed her eyes, took in a deep breath, then blew it out slowly. "Lizzie . . . I'll be there in a minute."

Lizzie slammed the door, and Sarah could hear her sister's feet pounding down the stairs.

But then the lantern in Sarah's head ignited, and she knew the one thing that she had that Danielle did not.

*Faith.*

Martha might drag Danielle to worship services on occasion, but Sarah knew that the girl didn't have much of a relationship with God . . . or so she'd heard from several folks, including Levi himself. And Vera. That's what Sarah would use to her advantage to make Levi see what a big mistake he was making.

And if that didn't work, Sarah had another idea . . .

*Ten*

DANIELLE FOLLOWED MARTHA'S LEAD AND SHOOK
the preacher's hand, grateful that the man had agreed to per-
form their wedding ceremony.

Danielle looked at her watch. In less than three hours, she
and Martha had reserved the church, hired caterers for the
reception to be held at their house, bought Danielle a dress,
and ordered a small bouquet and boutonniere for the occasion.

As she and Martha climbed into Martha's car, Danielle
touched her stomach. She'd been surprised that she had to get
a dress one size larger than usual. But she was pleased with
the simple ivory, knee-length dress that she and Martha had
surprisingly both loved. Danielle hoped Levi would like it too.
Right now, everything in her life seemed surreal.

"You and Levi will go get your marriage license tomorrow, right?" Martha pulled out of the church parking lot, and
Danielle settled back against the seat.

"Yep."

"And, Danielle ... you're *sure* about all this?" Martha twisted
briefly to face her, pushing some hideous red sunglasses up on

her nose. The woman asked her the same question at least four times a day.

"I'm sure." Danielle kept her eyes in front of her. Martha's driving made her nervous. And Martha had the same complaint about Danielle's driving. They always battled over who would drive, but Martha won this morning. "Did you hear any more from Vera?"

Martha tapped her thumbs against the steering wheel. "Hmm . . . funny you should mention that. I haven't heard a word from her, which means she must be up to something. You and Levi marrying has rocked her world, and I doubt she's sitting around sewing you a wedding quilt."

Danielle leaned against the headrest and closed her eyes. Her future mother-in-law would undoubtedly make life miserable for her, but she sure hoped that things would somehow be okay between Levi and his mother. By now, his sister Emily and her family knew about the wedding, and Jacob and Beth Ann knew too. Everyone would likely be polite about it, but Danielle knew they all had to be upset that Levi was marrying outside of the faith. Danielle thought about her own mother. She'd toyed with the idea of calling her, telling her that she was getting married, that she was going to be a grandmother. But an unfamiliar sense of protection washed over Danielle for the life growing inside her. She didn't want her mother around her child.

"Danielle, I'm going to tell you something. And I hope you're listening."

"I'm listening." Danielle opened her eyes and turned to face Martha.

"Levi has a strong faith, and—"

"Martha," Danielle interrupted, slapping one hand to her

knee. "I *know*. We've had this conversation already. I'm not going to do anything to mess up Levi's faith."

They were quiet for a few minutes before Martha spoke up again. "God is here for you. Even in the middle of all this messiness. You just have to reach out to Him." She turned to Danielle again as they pulled into the driveway at home and gave her a pat on the leg, smiling.

*Then where has He been for the last eighteen years? Standing on the sidelines while my mother beat me? When my father died? When Matthew got me pregnant?*

Levi could believe what he wanted to. But if that was all that God had to offer, Danielle didn't need any more from Him.

VERA SLAMMED THE dinner plates down on the table Tuesday night, fury building inside of her. Surely Anna Marie had gotten hold of her son by now and talked some sense into him. But just in case, Vera's backup plan was on her way. She'd just put the last plate on the table when Betsy walked into the kitchen.

"Is Sarah coming for supper so she can try to talk Levi out of marrying Danielle?" Betsy opened the refrigerator and stared inside.

Vera stopped what she was doing and eyed her daughter. "Betsy, don't stand there with the refrigerator open. And what in the world made you say that?" Vera moved toward the stove and stirred the pot of stew she had simmering, taking a deep breath, hoping that Betsy wouldn't say such things over supper. Sarah was her last hope, and she'd already figured it out. The way to Levi's heart was through his faith.

"I know you don't like Danielle, and you want Levi to marry Sarah. But I really like Danielle." Betsy pulled the rhubarb jam and a jar of chowchow from the refrigerator and placed them on the table. She twisted the top from the chowchow and made a face the way she always did. Her youngest daughter didn't like the pickled vegetables that were served with lunch and supper.

Vera put the lid back on the stew before turning to face young Betsy. "I have never said that, Betsy. And you best mind your manners tonight. Saying such things will only upset your *bruder.*"

"Did you know that fifty percent of first marriages in the *Englisch* world end in divorce?" Betsy tapped a finger to her chin and smiled. "But I don't think that will happen to Danielle and Levi."

*Lord, give me strength.* Vera closed her eyes for a moment, sighed, then opened her eyes and stared at her daughter. "Betsy, where on God's green earth do you learn of such things?" She shook her head, walked to Betsy, and straightened her *kapp,* which was lopsided.

Betsy eased away frowning, pushing strands of blond hair away from her face. Then she shrugged. "I heard it from Mr. Parsons at the hardware store."

"Don't believe everything you hear," Vera mumbled as she checked the rolls in the oven. Although, she suspected such a statistic might actually be true.

"Are you saying Mr. Parsons lied?"

Vera closed the oven door and spun around. "I didn't say that."

"Then how do you know it's not true?"

"Betsy!" Vera stomped a foot, but then was thankful for a knock at the door. "That must be Sarah. She offered to come a bit early to help me with supper. Betsy, go let her in." She gave Betsy a gentle push toward the living room. "And remember what I said. Mind your manners tonight."

A minute later, Sarah walked into the kitchen carrying a chocolate pie.

"Are you comfortable with what we discussed?" Vera felt guilt flood over her like a rushing river.

But Sarah smiled. "*Ya.* I am."

LEVI WAS SURPRISED to see Sarah in the kitchen when he and his father walked in after work. "Sarah. How'd you get here?"

Sarah smiled at him as she placed a pan of rolls on the table. "*Ach, mei bruder* brought me. I saw your *mamm* earlier today, and she invited me to supper."

His mother rounded the table, kissed Levi on the cheek, and said, "I told Sarah you could drive her home after we eat. No need her traveling in her buggy alone at night when it's not necessary."

Levi forced a smile. The last thing he felt like doing later was getting the horse and buggy back out and driving Sarah home in this cold weather. "Sure."

He pulled out his chair at the kitchen table and sat down. It didn't take an overly smart man to figure out what was going on. It was likely *Mamm's* plan to get Levi to cancel the wedding. That was never going to happen, but Levi figured he'd play along. He loved his mother, but sometimes she didn't know when to stop meddling. Levi had thought that maybe she was coming to accept the idea that he and Danielle were going to be a family. *So much for that.*

Sarah sat down beside Levi. Betsy sat across from them, and his parents were at each end. After the blessing, Betsy was the first one to speak. "Are you going to Levi's wedding?" Betsy smiled across the table at Sarah, whose cheeks flushed a rosy pink right away. Levi quickly stuffed a piece of roll in his mouth so he didn't burst out laughing. *This is what you get, Mamm.*

"I . . . uh . . ." Sarah dabbed at her mouth with her napkin, then *Mamm* rescued her.

"Betsy, it'll just be family at Levi's small wedding." *Mamm* was three shades of red as she spoke, and she aimed for control of the conversation. "So, Sarah, how are things going at the bakery? Aren't you working at Abbey's now?"

"*Ya.*" Sarah flashed a perfect smile in *Mamm's* direction. "Only five or ten hours per week, but I like it. I love to bake."

"I know we're looking forward to that chocolate pie you brought." *Mamm* grinned, winking at Sarah.

Levi shifted uneasily, wondering what the two women were plotting. He looked at his father for any hint of what was to come, but his father just shrugged.

SARAH WAS THANKFUL when Vera sent Betsy upstairs to bathe and dress for bed. It had become quite obvious how much Levi's little sister liked Danielle, especially when she said that Danielle was the prettiest girl she'd ever seen. She'd mentioned the wedding three more times too, and Sarah found herself wondering what she was doing here. *Am I crazy? Is this right?* But every time a doubt shot through her, confirmation soothed it. It was best for them all if Levi stayed where he belonged. It was her duty to see this through. Still, she was glad to say good night to busybody Betsy.

"I guess I should be heading home." Sarah stood up, and when she did, so did Levi and his father. She turned to Levi's mother. "*Danki*, Vera, for such a *gut* meal. I'd like to help you clean up before I go."

"*Nee, nee.*" Vera waved a hand in the air. "Let Levi drive you home before it gets any colder outside." She stood up, walked to Sarah, and gave her a hug. "We're so happy you came for supper. Give *mei* best to your *mamm* and family."

LEVI FOLLOWED SARAH to the hat rack by the door and waited for her to get her black bonnet and cape on, then he bundled himself up in his black coat and gloves. This first day of June had been in the 50s. Levi would be glad when the nights started to warm up like the days were slowly doing.

"I hope you don't mind taking me home." Sarah tied her bonnet strings under her chin. "Your *mudder* seemed so excited for me to come for supper." Sarah smiled, dropping her arms to her sides. "I just couldn't say no."

"No problem." Levi opened the door but then turned. "You might as well wait here while I get the horse hitched to the buggy. No need for you to be out in the cold."

"I don't mind."

Before Levi had time to argue, Sarah followed him to the barn. She even helped him get Chester hitched to the buggy.

After he'd helped Sarah into the buggy, Levi walked around

and got in himself. All the while, he couldn't help but wonder if he'd ever ride in a buggy again after Saturday. Would he purchase a car? Would Danielle drive them around everywhere? Would he wave to family and friends traveling by buggy as he zipped by them in a heated automobile? Could he keep his buggy and Chester? Did everything have to change? So many things that he hadn't had time to think about . . .

Levi looked up through the plastic weather shield in front of him, thankful for the protection from the wind. He wondered how many billions of stars were out there, but at least a few million seemed to be shining down on Canaan tonight. He was going to miss the peacefulness of buggy rides and stargazing, except maybe when the temperatures dropped well below freezing.

He lost himself in the *clippity-clop* of Chester's hooves, a sound so familiar that Levi knew he would hear it in his sleep for the rest of his life, even if he were traveling by car in the future.

"I love this time of year," Sarah said softly as she leaned forward to look at the stars. "I love when the seasons change. And soon it will be summer." She leaned back against the seat, closer to Levi than ever. And when he turned to glance at her, she lifted her chin, clearly offering her lush lips for a kiss. She was so close, he could feel her sweet breath on his face. He quickly faced forward, blinking rapidly. He'd never kissed Sarah, but he probably would have in time. *Sarah would have seen to that.* He fought a smirk. He'd met few Amish girls so forward.

His life would have been much simpler if he'd just stayed on course and followed his Amish upbringing. Even if he hadn't married Sarah, he was certain there would have been another Amish woman in his future. They would have married the way his parents had, in an Amish ceremony that would have lasted all day, then had lots of *kinner* and raised them all according to the *Ordnung*. Levi wondered how he and Danielle would raise the baby. Would the child adhere to any of the Amish traditions that Levi cherished? There was nothing more glorious than an Amish barn-raising. Would their child ever have an opportunity to participate in one, to know how it felt for an entire community to erect a barn in one day? Would their children have a love of the land, run barefoot through the fields, milk cows, take turns cranking the handle for homemade ice cream, churn their own butter, and still keep things simple, even though they weren't Amish? His mind was awhirl when Sarah touched him on the arm.

"Are you hearing me, Levi? You seem a million miles away." She rubbed his arm for a moment. "But I guess that's to be expected when your wedding is only a few days away."

Levi's heart flipped in his chest. He and Danielle were supposed to get their marriage license tomorrow, and by this time next week, he'd be a married man. A married man living in the *Englisch* world. It gave him a strange sort of comfort that their house wouldn't have electricity for a while, even though he knew it was a disturbing thought for his bride-to-be. But Levi knew he was going to need to ease into the sort of comforts that Danielle was used to. He just hoped she'd be patient with him.

Sarah sighed petulantly and edged away, dropping her hand.

"I'm sorry, Sarah. You're right. I am a bit lost in my own thoughts. What did you say?" He glanced in her direction. The headlights on the buggy cast enough of a glow that he could see her ivory skin, her pink lips slightly parted in a smile, and her eyes searching his. She was a beautiful woman, no doubt. Levi had wondered, particularly over the past few days, why he didn't feel anything when he was with her. Not the way he did around Danielle. With Danielle, he'd always been comfortable, loved her as a friend . . . but now that they were getting married, his stomach flipped every time he thought about her. He couldn't quite get a handle on why that was, since they'd always just been friends, but Levi could feel something changing. Or was it just fear? Was he really interpreting God's calling correctly?

*All I know is that my stomach never flips around Sarah.*

"I was just thinking about you leaving here." Sarah eased her hand around his arm and lowered her chin. "I'm happy for you, Levi." She paused as she looked back at him, and Levi glanced at her again. She blinked several times before she spoke, and Levi could see the tears in the corners of her eyes. "I'm just incredibly sad that you're leaving your faith."

Her words were like a punch to the gut. Levi sat taller. "I'm not leaving my *faith*. I can take it with me wherever I go." He stared at her, needing her to agree with him. She—and his mother—made it sound like he was walking away from God and everything he'd ever believed in. Instead, he felt closer to Him than ever.

Sarah lowered her head again and dabbed at one eye with the back of her glove. Then she looked back up at him, smiling a little. "Okay."

"What do you mean? You say 'okay' like you don't agree. Just because I'm not going to be living among the Amish, that doesn't mean I won't be Christian, love God with all my heart, and do my best to live by His will."

"I know, Levi." She sniffled, offering him a weak smile.

*Why do I need to defend my choices to you?* He gave a gentle snap of the reins and picked up the pace.

He tensed when he felt Sarah's hand squeeze his arm again.

"I'm sorry if I upset you." Sarah leaned her head down on his shoulder, but quickly lifted back up and twisted to face him, putting her face within inches of his. "I'm sure you and Danielle will be very happy. But please understand that this came as a shock to me since you and I had been going to Sunday singings together, and . . ." She shrugged, sniffling again. "I was just surprised."

Levi took a deep breath, realizing that he hadn't given enough thought to Sarah's feelings. She'd probably had the wrong idea for a while now. "I'm sorry, Sarah. I don't know how to explain. I just feel called to marry Danielle and take care of her and the baby." Levi assumed that Sarah knew about the baby. His mother would have made sure of it. "But I will take my beliefs with me. Some things won't change; my faith, my love of the land, daily devotions, and trying to be the best man I can, the man the Lord wants me to be."

"But you will be separated from our people. And maybe you can carry those things with you, but it won't be the same, Levi. Your *fraa* will not cover her head or wear our conservative clothing. You'll be connected to the world through modern conveniences. And there's no way you can stay true to the *Ordnung* if you are not living the way the *Ordnung* tells us to live. You can't have it both ways. You're in or you're out. And that makes me sad."

Levi took a deep breath and let it out slowly, remembering that Sarah was a woman. Yelling at her would be unacceptable.

"I'm going to love God and stay true to my faith, even if that means that some things will have to change."

SARAH HAD UNDERESTIMATED Levi. And so had Vera. She could tell by the firm way Levi spoke to her that he was going to go through with this ridiculous wedding if she didn't do something to stop it.

They were quiet for a few minutes, and Sarah tried to speculate how Danielle had brainwashed Levi into this. God would never call a man away from his home and his life to marry outside the faith and to take on an *Englisch fraa*, a sinner who'd allowed herself to get pregnant by another man. Levi wasn't thinking straight, and Sarah wondered what kind of strange hold Danielle had over him. She assumed it must be physical. Did she tease him with her womanly ways? That had to be it. Sarah put her hand on Levi's strong leg. His muscle tensed, but she left her hand there. Two could play that game.

*Time to put a halt to this silly wedding once and for all.*

# *Eleven*

VERA FINISHED CLEANING THE KITCHEN BEFORE she walked into the living room. Elam was sitting on the couch reading the Bible, and Betsy was already upstairs in bed. Vera turned up the propane lamp on her side of the couch, and she eased down beside Elam. She was reaching for her Bible when he cleared his throat.

The scowl on his face as he looked at her above his wire-rimmed reading glasses told her she was about to get a talking to. She went ahead and pulled the Bible to her lap, then faced him. "What is it, Elam?"

"You and Sarah are up to something, and you better be careful. We might not approve of Levi's choices, but we can't control them. Only God is in control."

Vera crossed her legs and nervously kicked her foot. "I know that, Elam. Sarah is just going to talk to Levi and make sure he understands what he is giving up. I think he'll listen to her. I'm sure he has some sort of feelings for the *maedel*, and she might be able to get through to him where we failed."

Elam groaned, but she pressed on. "Levi doesn't want this

marriage, this *boppli*, Elam. He just *thinks* he does. God bless our Levi; he is an honorable man. But the wrong man is taking responsibility for this *baremlich* situation."

"Again, be careful, Vera. A child is a blessing. The situation might not be ideal, but I doubt the Lord would approve of you calling it terrible." Elam ran a hand down his brownish-gray beard, studying Vera as if she'd done something horrible.

"I know you think I'm meddling, Elam, but this is our *sohn* we're talking about. I've done nothing more than encourage Sarah to speak with Levi, to help him to understand what leaving our community will mean." She uncrossed her legs and waved a hand in his direction. "It didn't take much to encourage Sarah to talk to Levi. The girl is crazy about him, and I know his choices are hurting her." Vera shook her head. "How can he not see it? The two of them are perfectly suited. How could he choose Danielle over Sarah?"

"Vera, I'm not happy that Levi has made this choice. But I will tell you again . . . it's Levi's choice to make."

"Elam." Vera folded her hands in her lap. "Did you even talk to the boy? Did you tell him what a mistake he is making?"

"*Ya.* I talked to him. I wanted to be sure that he was clear how his life would change if he makes this decision. He knows it saddens us both, Vera. But Levi has a *gut* head on his shoulders, and an even better heart. And if he feels called by God to make this honorable step onto another path, regardless of the cost, who are we to question that calling?"

Vera took a long, slow breath, trying not to snap back at Elam. "Levi isn't being *called* to do anything. He is being manipulated by a pregnant *Englisch* girl who doesn't want to raise a *boppli* on her own."

"*Ya*, well, if you're wrong . . ." Elam put his glasses back on and buried his head in the Good Book.

"If I'm wrong?"

He looked at her over his wire rims. "Then you'll be praying for forgiveness for your meddling."

"Asking Sarah to just talk it through with Levi is not meddling. It's simply giving our boy yet another opportunity to see if this is truly the Lord's will." She opened up her Bible and flipped to the book of Job, realizing that Job too had to suffer loss but that it was allowed by God's grace. *Is this what's happening to me? Will this be a blessing down the road?*

It was hard for Vera to believe that.

LEVI SHIFTED HIS weight on the seat and hoped that Sarah would remove her hand from his leg. He'd done this twice before with no luck, but this time she eased her hand away. They were almost to her house, and she'd done most of the talking on the way. Thankfully she didn't bring up Danielle or the wedding again. She'd talked about her job at the bakery, an upcoming quilting party, and things that didn't really interest Levi, but he'd nodded and made a comment every now and then and tried not to yawn.

He and his father had installed solar panels at four different homes today, and he was exhausted. But at least he was off work tomorrow and could sleep in. Danielle was picking him up at seven thirty to go eat breakfast, then they were going to the courthouse to get their marriage license. He couldn't believe that he'd be a married man in just a few days. His mind was wandering again when Sarah twisted in her seat to face him and cupped his cheek with one hand. It caught him a bit off guard, but he didn't jerk away. He felt like he'd already hurt Sarah's feelings enough.

"*Danki* for bringing me home." Sarah's brown eyes captured his as the waxing moon lit the area around the buggy. Long lashes swept across high cheekbones as she blinked. She looked up at him again, tears in her eyes. Maybe if things had been different, he might have kissed her on this night, if for no other reason than to comfort her. But he gently eased her hand from his face.

"Sarah," he whispered. "You'll find the man you're to be with. In time."

She smiled, sniffling. "I thought you to be that man, Levi."

Levi lowered his head in shame. He never should have taken her to the Sunday singings, should have known that she'd think it meant more than it did. But at the time, Levi didn't know if his feelings for Sarah might have blossomed. He never could have foreseen God's calling or known how deep his feelings for Danielle really went. "I'm sorry," he said before he stepped out of the buggy. He wound his way around to her side and opened the door, then offered her his hand, the way he would any woman. Once she was standing in front of him, she slowly wrapped her arms around his waist. Levi didn't move and kept his hands at his sides, even though his heart was racing.

"Just hold me this one time," she said, her voice breaking, "before you're a married man." Sarah's head rested on his shoulder.

Levi slowly wrapped his arms around her. They were both shivering out in the cold, and he was ready to get home. But Sarah was clearly upset, and he couldn't just drop her off in such a state. So he held her for a few moments. Finally she eased away, but her eyes, still glistening with tears, swept across his face before she leaned in and pressed her mouth to his. Her lips were soft, her touch tender, and Levi found himself returning the kiss as if his body were making its own decisions.

Danielle's face flashed in his mind's eye, and as if pricked by a needle, Levi pulled away from her. "No, Sarah. I can't."

"But you did. You kissed me back, Levi. Don't you think that means something?" She leaned her head on his shoulder again, and this time he was more forceful as he pulled away.

"I'm marrying Danielle. That . . . the kiss . . . it shouldn't have happened." Levi pulled off his black hat and scratched his head. He'd kissed a few women during his *rumschpringe*, but none of them had ever initiated it. "I have to go." He waited for Sarah to head toward her house. Levi wouldn't leave until he saw that she was safely inside. But she covered her face and started to cry hard.

"Ahh, Sarah, please don't cry." Levi gently placed a hand on one of her arms. "Please." He couldn't stand to see her so upset. And knowing he was the cause of it made it worse.

"I shouldn't have kissed someone who is promised to another. I'm sorry." She moved her hands away and tucked her chin. Levi could barely see her face beneath the rim of her black bonnet. "I'm so ashamed."

Levi lifted her chin and found her eyes. "I'm sorry too, Sarah. I'm sorry if you thought that there was more between us than . . ." He moved his hand from her chin when he saw her blinking her eyes, her lips parted. He couldn't risk another kiss. The first one had been wrong enough, and to allow it to happen again would be unforgivable.

She ran a soft finger along his cheek, and despite how he longed for her to go into the house, he couldn't deny a sudden urge to have her stay. She was so beautiful . . .

"You're making a mistake, Levi." She spoke softly as her finger trailed down and across his lips.

Levi swallowed hard as he stepped back and away from her touch. "I hope not." As soon as he said the words, he regretted them, knowing he should have spoken with more conviction.

"There's still time . . . you know, for you to change your mind." Sarah pulled a tissue from her apron pocket and dabbed at her eyes for a few moments, sniffling. "You kissed me back. Think about that tonight, Levi."

Without any warning, she quickly stepped forward and kissed him on the mouth, then turned and ran toward her house. Levi could hear her crying as she stood on the porch, trying to get ahold of herself before entering. And he felt like a big heel.

DANIELLE PULLED UP to what she'd come to call "my little church" at seven fifteen Wednesday morning. She flung herself out of the car, marched up the steps, and pulled the heavy wooden door open. She hurried to the front pew and sat down. She stared at Jesus hanging on the cross, took a deep breath, and asked herself what she was doing here. What was it about this place that made her angry, yet seemed to pull her in at the same time?

She looked around, making sure she was the only one in

the church. She assumed God could read her thoughts. If there was a God. But she found herself whispering what was ringing through her mind. "I'm not sure what I'm doing here."

She waited, although she had no idea what she was waiting for. A response? A "word from the Lord"? Breathing in the silence, she crossed her legs and recalled the many Amish worship services Martha had dragged her to. Sometimes, despite the language barrier, she'd felt something . . . something peaceful. Maybe it was just because the Amish were loving, kind people, and with a whole room of them, the love just soaked into your heart somehow.

Danielle uncrossed her legs and leaned forward. It came to her then. She knew why she was there and what she had to say. "God, I don't want to ruin Levi's life. I love him enough to not do that. So, if You are there, and You do hear people's prayers . . . could You maybe just give me some kind of sign? And I'll try to be a better person." She paused. "Amen."

She got up and hurried out of the church. It was exactly seven thirty when she pulled up at Levi's house, and she was glad to see him sitting outside on the porch. The last thing she needed this morning was to face Vera. She'd already had a bout of dry heaves this morning, and she was sure seeing Levi's mom would bring on another wave of nausea.

"Hey," Levi said as he got into her car. He leaned over and kissed her on the mouth, and Danielle wasn't sure that anything had ever felt more awkward. *Was that a sign from God?* She should have never asked for a sign. She wasn't even sure if that was how God worked, or more importantly, if He even listened to anything she had to say. *Great. Now I'll be thinking everything is a sign.*

By the time they got seated at the Parkview Café for breakfast, it felt like old times. Just her and Levi, two best friends having breakfast. She even managed to get down two pancakes without feeling like she might hurl. But coffee remained out of the question. Just the smell made her tummy queasy. When she was done eating, she stared at the handsome man across from her who would soon become her husband. She tipped her head to one side.

"Why are you staring at me like that?" Levi's sandy blond hair was flat on the top where his hat had been. He'd placed it on the bench seat beside him when they'd arrived. But his brown eyes twinkled, and to Danielle, he looked happy.

"You know . . . I used to be able to tell you anything."

The left corner of Levi's mouth curled up, which seemed even cuter now than it used to. "You still can. Nothing's changed."

"Everything has changed. We're going to be married. Husband and wife." She leaned back against the seat. "Now it feels weird to tell you what's on my mind."

"Danielle, what is it?" Levi raised one eyebrow.

"Does it feel weird to you when we kiss?" She held her breath as she waited for him to answer.

"A little." He grinned. "But in a *gut* way." He reached over and patted her hand. "Don't worry. It will all come naturally. I'm sure that I love you and that I want to be with you forever."

She smiled. "I'm sure too." *Maybe this is my sign from God, the warm feeling that I have all over?* Tossing her hair over her shoulders, she knew she had to quit seeing everything as a sign. It was far-fetched. If that were the case, God would have helped her years ago.

"You ready to go get our license?" Levi put some cash on

the table for the waitress and reached for his hat on the seat beside him.

"Yes. I am."

She smiled when Levi reached for her hand as they left the café. Amish weren't big on public affection, so she knew it was a big step for Levi. And there it was again . . . that warm feeling. His fingers felt good, intertwining with hers. *If this is a sign, Lord, I'll take it.*

SATURDAY MORNING, DANIELLE didn't feel sick to her stomach for the first time in days. Ironically. She would have thought that wedding-day jitters might have brought on an extra dose of morning sickness, but she felt great today. *Another sign from God?*

Martha had already gone to the church earlier that morning and returned home. She'd wanted to put up a few decorations and to make sure everything was all set. There wasn't really that much to prepare for, but Martha had insisted on doing it while Danielle got ready. Danielle had been particularly happy to see that Martha had dyed her hair again, and it had turned out a lovely, soft brown. No more purple. Danielle didn't want purple-haired Martha in her wedding pictures.

As she pulled a section of hair through her flatiron, she wondered what kind of wedding pictures she would have. The majority of the people attending were Amish, and they didn't believe in posing for pictures. Would Levi pose with her, at least? They hadn't discussed it.

She took a final look at herself in the mirror in her ivory dress and thought about her mother. Blinking her eyes a few times, she was determined not to cry. Her mother had lost the right to attend her wedding a long time ago. She placed her hands on her tummy. *Or to be a grandmother.*

Martha would be the baby's grandmother. And Vera, she supposed. She'd watched the way Vera was with Levi's younger sister, Betsy, and with all the little ones in the Amish community. She'd be a wonderful grandmother too. In time. Once she accepted their marriage.

She dabbed on a bit of lip gloss, opting to wear almost no makeup. It seemed important to make this day as easy as possible for Levi and his people, even if his people wouldn't *be* his people after today. That thought still troubled her, how much Levi was giving up. She heard Martha bellowing from downstairs that it was time to go, so Danielle leaned close to the mirror, had a final look, and went down the stairs.

Martha was grabbing her purse from the couch when Danielle hit the landing, and Arnold was putting on his black hat, the one he always wore to church.

"You sure look spiffy," she told Arnold, then gave him a hug.

"As do you. A beautiful bride." He pulled her into a hug and kissed her on the cheek. "Are you ready?"

"Yes. I'm ready. And, Arnold . . . thank you for helping Levi, his brother, and friends work on our house for the past couple of days."

"It felt good to step out of retirement." He pushed his outdated hat into place. "Does an old man good."

Arnold had been a carpenter when Martha had first met him, helping to build a school for the Amish children.

Martha huffed. "If you're old, I'm old, and I choose not to be old." She turned off the television and flipped off the lights.

"We're not going to have any electricity or solar panels for a while, but otherwise, Levi said it's cleaned up and livable." She looked to Arnold for confirmation and with some relief saw him purse his lips and nod. "Though I'm not sure how it can be livable without me being able to charge my cell phone."

Arnold chuckled. "Well, that will give you a good reason to come visit. To charge your cell phone, straighten your hair, or whatever else you might need." Then he whispered, "And I know you'll miss Martha's cooking."

Truth was, Danielle couldn't cook much better than Martha. "You can eat my share," she whispered back.

They both were laughing, but stopped when they heard a knock at the door.

"I'll get it." Danielle walked to the door and pulled it open, surprised to see Sarah standing on the porch. She'd been around Sarah a few times and saw her at the Amish worship services, but she didn't know her well at all. But she did know that Levi had taken her to a few of their Sunday singings. She tensed. "Hi, Sarah. What's up?"

Sarah bit her bottom lip for a moment, then blew out a breath. "I need to talk to you."

"Okay." She stepped aside and gestured toward the den.

"Alone?" Sarah whispered after she'd nodded in Martha and Arnold's direction.

Arnold moved past them, gently pulling Martha by the arm. "We'll be outside, ladies, enjoying the sunshine."

"Make it quick," Martha said. "We need to leave shortly."

After they were outside, Danielle motioned for Sarah to sit down, but Sarah folded her hands in front of her and shook her head.

"I can't stay. I just came here . . . I came here to . . ." Sarah dropped her gaze to the floor.

Danielle took a step toward her. "What's wrong? Is something wrong with Levi? What is it?"

"No, Levi is fine." Sarah looked up at her. "And I'm so sorry to come on your wedding day, but, Danielle . . ." She moved closer and touched her arm. "I couldn't have lived with myself if I didn't come." Pulling her hand away, she blinked back tears.

"It's Levi, isn't it?" Danielle's heart was racing, wishing Sarah would get to the point.

Sarah nodded. "Levi is so confused, Danielle. This wedding will pull him from his people. I was with him Tuesday night, and—"

"This past Tuesday?" Danielle put a hand on her hip. "Where?"

"I had supper with the family and Levi drove me home. We talked a lot, and he just isn't ready for all of this . . . the wedding and everything." Sarah looked at the floor and shook her head.

Danielle folded her arms across her chest. "Really?" Or maybe Sarah just wanted Levi for herself and this was her last-ditch effort to keep Danielle from marrying him. "He seems fine to me. He loves me." *But did Levi really confide in Sarah? Does he still have reservations?*

Sarah's tears in the corners of her eyes dried instantly as she locked eyes with Danielle, a smirk on her face. "If he loves you so much, why was he kissing me?"

Danielle felt her knees giving way beneath her. "I don't believe you."

"Ask him then." Sarah flashed a thin-lipped smile at Danielle. "Because you know Levi can't lie. He'll tell you the truth. Just a few days ago, he was kissing *me*. I think that should tell you something. He's not ready to be pulled from his faith, from all that is familiar to him . . . or from me. He doesn't belong with you, Danielle. Do the right thing, and let him go."

Sarah spun around and marched to the door.

Danielle stood with her jaw hanging open as she watched Sarah leave in her buggy.

Martha and Arnold came back inside.

"What was that about?" Martha walked up to Danielle and stood in front of her.

Danielle couldn't control the tears from falling. Sarah had been right about at least one thing. Levi couldn't tell a lie. He'd surely kissed Sarah recently. Danielle already knew what the answer would be if she asked him about it.

"The wedding is off!" Danielle fled the room and hurried upstairs.

*I wanted a sign from God. And now I have it.*


VERA FACED OFF with Elam in the living room, her bottom lip trembling. A combination of anger and hurt swam through her veins. "I'm not going, Elam. And there's nothing else you can say to me."

"How about I am the head of the household and you have to do what I say?" Elam looped his thumbs beneath his suspenders and stood taller. But only for a moment. "*Ach*, Vera . . . come on, *mei lieb*. He's our *sohn*. And it's his wedding day."

Vera placed her hand over her heart. She hadn't heard from Sarah or Anna Marie. How could both efforts have failed? Sarah was evidently not able to talk Levi out of the wedding, and Anna Marie couldn't get her irresponsible son home either. "I cannot go and watch Levi ruin his life. I just can't. 'A wise son maketh a glad father: but a foolish son is the heaviness of his mother.'"

Levi had left twenty minutes ago while Vera was upstairs. But as she'd watched Levi and Betsy leaving the house from her upstairs bedroom window, she was sure she'd felt her heart crack in two. Why was God letting this happen? She knew in her mind and heart that the Lord always had a plan for everything and that His will was to be done . . . but something was terribly amiss here, and Vera just couldn't accept it as right.

"Well, I'm going then." Elam pointed a finger at her, and Vera held back the urge to slap his hand away. "I think you are making a mistake."

"Then it's my mistake to make." She turned and walked toward the stairs before Elam could see the tears spilling down her cheeks.

LEVI PULLED UP at the small church. He recognized Martha and Arnold's car. He saw Jacob's gray buggy with the long scratch down the side, a reminder from when his brother's horse had gotten away from him one day and sideswiped a hitching post in town. His sister Emily and his brother-in-law David had also arrived, their buggy recognizable by the fine black horse hitched to it.

"Am I still going to see you?" Betsy tugged on the sleeve of Levi's black jacket. "*Daed* said you aren't shunned, so I'll still see you, right?"

Levi pulled his buggy next to Emily and David's. "Of course. You'll see me all the time." Once he was stopped, he twisted his head over his shoulder and searched the road, hoping his parents would be along soon. He knew this was hard on his mother, and she'd said very little, but maybe *Mamm* would come around when she saw Levi take vows with Danielle. Then she'd know in her heart, the way Levi did, that this was God's perfect plan.

He stepped out of the buggy, feeling a refreshing spring in his step. He'd wondered if he might be nervous today, but he wasn't at all. Grabbing Betsy's hand, he helped her out of the buggy. "Go on inside. I'll be in there shortly, after I get Chester settled. Some of your *aentis* and *onkels* are already here."

Levi whistled softly as he tethered Chester to the post. *Thank You, Lord, for this day, for guiding my steps to do Your will. I pray that I will be a loving, yet strong and protective husband and father.*

Excited to see Danielle, he made the last loop on the hitching post, gave Chester a quick pat on the head, then headed for the church. He was halfway to the entrance when the door flew open. Levi didn't think he'd ever seen Martha move as fast as she was moving now. Her face was red as a beet, her jaw was clenched, and half her hair was falling from her clip.

Levi stopped where he was in the parking lot, but Martha didn't. She kept coming like a bull until she'd grabbed both sides of his open jacket and yanked him with the force of three men.

"You . . . you scoundrel! How could you do this to our girl?"

Levi didn't move away. "What are you *talking* about?" He could see Emily, David, Beth Ann, and Jacob over her shoulder heading toward them. Arnold was trying unsuccessfully to coax Betsy into the church.

"Why would you go through this charade only to break Danielle's heart?" Martha finally let go of him and took a step backward, wiping quick, angry tears from the corners of her eyes.

Levi straightened his jacket, glanced over Martha's shoulder again at his family, then back at her. "Martha, how am I *breaking* her heart? I love her!" His own heart was pounding against his chest.

Martha pointed a finger at Levi. "Your *friend* Sarah came calling this morning and informed Danielle about your hanky-panky."

"What?" Levi's stomach roiled as he took a deep breath.

"Don't look so innocent there, mister. Danielle knows all about what you were up to *a few nights ago*." Martha shoved her finger into his chest, glaring at him. "I'm going home now, to check on Danielle. We just came to let you and your family know that the wedding is off." Then she marched to her car, hollering for Arnold to follow her.

Levi didn't move as his family came around him. He could feel the heat in his cheeks despite the sting of the cool wind.

He had to get to Danielle . . . to make her understand.

# Twelve

Levi pawned Betsy off on his stunned family before he went directly to Martha's house. But Martha wouldn't even let him step one foot inside.

He stood outside and bellowed up at Danielle's window. "Danielle! Just give me a minute! I need to talk to you!"

Arnold came out to the porch, arms folded in front of his chest. "Best give it a rest, son. Give her some time. Give us all some time."

Levi closed his eyes and then rubbed his face. Slowly he turned away and climbed into his buggy, staring up at Danielle's window, watching as Arnold slipped back inside. He didn't blame them. He was an idiot. How could he have allowed himself to be in that position with Sarah? So soon before his wedding?

His heart was split in two—broken over losing Danielle, and splintered with anger that Sarah would stoop so low as to try to keep him from doing what he believed he was called by God to do. He was sure his parents had shown up at the church, heard what happened, and were back home by now.

By the time Levi pulled up at his house, the anger had built to a point that he probably should have gone somewhere else to cool off, but he wanted *Mamm* to know exactly how much she'd hurt him. Because she was behind it all. He was as sure of it as he was of the sun rising in the east.

"How could you do this?" he said to his mother as soon as he walked in. She halted the sweeper she was running across the floor. "Levi, I'm so sorry this happened, but maybe—" She reached out to stroke his arm, but Levi jerked it away.

"Sorry? Are you kidding me?" He took another step back.

His father and Betsy were on the couch, and *Daed* quickly stood and sent Betsy upstairs. He turned back to Levi. "You watch the way you talk to your *mudder* in this *haus*."

Levi locked eyes with his father. "Did *you* know about it too? That Sarah was headed to Danielle's to convince her not to marry me?" His father's frown told him what he needed to know. Levi turned to his mother. "But I'm sure *you* were in on it."

His mother stepped forward. "Levi, I promise you. I only asked Sarah to make sure that you had fully considered what you were leaving behind. Our community. Your faith. I never knew she planned to go and see Danielle."

*Daed* walked closer and cleared his throat. "You may wish to lay blame at your mother's feet, but tell us, *sohn* . . . why were you kissing Sarah, if you were planning to marry Danielle?"

Levi rubbed his forehead, avoiding his father's eyes. He felt bad enough about the kiss with Sarah, but he knew he couldn't stand to be under the same roof as his mother. He didn't want to have to explain anything to anyone at the moment. He rushed past them both and up the stairs, knowing he wasn't spending one more night here. Married or not.

MARTHA SAT UPSTAIRS on Danielle's bed, doing her best to comfort the girl. She was shocked that Levi would promise himself to Danielle, then do something like this.

"Honey, you need to catch your breath and stop crying." Martha wrapped an arm around Danielle's shoulder and pulled her close. "I have a feeling there is more to this than meets the eye."

Danielle blew her nose, then twisted out of Martha's hold to face her. "Like what?"

"This sounds like a huge setup." She raised her hand. "Don't get me wrong . . . I'm mad as all get-out at that Levi, but this just doesn't sound like him. Sneaking off for a little hanky-panky right before he gets married? I'm guessing Sarah threw herself at him." Martha shrugged. "Women have been known to do worse things."

"They're Amish, Martha. You always talk about what good and righteous people they are." Danielle rolled her eyes, then walked to the mirror and stared at herself in the ivory wedding dress before covering her face with her hands and sobbing. Again.

Martha wanted to slap that Levi silly. And if she found out that Vera had anything to do with this, she'd give her a talking-to that would be as good as any lashing. "Honey, please don't cry." She walked to where Danielle was standing and stroked her hair until Danielle turned around and fell into her arms.

"God hates me, Martha. He hates me."

Martha eased her away, brushed away her tears with her thumbs. "No, baby girl. He doesn't hate you. God loves you."

"Then why can't I seem to catch a break? Every time I think that someone might love me, it turns out not to be real. Like my mom . . . she couldn't possibly have loved me."

Martha could hardly stand to think about the beatings that Danielle had suffered at the hand of her mother. But right now, Danielle needed to hear that her mother loved her. Martha could see the longing in her eyes.

"Honey, your mom loves you. But she's messed up in the head, and she doesn't know how to show it." She smiled. "I love you too. And God loves you."

"God, God, God! Whatever!" Danielle threw her hands up in the air and walked back to the bed, plopping down before she kicked off a pair of ivory heels. "I'm sick of hearing about Him."

Martha decided this wasn't the time to push the issue. Danielle was growing more bitter by the moment. "I have an idea." She sat down beside Danielle, snapped her fingers, and grinned. "How 'bout I go beat the snot out of Sarah for you? Or maybe Levi? Or even Vera, in case she had anything to do with this. You pick."

The result was a slight smile. "Don't try to make me laugh, Martha." Then she started to cry again, and Martha just reached over and pulled her close.


VERA FOLLOWED LEVI to the door as he carried out the last few items from his room, things he'd previously said he would leave or get later—like his old baseball cap and other memorabilia that would have given Vera comfort down the road if he'd gotten married.

"Please, *sohn*. Don't leave like this." She reached for his arm, but like he'd done earlier, he pulled away, and Vera brought a hand to her chest as she turned to Elam. "Do something."

Levi turned before he got to the door. "*Mamm*, it's time I move out anyway. And I've already put money down on the *haus* for me and Danielle. My things are already there. I'll still close on it, whether or not I can convince her to take me back." He looked at Elam. "Do I still have a job with you, *Daed*?"

Elam nodded, tucking his thumbs into his suspenders. "Of course. And we wish you well, Levi, however all this turns out."

"But you don't have to move out right now, Levi," Vera said.

"Let the boy go, Vera." Elam spoke with an authority that Vera didn't like, but she took a deep breath and held her tongue. How had this situation blown so completely out of control? And one thing hung in her thoughts like fog in the air.

"Will you be keeping up with your Amish ways?" She pinched her lips together, fighting tears, as she waited for Levi to answer.

With tears in his eyes, her son glanced at her. "Wherever I go, whatever I do, *Mamm* . . . my beliefs in God and His plan will not change."

Vera wanted to tell him that he didn't answer the question, and that now that his marriage to Danielle was off, he could continue on his path, find someone to marry among their people, and raise his *kinner* according to the *Ordnung*. But she'd heard him say that he was going to try to get Danielle back. *Does he love her that much?*

Sarah had certainly taken things past what they'd discussed

by kissing Levi and telling Danielle about it. But it had worked. The wedding was off. So even though she couldn't fault Sarah for her actions, it seemed more manipulative than Vera ever intended.

She watched from the window as her son loaded up the last of his things, barely aware that Betsy had come downstairs and was speaking to her.

"Why is Levi moving out if he's not marrying Danielle?" Betsy frowned. "I don't understand why they didn't get married."

Vera pulled her eyes from the window, glanced at Elam, then down at her daughter, glad Betsy didn't know all the details. "He feels it's time to be on his own. And things just didn't work out between him and Danielle."

"He's sad. I can tell." Betsy twirled the string on her *kapp*. "He said good-bye to me upstairs, and he looked like he wanted to cry."

"Everything is going to be fine." She leaned down and kissed Betsy on the forehead. "You'll still see Levi all the time."

*But who will cook for him?* Her son had never cooked a meal in his life that she knew of. *Who will tend to his clothes? Pack his lunch? Mend his socks?* It just wasn't normal for a young man to go off on his own without a *fraa* to tend to him. Perhaps the lesser of the evils would have been for him to marry Danielle. At least Vera would have known that he wasn't alone.

"Betsy, go play outside on the porch for a few minutes so I can talk to your *mudder*. The sun is shining, and it's a beautiful day." Elam pulled the door open and Betsy marched outside, huffing slightly but not arguing with her father.

"I can't believe this is happening." Vera walked to the

window again just in time to see Levi's buggy rounding the corner. "He shouldn't be alone, on his own."

"He's twenty-two years old, Vera. He'll be all right." Elam ran his hand the length of his beard. "His heart must heal, though, and that will take some time. Unless he's able to win the *Englisch* girl back, which seems to be what he wants."

Vera stayed quiet, but she was sure that being alone was better than living a life in the outside world. For now, she'd just have to travel to his house and tend to him. Take him food, carry his clothes back and forth for laundering, and whatever else he needed.

LEVI WALKED INTO his new home, dropping his few trinkets inside the doorway. He knew that taking his baseball cap and other things was an immature thing to do, a way to let his mother know that he was never coming back, but it was better than losing his temper with her. He glanced around the living room.

The house looked better, but there was a long way to go. He'd had a bed, two rocking chairs, and kitchen appliances delivered. He'd figured that he and Danielle could take the little bit of savings that he had and go buy dishes, linens, and other things that they needed.

What had he been thinking? As he looked around, he mentally tried to calculate the hours he would have to spend fixing the place up, which had all seemed worth it, knowing he was doing it for Danielle and the baby. Now the house represented what he'd lost.

As he walked from room to room, his heart ached. Not

only had he lost his future wife but his best friend as well. When he walked back into the living room, Jacob was standing in the doorway.

"Can I come in?" His older brother waited until Levi motioned for him to do so.

Levi rubbed his forehead. "What brings you here, *bruder*?"

"Checking on you."

"I'm okay." Levi walked to one of the only two pieces of furniture in the living room and settled into the bentwood rocker, motioning for Jacob to have a seat in the other one. "I would offer you something to drink." He lifted one shoulder, then dropped it. "But I don't have anything." He rubbed his nose when it started to run, blinking his eyes a few times. "I figured Danielle would stock the kitchen after we were married, or we'd do it together."

"I can see you're hurting. But do you think . . . Could it be that this is for the best?" Jacob tipped back the rim of his black felt hat, then rested his elbows on his knees as he tucked his hands under his chin. Levi assumed the same position, and both men stared at the wall in front of them.

"If it were for the best, it wouldn't feel so wrong. I've stepped off of God's path, Jacob. I can feel it."

They were both quiet for a moment before Jacob spoke up. "This place still needs a lot of work." He turned to Levi. "I can help you for an hour or two in the evenings after I close the store."

"*Danki*, Jacob." Levi tried to smile, knowing his brother was trying to distract him. But how could he think about anything else? He'd let Danielle down. His parents, for sure. And God. Maybe even Sarah in some way, although he was having trouble feeling much of anything for Sarah right now.

He appreciated Jacob's visit and his offer to help, but mostly he just wanted to be alone in prayer. If God was calling him to marry Danielle, how had He let things get so messed up?

"Danielle agreed to live here without electricity?" Jacob glanced around the walls that were void of electrical outlets.

"*Ya*. I'd told her that I would get some solar panels when I could afford it." Truth was, Levi had been hoping to ease into all the luxuries that Danielle was used to, even though lots of Amish folks were adding solar panels, especially for heat and lighting.

Jacob stood up and stroked his beard. "It's a *gut haus*. You will make it into a fine home, I'm sure. And I'll help you as much as I can."

"What does Beth Ann think about all of this?" Levi knew his sister-in-law had a large opinion about things that didn't go as she thought they should.

Jacob shrugged. "She was relieved that the wedding didn't happen." His brother eyed him. "We all were." He paused, glancing down at the ground. "I'm sorry, *bruder*, if that hurts you. But watching you leave the faith to marry . . ." Jacob shook his head and stopped, but Levi knew what he'd wanted to say . . . *a woman from the* Englisch *world carrying another man's child.*

When Levi let the thought sink into his mind, it did sound crazy. He closed his eyes. He couldn't get a grasp on what he was supposed to think. His whole world seemed topsy-turvy.

"I have some time now," Jacob said, stuffing his hands into the pockets of his black jacket. "Do you want me to help you work on this place for a while?"

Levi thought about accepting his offer, but his need to be alone was too great. "*Nee*, but *danki*. I'd like to spend time in prayer for a while."

Jacob nodded. "I'll come by Monday after work."

Levi smiled, knowing his brother was risking Beth Ann's wrath for coming home late in the evenings. But it'd be both a help and good to spend time with him. "*Danki.*" He walked with Jacob to the front door, shook his hand, then closed the door behind him, having to give it an extra push for it to click into place.

He sat down in the rocker again and begged the Lord for guidance. *I thought I was doing what You wanted me to do . . .*

As he tried to focus on prayer, his stomach rumbled, and he realized he hadn't eaten since breakfast. And he'd missed the big meal planned after the wedding. He briefly wondered what happened to all the food, but shook his head to clear the selfish thought, fueled by more stomach growling. He tried to think about something else, like how he planned to tend his ten acres. In Canaan, they had to make the most of their short growing season.

He forced himself up and went out the back door, which also stuck, and came back in with an armful of firewood he'd gathered earlier in the week. Building a fire in the roomy fireplace, he pictured Danielle sitting beside him, warming her hands, and he wondered if she could have lived in these conditions for a while. He swallowed hard, realizing that this would have been his wedding night. Instead he was alone. For the first time in his life. He already missed Betsy's busy steps running up and down the stairs and the smell of his mother's kitchen.

The old house was damp, dusty, and empty. Soon there wouldn't be a need for a fire, but it was still chilly, and he was glad he'd cut wood a couple of weeks ago. Squatting, he watched as the timber caught fire, orange sparks shimmying up the chimney. As the oak began to crackle and pop, he knew he'd be warm on the outside tonight, but inside he felt cold and alone. And despite his misery, he was hungry as a man could be. He stood up when he heard a knock at the door, half hoping it was his mother with a basket of food. Even if it meant they'd have to have another conversation, hunger would undoubtedly win out.

But it wasn't his mother waiting on the other side of the stubborn door.

# Thirteen

DANIELLE BALANCED THE BAG OF FOOD ON HER HIP, shaking from head to toe. Partly from the chilly weather, but mostly because she was nervous. Levi's jaw dropped when he opened the door, but Danielle focused on the dark circles underneath his weary eyes.

"I miss my best friend," she said, swallowing hard, determined not to cry. She pushed the bag of wedding food toward him. "I need to talk to him because my husband-to-be did a very bad thing and I had to call my wedding off." She blinked her eyes a few times and gave the bag a shake until he finally took it.

"Danielle . . ." Levi hung his head, shook it, and then sighed.

"Can I come in? I'm cold."

"Uh, sure. I'm sorry." He stepped back and yanked on the wooden door until it opened enough for her to step inside. She glanced around, feeling the warmth, but unable to fathom how she might have lived in this house. Until she looked into Levi's glassy eyes. *Him.* That's how she would have lived here, and together they would have made it into a home.

She looked at the two rocking chairs along the wall, the

only furniture in the room, then stared at the fire glowing in the hearth.

"I figured you hadn't eaten either." She pointed to the food. "So there's enough for both of us, if you feel like it. But first I'm hoping you can give me some sort of explanation as to why you were kissing Sarah." She folded her arms across her chest and kept her chin raised as her bottom lip began to tremble. "Do you love her, Levi?"

He put the bag in one of the rockers and placed gentle hands on her shoulders. "No. I don't, Danielle. *Mei mamm* invited her to supper, then I had to take her home . . ." He paused, his mouth opened, but no words came out for a few moments. "Then she kissed me. She was crying, but . . . I shouldn't have let it happen."

Danielle gazed into his eyes as she weighed his words, knowing in her heart that Sarah had set him up, just as Martha suspected.

"I love you," he said. "I want to marry you. And I'm so sorry that this happened."

She eased out of his firm grip, walked to the empty rocker, and sat down. "As my best friend, how would you advise me about this situation?"

Levi paced for a moment, not looking at her. "That's not fair," he mumbled.

"Because . . . ?"

He lifted a hand in the air. "Because I'd probably tell you to stay away from a louse like me. But as the man who wants to marry you, I beg you to forgive my part in this." Levi dropped to one knee, and Danielle kept her eyes on his as he leaned close. "The kiss with Sarah meant nothing."

Danielle thought about the few kisses she'd had with Levi, and she couldn't help but wonder if Levi's kisses with Sarah felt more romantic, not so awkward. She wanted to ask, but she didn't want to know the answer.

"Can you forgive me, Ladybug?" He ran a thumb along her cheek, but she pulled away from him.

"It's not fair to call me that." She let out a huff. "Not today." Nervous because of his proximity, she glanced around the house, dimly lit by the little bit of sun that was left outside. *This was supposed to be my home.*

But Levi remained where he was, directly in front of her. Gently, he cupped a hand behind her neck and pulled her closer. "Ladybug . . . ," he whispered. Then he leaned down and as their lips met, something was different. More exploratory, still awkward . . . but in an okay way. If Danielle hadn't been sitting, she might have gone weak in the knees. When he finally eased away, he lifted her hands in his and gently kissed them, still watching her.

"Wow," she said, breathless, when he stilled. "That was quite the apology kiss." She'd known when she came here that Levi would have an explanation and that she'd forgive him. She'd had several hours to think on it, and she just didn't think he would have been so insistent on marrying her if he truly loved Sarah.

"Please marry me, Danielle. Be my *fraa*." He lowered his head. "Otherwise, I might not ever have a decent meal again."

She laughed, slapping him on the arm as he looked at her with an exaggerated pout. "I don't know what makes you think you'd have a decent meal if we were married, Levi! You know I don't cook." She rolled her eyes, still smiling. "I've told you that."

He reached for her hands and pulled her from the rocker, then pulled her close to him. "I really am sorry this happened. I'll never do anything to hurt you again."

She let him hold her tight, but said, "Sure you will. It's the people who love us the most who can hurt us the most."

He ran a hand through the back of her hair, then kissed her on the forehead before he eased her away. "Let's get married now."

She scowled. "What? Now? Where? How would we . . ."

Levi grabbed the bag of food from the rocker and headed toward the kitchen. "We'll eat this when we get back. I'll put it in the refrigerator."

"We have a refrigerator?" she asked, following him.

"*Ya*, propane." After he stowed the bag, he checked on the fire in the fireplace, then pulled her by the hand out to her car. And she didn't put up a struggle.

She was apparently going to be Mrs. Levi Detweiler before anyone else tried to come between them.

AN HOUR LATER, Danielle and Levi stood facing each other in the Sangre de Cristo Chapel. Levi still had on the clothes he'd planned to be married in earlier—black trousers, a long-sleeved dark blue shirt, and a black jacket. But Danielle was wearing blue jeans, a white blouse, and her tennis shoes. Her hair was pulled into a loose side braid, and her green eyes glistened with anticipation. Levi didn't think she'd ever looked more beautiful.

There was no one but the pastor and his wife in the church. And God. Levi expected to be nervous, to sense that Danielle was anxious too. Instead, a peace surrounded him as he and

Danielle exchanged vows with an ease that could only mean that they were stepping onto the path that God paved for them.

"I now pronounce you man and wife." The elderly pastor smiled. "You may kiss your bride."

And Levi did, knowing that he would spend the rest of his life loving Danielle. Taking care of her. And the baby.

IT WAS NEARING dark, and Martha was starting to get worried about Danielle. She suspected that those kids would fix things, but she hadn't heard from her in a few hours. Even Martha's anger at Levi had fizzled with time. He just didn't seem like the type of kid to betray Danielle, and Martha suspected that Sarah or Vera had a heavy hand in this little setup. Martha was pacing the living room when Danielle called. She listened with a smile on her face as Danielle described their very private and small wedding that had taken place an hour earlier.

"I'm so sorry you weren't there," Danielle said after sharing the details. "It was just us, but it was perfect. And I'm happy."

"That's all that counts, sweetheart. You enjoy your honeymoon night, and we'll worry about getting all your things to your new home tomorrow. Do you need anything?"

"Nope. My husband and I are going to curl up in front of the fireplace and eat the wedding leftovers that I brought."

Martha laughed. "We are all going to be eating Swedish meatballs, mini quiches, and stuffed mushrooms for a long time to come. So let me know when you need some more."

After they hung up, she turned to Arnold who was sitting in his recliner. "Well, they did it, went to the church on their own and got married."

"Splendid," Arnold said. "As long as she's happy."

Martha eased into her own recliner and propped her feet up on the worn ottoman. Smiling, she said, "Yep. I can hear it in her voice. She's happy." She shook her head. "Although I'll bet Vera is going to flip her lid."

LEVI HAD LAID a thick brown and yellow quilt on the floor in front of the fireplace, and after they'd eaten, he and his new bride had kissed a few times, but as much as Levi wanted to love Danielle the way a man loved his wife, there was something bothering him.

So instead of consummating their marriage, Levi had pulled out a bag of memories, and for the past couple of hours, they'd been digging through it, both of them recalling things that had happened since they'd known each other over the past year. Levi was surprised at how much they'd done together and shared with each other in such a short amount of time. No wonder she was his best friend. He corrected his thought . . . *fraa*.

They were facing each other on their sides, their heads propped up on their elbows.

Danielle laughed, a sound that was familiar, and it brought a smile to his face. "Remember that time we flew kites out in the field?" she asked.

Levi put his face down on the blanket for a moment and grunted before looking back up at her with fond recollections. "*Ya*. I felt *dumm*, but you said I should be more playful, and you couldn't believe I'd never flown a kite."

"We bought those cheap kites, and mine kept crashing to

the ground." She smiled again as she reached over and intertwined her free hand with his.

They were quiet for a few moments, and as Danielle bit her
bottom lip, he could almost see her mind whirling like the winds
on a stormy day. "What are you thinking about?" he asked.

"Just that this is all . . . different." She glanced around the
room, lit only by the glow of the fireplace. "And I was just
wondering if you . . ." She shrugged. "If you've ever . . ." She
captured his eyes with hers. "You know."

"No." Levi had been saving himself for marriage, and now,
after twenty-two years, his bride lay beside him, and there was
nothing that he wanted more than to take her in his arms. But
something held him back.

She eased her hand out of his, touched her stomach, and
avoided his eyes. "Obviously I have." With teary eyes, she
looked up at him. "Does that make me bad?"

Levi studied her beautiful face, and she'd never looked
younger to him than at this moment, a child seeking approval.
He cupped her cheek. "No, Ladybug. There is nothing bad
about you." He put his hand on her stomach.

"But you believe that sex should only come after marriage."

It was true, but Levi wanted to tread carefully. "I believe
God wants people to share His eternal and unconditional love
through the act of marriage." He paused and then placed a
hand on her belly. "But this child remains a gift, no matter
the circumstances. God blesses us all in different ways. And
together we will be *gut* parents. A baby is the greatest gift God
can offer. I'm thinking it's our best wedding present."

She smiled. "Your people—especially your mom—are never
going to accept us being together."

Levi worried about the same thing but shoved it away. "Sure they will."

They were quiet again, the only sound the crackling of the fire. He snuggled up close to her, wrapped an arm around her, and kissed her lightly on the mouth. "I love you, Danielle."

"I love you too." She leaned forward and kissed him this time, and each kiss came more naturally and with a passion that Levi had only imagined. Danielle was as tender and loving as he knew she would be, but he gently eased her away and yawned.

"Are you sleepy?" Danielle grinned, as if she expected him to say no.

"*Ya*. You ready to go to sleep?"

"Uh . . . okay." She bit her bottom lip, and Levi turned and lay on his back before there could be any more talk about it. A thought needled at him, so tonight he would be content just cuddled next to his wife.

Sunday morning worship was held at Jacob and Beth Ann's house, but when Vera didn't see Levi there, worry filled her heart. Levi never missed worship service unless he was ill, and she knew that yesterday had been a hard day for him. She managed to stay through the entire church service, but convinced Elam that they needed to skip the meal. He'd grumbled a bit, but Vera promised to make him a meal after she went to check on Levi, so she took Elam and Betsy home before she headed to Levi's.

Vera made her way up the porch steps of her son's new home, noticing a few boards had recently been replaced. *So much work to do.* She eyed the chipped paint, cracked pane of glass, and cobwebs hanging in the corners. Their people were all about hard work, but it was going to take a team effort and many long hours to get this place in order. She hoped the inside was better.

Vera couldn't stand the thought of Levi living here alone with no one to tend to him. She'd take inventory when she got inside and see what all she could do to lend a hand.

She peered through one of the cracked windows and let out a small gasp. Her poor boy was curled beneath a blanket in front of the fireplace, with only a few embers still glowing at his feet. In a beam of sunlight, she could see one of Levi's feet poking from beneath the covers. She'd never known him to sleep this late.

Shaking her head, she tapped on the door, which wasn't entirely closed. It appeared stuck. "Levi?" she said, shoving it farther open.

"Levi? *Sohn?*" Vera pinched her lips together in a frown as a musty smell wafted up her nostrils. She shook her head. Men didn't know a thing about cleaning. "Levi?" She squeezed through and stepped into the warmth of the living room. At least he hadn't been cold during the night. She took a few more steps toward the bundled mass in front of the fireplace and gently tapped him with her black leather shoe. "Levi?"

When Danielle's head popped out from beneath the covers, Vera brought a hand to her mouth and gasped. Then Levi raised his head too. "*Mamm?*"

"What is going *on* here?" Vera kept her eyes on her son as he sat up and ran a hand through tousled hair before rubbing his eyes. Try as she might not to look, her eyes veered

165

to Danielle, whose long blond hair was a tattered mess. They were both dressed, and for that, Vera thanked the Lord.

"*Mamm*, what are you doing here?" Levi stood up, dressed in black slacks, white undershirt, and black socks. Danielle stood up beside him, pushing back loose strands of hair from her face. Her white blouse was wrinkled, and she was wearing *Englisch* britches.

Vera could feel her face turning three shades of red, unsure which emotion was in the lead—embarrassment or anger at finding her son in this position. "You don't get married, but you have a sleepover?" She pressed a palm against her chest.

"We *are* married." Danielle actually smiled as she spoke.

Vera's heart stopped for a moment, then painfully pounded. "Is—is this true, Levi?" She took a step backward, hoping she didn't fall.

"*Ya*. We got married late yesterday afternoon."

Vera swallowed hard and blinked back the tears that threatened to spill as Levi latched on to Danielle's hand. She glanced at Danielle again, trying not to look at her stomach. The deed was done. They were married. And Vera had lost.

"I—I was worried because you weren't at worship service this morning."

Levi hung his head. "*Ya*. I feel badly about that, but I didn't think to bring any towels to use for bathing, and Danielle doesn't have her toiletries here. I think we'll probably go shopping for things we need and groceries today."

"On a Sunday?" Vera swallowed hard. It was already starting, his slow departure from their world. "I suppose you will be going in luxury, taking Danielle's car?"

"I don't know how luxurious my old clunker is," Danielle

said with a smile, and even with her hair in such a tangled mass, Vera had to admit that she was a pretty girl. But Danielle had used her beauty from the first day to woo Levi into a friendship, and now this entrapment.

"*Ya*, we'll go in her car," Levi said, avoiding Vera's eyes. Then he smiled. "But no electricity." He waved his arm around the room. "Maybe some solar panels, though, when I can afford it. I guess I'm still part-Amish."

*Uh, no, my son, you're most definitely not.* "I must go."

"Don't you want to see the rest of the *haus*?" Levi stepped forward, still holding Danielle's hand.

"I will see it another day." She moved toward the door, knowing her son expected her to say or do something, but she simply waved as she hurried toward her buggy.

It was everything she could do to hold her tears until she'd made her way out of the driveway.

"SHE HATES ME." Danielle watched from the window as Vera turned the corner in her buggy.

Levi came up behind her and put his arms around her waist, which felt strangely familiar, but weird at the same time. "She doesn't hate you. It's just going to take her some time to get used to the idea of us together. Forever."

Danielle twisted to face him. "Do you really think she will come around? Because I don't. She will always see me as the girl who pulled you from your Amish roots."

He kissed her on the nose. "She will grow to know you and love you like I do."

Danielle sighed. "I don't know about that." She nudged

him playfully when she heard his stomach growling. "I bet you're going to miss your mother's cooking, especially the homemade bread. Katie Ann would bring us bread, and it was always so good."

Levi smiled. "Well, uh . . . maybe you could make bread for us?"

Danielle chuckled. "I can make a mean piece of toast. But I've told you, I don't really know how to cook anything that doesn't come out of a box with specific instructions." She poked him on the arm. "And Martha said it's hard to make bread. She grew up watching her grandmother do it. You have to smash it over and over again, let it rise, then smash it some more."

"I think you mean *knead*. You knead the bread." Levi licked his upper lip. "If there was one thing I could have every day from my parents' house . . . it would be *Mamm's* bread."

Danielle watched him, thinking, *Someday I'm going to make him a loaf of bread that will make him forget about his mother's.*

Vera trudged up her porch steps with the weight of the wedding news causing her to feel two inches shorter. She reached a hand to her left shoulder blade and rubbed before she opened the door.

After crossing through the living room, she found Elam in the kitchen with Betsy, each eating a piece of shoofly pie. She waited until Betsy had taken her last bite before asking her young daughter to go play upstairs.

"They did it." Vera slid into a chair at the table, propped her elbows on it, and covered her face with her hands. "Levi and Danielle got married late yesterday afternoon. Danielle was there when I arrived." She clenched her jaw to kill the sob in her throat, then looked up to gauge Elam's reaction. He finished chewing a bite of pie and sat back against his chair as his brows lowered. Vera held her breath as she waited for any words of comfort her husband might share.

Elam pushed his plate forward on the table, then stroked his beard. "Vera . . ."

She let out the breath she was holding and folded her hands on the table. Elam was about to tell her that she had to accept this marriage. She knew him well enough to know his thoughts. She tapped a finger on the table and waited.

"This isn't what either of us wanted, *mei lieb*, but if you want to have a relationship with your *sohn*, you're going to have to find some way to make peace with this. God is in control. Not us. If Levi felt called to marry Danielle, then who are we to question it?"

Vera couldn't bear the thought of not having Levi as a part of their lives, but she couldn't shake the feeling that Danielle had tricked him somehow. Pushed him into a corner. Until he believed it was God telling him to marry her.

"It's not right for you to practice your own personal shunning, Vera, when the boy hasn't been baptized. We've always known this was a possibility with any of our *kinner*."

Maybe Elam had thought it was a possibility, but Vera never had. It was a distant fear, but never a real possibility. She remained quiet, blinking back tears as she drummed her fingers on the table.

"I suggest you get to know this girl. Whether you like it or not, she is now the number one person in Levi's life, after God." Elam pushed back his chair and carried his plate to the sink. He turned to face her, leaning against the counter. His eyes warmed, a slight smile on his face. "You will do the right thing." He walked to her, leaned down, and kissed her on the cheek.

# *Fourteen*

DANIELLE PULLED BOTH LOAVES OF BREAD FROM the oven, slammed them down on the top of the stove, and stared at the mounds that had refused to rise—for the third time.

Today was Sisters Day, and Levi had been insistent that Danielle accept the invitation from his sister Emily, who was hosting it at her home, so Danielle had taken the day off from work. Danielle had been around the Amish long enough to know that a Sisters Day was a monthly gathering when all the women got together to do quilting, canning, or some other sort of project. Sometimes they cleaned house for an elderly person or shut-in. Everyone brought food. Danielle had known not to count on bringing bread following her first two failed attempts, so she'd bought some cookies from the grocery store the day before.

She dreaded going to the event, and the only saving factor was that it was being held at Emily and David's house. Her sister-in-law and her husband had always been kind to her, and when Emily showed up and asked Danielle to come, Danielle knew she wouldn't be able to get out of it.

It had been over two weeks since their wedding, and she and Levi weren't living any more like husband and wife than when they first got married. They'd moved from the floor in front of the fireplace and to the bed on the second night, but there wasn't anything physical going on. Twice she'd tried to initiate more than just a few kisses with Levi, and both times he'd said he was tired. Danielle wondered if maybe Levi wasn't attracted to her. She reached down and touched her belly, knowing it protruded a little more than she'd like. She wasn't even four months pregnant yet, but the way she'd been eating lately, the pounds were coming on quickly.

They hadn't gone to the Amish worship service yesterday because Danielle had been sick to her stomach. She'd told Levi to go without her, but he'd insisted on staying home with her. Danielle figured Levi might be nervous to face his family, even though Danielle knew that he'd always be welcomed at church. Either way, she'd been relieved to get out of it herself.

She dumped the loaves of bread into the garbage. Again. Levi had left for work hours ago. He never said anything about her not getting up to make him breakfast, even though she knew that Amish women did that . . . rising at four or four thirty to send their men off with a full stomach. Best she'd likely ever be able to do for Levi would be to pour him a bowl of cereal, and she doubted he needed her to do that. She'd been working the afternoon shift, but her hours had been cut. Both she and Sue suspected a layoff was coming. Business had declined since the new owners took over a few months ago and changed the menu.

She looked around her simple kitchen. Levi had purchased a small oak kitchen table with four chairs, promising to get a bigger one when they could afford it. They hardly had any furniture—two rockers in the living room and a queen-size bed in their bedroom. She wondered how they would afford all the things necessary for a baby. Thankfully, Martha would make sure the baby had everything he or she needed. She'd said so plenty of times. Levi was insistent that Danielle keep her little bit of savings for now, something in case of an emergency.

Her surrogate mother had been by to visit daily, sometimes alone, sometimes with Arnold. Danielle tried to make excuses for the condition of the place. In addition to the rundown state of the house, Danielle knew she wasn't the best at cleaning. Martha had eyed their sink full of dishes several times when she'd visited. But it just seemed easier to let them all stack up and do them when the sink was full. There was no dishwasher, so she had to fill the sink up with soapy water and do them all by hand. Plus, Danielle had been working in the afternoons and by the time she got back, she was tired.

She glanced at the clock on the wall in the kitchen, took a deep breath, and went to get dressed for the event. After she put on the most conservative thing she owned—her knee-length navy skirt, pullover white blouse, and tennis shoes—her heart pounded, wishing there was some way to get out of going. But Emily had been so sweet when she came to invite her, and Danielle suspected Katie Ann and Lillian would be there—and she really liked both of them.

It was Vera and Sarah she was mostly worried about.

She wound her hair into a loose side braid, something she'd been doing most of the time, since she didn't have electricity to use her flatiron. She'd gotten used to using lanterns in the evening, and even found it a bit cozy—and romantic—even though romance didn't seem to have a big claim on their lives at the moment. Levi had even stopped kissing her with the passion of their wedding night. It was hard not to be depressed, and there wasn't even a television or radio to take her mind off things. So she'd tried bread making a few times and played games on her cell phone in the mornings until time for work. When Martha came to visit, Danielle took advantage of that time to charge her cell phone in Martha's car.

She'd also found a new love of pickled okra, something she didn't even like before she was pregnant. Now she went to the market every other day for a new jar.

She picked up her box of cookies to take to Sisters Day, found her purse and keys, and made herself walk out the door. Maybe it wouldn't be so bad.

SARAH PULLED UP at Emily's house at the same time as Vera and Betsy. No matter how things had transpired, Sarah respected the sacrament of marriage enough not to do anything more to try to cause problems between Levi and Danielle. She had no choice but to go on with her life. But her stomach churned at the thought of having to be around the girl at all.

Sarah forced a bright smile to her face and climbed out of the buggy as Vera and Betsy walked past. "*Wie bischt*, Vera and Betsy?" Sarah balanced her container of whoopee pies and stepped into stride alongside Vera, who toted a cake plate covered in foil. When Betsy skipped ahead of them, Sarah whispered, "We haven't had a chance to talk since—"

"The Lord's will has been done." Vera kept her eyes straight ahead and moved faster toward the house. There was no mistaking Vera's sharp tone of voice.

"Well, of course it has." Sarah had failed to stop the wedding, but was Vera going to hold a grudge? "I—I hope that—"

"Sarah, now is not the time." Vera hurried in front of Sarah and up the porch steps with Betsy.

Sarah followed slowly, unsure what to make of Vera's attitude. She'd done everything she could do. What had the woman expected? And did she somehow *blame* her for how it ended?

"Emily, dear." Vera hugged her daughter, then Sarah did the same.

Sarah put her whoopee pies alongside the many other dishes on Emily's kitchen table, then made her way around the room greeting the other ladies. Lillian was sitting on the couch with her two daughters, Anna and Elizabeth, and Katie Ann was carting Jonas on her hip. Levi's sister-in-law, Beth Ann, was in the far corner. Beth Ann was another woman in their community who had been married ample time to have conceived a child, but like Emily, was still not pregnant. Sarah hoped Beth Ann didn't start whining about it the way she was sometimes known to do. Hannah, Ida Mae, Karen, Frieda, and Laura Jane were already there—all kin to Katie Ann through her husband, Eli.

The only person Sarah didn't see was Danielle. Emily had already told her that she'd extended an invitation to Danielle in an effort to make her feel welcomed into the family. Emily was like that. Always sweet. Sarah knew she should be more like Emily. Sometimes there was a bitterness that crept inside Sarah's soul, an unpleasant restlessness that she knew she brought on by her actions. She took a deep breath and once again resolved to be a better person.

But when Danielle walked in, Sarah felt her resolve melt like butter on a griddle. If there was anything to be thankful for, it was that Martha wasn't with Danielle. The older *Englisch* woman was obnoxious, and Sarah couldn't believe she'd been allowed into their circle. Martha had attended several Sisters Days in the past, arriving with Katie Ann, and she went to most worship services. Sarah was sure the Lord didn't approve of Martha and her place within their community. If she hadn't been welcomed in, surely Danielle wouldn't have been able to sink her talons into Levi . . .

Danielle's long blond hair was pulled to one side in a braid, and Sarah tried not to think about Levi running his hands through it while they slept side by side at night. At least Danielle had dressed conservatively today, not the trashy way she'd been known to in the past. Sarah couldn't help but feel a slight sense of satisfaction that Danielle's face was red as she shuffled into the room. And her satisfaction grew when she noticed the box of store-bought cookies in Danielle's hands.

LEVI WONDERED HOW Danielle was faring at Sisters Day, knowing he probably shouldn't have pushed her into going, but he longed for her to be acknowledged by his family. His mother hadn't been back to the house since the morning after the wedding. And according to *Daed*, *Mamm* refused to speak about his marriage. Jacob had been coming to help Levi work on the house in the evenings, but even his brother avoided conversation about Levi's marriage.

He missed the closeness of family, of community. He could tell that Danielle was doing her best to be a good wife, but their married life wasn't anything like he'd expected. Things started out awkward, and there hadn't been much change. They weren't intimate like husband wife should be. Levi knew that was his fault, and he prayed daily that he'd done the right thing by marrying Danielle. The calling had seemed so strong before, but he worried that he'd misread God's plan for him.

If there was a saving grace today, it was Emily. Levi knew that his sister would be good to Danielle and do her best to make her feel included.

Levi walked to the buggy and got his lunch pail, as well as his father's. *Daed* had been picking him up for work every morning around six o'clock. Levi missed his mother's hearty breakfast before he set out for work; Danielle was still sleeping when he left. He was grateful for the lunch Danielle always made for him the night before, but the store-bought chicken salad was nothing like his mother made. Same went for the apple pie that Levi watched Danielle pull from a box to heat up.

Today they were installing solar panels on an *Englisch* house that was still under construction. The panels weren't meant to power up the entire house, just parts of it to minimize the electric bill. Levi wound his way around several construction workers to where his father was leaning against a stack of lumber. He handed him his black lunch pail.

Levi was chewing on his first bite, trying not to frown, when his father spoke up. "How is married life?" *Daed* grinned.

Levi tried to return the smile, not sure how his father had intended the question. *"Gut,"* Levi finally said before he took another bite, wondering if he'd ever have homemade bread again.

They were quiet for a few moments, then Levi asked, "Has *Mamm* spoken of our marriage?"

"*Nee.*" *Daed* pulled a thermos from his lunch box and took a sip of what Levi presumed was iced tea. Levi glanced at his own thermos filled with grape Kool-Aid. *It couldn't be that hard to make tea.* "But that's probably a *gut* thing, *sohn*," his father added. "Your *mamm* is dealing with this the best way she knows how."

Levi doubted it. He reached into a bag of potato chips as he watched his father scoop out a spoonful of broccoli and raisin salad, Levi's favorite. His mouth watered just thinking about the taste.

*Daed* smiled as he handed the container and spoon to Levi, reaching for the bag of chips. "I don't even remember the last time I had potato chips. Your *mudder* says they're bad for my cholesterol." His father bit into one of the chips with the same passion that Levi felt as he scooped up a bite of broccoli and raisin salad. Levi savored the flavor, and he could tell his father was doing the same thing with the chips, a gleam in his eyes as he ate two at a time.

Levi had wanted to talk to Jacob about what was on his mind, but since his brother didn't seem interested in talking much about him and Danielle, *Daed* was second in line. But every time Levi tried, the words just wouldn't come. It would have been so much better and easier to talk to his older brother, but Levi suspected Beth Ann was putting distance between Levi and Jacob. Maybe he was wrong, but his brother's wife didn't respect Jacob's place as head of the household. Everyone knew that Beth Ann ran most aspects of their lives.

*Daed* wadded up the empty chip bag and handed it back

to Levi. "Can't let your *mamm* see the evidence," he said, followed by a chuckle.

Levi gave him the empty container and spoon, wishing there had been twice the amount inside.

"I woulda told your *mudder* to send a lunch for you too, but I figure no sense fueling her fire. She'd think your new *fraa* wasn't taking care of you."

"It's okay. She . . ." Levi paused. "She doesn't really know how to cook." He thought about the frozen pizza they'd had for dinner last night. *Mamm* would have fallen over. Levi had always thought that he'd marry an Amish girl whose mother had taught her to cook. Now he faced the possibility of never having a home-cooked meal again. But he thought about how Danielle had been trying to make bread. At least she was trying, even though Levi had no idea what she was doing wrong. How hard could it be to get bread to rise? *Mamm* and Emily did it daily, several loaves.

*Daed* gave him a sorrowful smile. "I've heard Martha say repeatedly that she doesn't cook, so I reckon the girl didn't have much opportunity to learn. Be patient with her."

Levi nodded and followed his father back to the buggy. They both put the pails on the backseat. Then Levi couldn't stand it anymore. "*Daed . . .*"

His father turned to him. "*Ya, sohn?* What is it?"

"Danielle and . . ." Levi pulled his eyes from his father's and shifted his weight. He looped his thumbs in his suspenders, thankful it was a warm and sunny day. He'd have done anything to be spared asking his father this next question, but he had to know. "Danielle and I haven't . . ." He shrugged, still not looking up.

"Haven't what?"

"Uh, you know . . ." Levi locked eyes with his father. *Read my mind*, Daed. *Don't make me say it.*

In some ways, Levi and Danielle were so close. But in other ways they were miles apart, and Levi's question was one that needed to be answered if he was going to narrow the distance between them.

"*Ach* . . . do you mean . . . you haven't been intimate?" *Daed's* expression was difficult to read.

Levi nodded. "I'm afraid . . ." He took a deep breath. "I'm afraid I'll hurt her."

*Daed* raised a brow, frowning. "Huh?"

Levi rubbed his forehead and sighed. "You know, because she's pregnant. I'm afraid for the baby."

A slight smile formed on his father's face. "*Ach*, I see. If there are no problems, married couples have relations usually until just three or four weeks before the baby is born." *Daed* paused, stroking his beard. "Or in the case of Jacob, all the way up until the day he was born."

Levi could feel his face turning three shades of red as he avoided his father's eyes.

*Daed* slapped him on the shoulder. "Go home and be a husband to your *fraa* tonight. I promise you, it will be fine."

Levi knew his face was still red, but he smiled ear to ear just the same, wondering if they would finish early for the day today.

VERA WASN'T SURE who she was trying to avoid the most. Danielle or Sarah. She could barely stand to think about

Danielle and Levi married, yet Sarah's attempt at seducing her son—then telling Danielle about it—wasn't settling well with her either. Vera didn't regret asking Sarah to try to talk Levi out of his marriage to Danielle. The boy needed to be reminded about what was at stake. His life. His faith. But Sarah took it a step further than Vera would have liked. Although, if she was honest, she couldn't help but wonder if she'd be finding fault with the girl if her plan had worked, which made Vera question her own morals a bit.

She longed to know how Levi was doing. Was he happy? Well fed? Did Danielle read from the Bible with him in the evenings? Did they share devotion time? She doubted it. And that caused a pain in her heart. She was lost in her own thoughts when Lillian gently nudged her.

"Vera, what do you want to contribute?" Lillian was holding a pad and pen in hand, smiling. The main purpose of today's gathering was for everyone to come up with a list of food items to take to a nearby homeless shelter.

"I'll make a lemon pie and bring a pot of my stew." Vera smiled, watching Danielle out of the corner of her eye. Both Katie Ann and Emily had stayed close to her. Probably to protect her from any bitter words from Sarah. Or Vera. She frowned as she thought about her own daughter having to protect Danielle from the likes of mean ol' Vera. *That is not who I am.*

Everyone was gathered in Emily's living room, plates in their laps, as Lillian continued to make the rounds. Vera had barely touched the sampling of everything she had on her plate. She stood up and weaved her way through the chairs and into the kitchen. As she tossed her plate in the trash, she noticed that none of the cookies Danielle had brought were gone.

181

Well, it was no wonder. Who would want to eat those cookies with all the homemade treats around?

She twisted her mouth from side to side, knowing how she would feel if no one ate something that she brought. Glancing back into the living room, she knew that most of the women had loaded their plates for the last time. She let out a heavy sigh, sure that Levi must be starving in his new household.

Vera stared at the box for a few more moments. As discreetly as she could, she grabbed a handful of Danielle's store-bought chocolate chip cookies and stuffed them into her apron pockets. The girl had brought about two dozen cookies, and Vera probably now had about a dozen in her pockets.

She hurried through the living room, found her purse, then excused herself to the restroom. After she closed the door, she stole one of her daughter's hand towels, wrapped the cookies inside them, and stuffed them in her purse. Betsy would eat anything.

DANIELLE DUMPED THE box of macaroni and cheese into the pot and set the timer. Levi would be home soon, and she wanted to have a hot meal for him. After the noodles had cooked exactly ten minutes, she drained them and added the cheese powder and a can of tuna. *Voila!* Dinner. She smiled as she recalled her day. Most of the ladies had been nice to her and included her in their conversations. Danielle hadn't said much, but she had to admit that she felt the glow of a new bride when several of the women had congratulated her. No one brought up the baby, though, and that made her kind of sad. Vera and

Sarah had nodded when Danielle arrived, but then stayed away from her. And that was fine by Danielle.

She gave the noodles and tuna a final stir, pulled the pot off the stove, then glanced at her box of cookies. At least a dozen were gone, so she felt good about that. And she could send the rest with Levi for his lunches. She glanced around the kitchen. The sink had last night's dishes in it, but she'd been gone a good part of the day. She'd get to them tomorrow.

A few minutes later, she heard Elam's buggy pull up, and she knew Levi would be coming in. She smoothed the wrinkles in her skirt and waited for him, looking forward to a kiss and hug after a long day. Levi burst through the door just as she leaned down and picked a stray noodle from the floor. His face was flushed and he seemed out of breath.

"I made dinner." She straightened and smiled. "Something cooked. I mean, it's probably nothing like—"

Levi's mouth shushed her with a kiss like she hadn't experienced since her wedding night. He swooped her into his arms, kissing her all the while as he carried her directly to their bed. And as he leaned over her, looking at her with such passion as he unwound her braid, Danielle had one thought.

*I should have cooked a hot meal a long time ago.*

# Fifteen

LEVI HAD NEVER FELT MORE UNCOMFORTABLE IN his life, and he wasn't sure how or why he'd agreed to this. He glanced around the waiting room filled with pregnant women. *This is no place for a man.*

Danielle latched on to his hand, and he didn't pull away, even though public affection made him a little uncomfortable. But he knew why he was here.

Ever since he'd spoken with his father a couple of weeks ago, Levi and Danielle had spent a lot of time in the bedroom. And it seemed like Levi would agree to most anything while they were in there. He scratched his chin with his free hand as he recalled their conversation last week when Danielle had asked him to come to the doctor's office with her.

Danielle waited until today to tell Levi that he would come in for her examination, then they'd run a machine over her stomach and tell them if the baby was a boy or a girl. If the first part wasn't frightening enough, the second part seemed downright unnatural. He glanced down at his black slacks and long-sleeved blue shirt. The only part of his Amish attire that he'd shucked was his hat. His hair was still in the traditional cut, and he wasn't sure he could keep his britches up without suspenders. Danielle had suggested a belt, but Levi kept the suspenders. He wondered if everyone could tell he was Amish.

He reminded himself that he wasn't actually Amish, even though he and Danielle had attended worship service recently. But it wasn't the same, and Levi was working on feeling at peace about all that.

His mother still hadn't been by for a visit, but Emily had come by twice. God bless his sister. She'd brought homemade bread, cookies, a pot of stewed chicken, and a batch of creamed celery. Danielle hadn't seemed offended at all, and for the next three nights they'd eaten the way Levi was used to eating. He was praying every night that Emily would find time to teach Danielle to cook. Emily had learned from the best. Their mother.

"Don't look so nervous." Danielle squeezed his hand as she leaned over and whispered to him.

"I'm not nervous," Levi finally said as he asked God to forgive the small lie. He forced a smile, wishing he were anywhere but here. He was sure his father had never had to do this before. Jacob and Emily were delivered by a midwife, and Levi had often heard his father tell of how he waited on the front porch until they were both born. And even though Levi and Betsy were born in a hospital in Middlefield, *Daed* had been outside in a waiting room, and to Levi's knowledge, he'd never been to a doctor's appointment with their mother.

Levi swallowed hard. "I just don't know why you'd want me in there when they . . ."

Danielle smiled. "Okay, listen. You don't have to come in for the exam, but I really want you to be in there to hear the baby's heartbeat. Remember the other day, when the baby kicked and you got to feel it? That was cool, huh?"

"*Ya.* That was cool." He smiled at the recollection, feeling relieved that he wouldn't have to go in while the doctor examined her.

"Then that's that. I'll come get you when it's time for the ultrasound."

"And they will be able to see if it's a boy or a girl?" Levi took a deep breath. "Or if anything is wrong with the baby?"

Danielle gave his hand another squeeze. "Don't worry. I'm sure nothing is wrong with the baby." She paused. "I don't care if it's a boy or a girl. I just want a healthy baby."

The whole process made Levi nervous, but he nodded. His wife's beautiful face was aglow, and if it would make her happy, he'd suffer through it.

It was about ten minutes later when they called Danielle's name. *Danielle Detweiler.* He liked hearing that.

About a half hour later, a nurse came out and called Levi's name, motioning for him to follow her. And he did. On shaky legs.

Danielle was lying on her back, her head propped up with a few pillows, with electronic gadgets all around her. He frowned, thinking she looked sick.

"I'm fine, Levi," she said as the nurse left them alone, promising to be back shortly with the ultrasound machine. "The doctor said everything is okay, but I've kinda gained a little too much weight. So I'll have to watch that." She frowned, but Levi thought she was perfect. And how could she be gaining weight when he was sure he'd lost weight? His appetite just wasn't what it used to be. Except maybe when Emily came calling. He smiled to himself, wondering when his sister's next visit would be.

A few minutes later, the nurse lifted Danielle's shirt to reveal her slightly enlarged tummy. Levi felt his cheeks warming, but he reminded himself that *Englisch* men watched this kind of procedure all the time. That's what Danielle had told him.

He thought about the life she was carrying and how he'd be raising this child as his own, and suddenly he couldn't wait to find out if the baby was a boy or a girl. But it feared him that something might be wrong with the child, and Levi knew that the machine would tell them that too. He held his breath as the older woman doctor squirted a thick goo over Danielle's belly, then ran a round piece of equipment over her stomach. He watched the screen as gray images moved around. There was only a slushy sound, and Levi wondered if that was normal. Within a minute, there was a faint rhythm that got stronger as the doctor moved the wand.

"There it is," the doctor said. "A good, steady heartbeat." She looked up at Levi and pointed to the monitor and circled a pulsing image. "Do you see this, Daddy?"

Levi blinked a few times. *Daddy.* That sounded nice. He nodded as he watched the tiny life inside of his wife, a miracle, a blessing from God. Then he looked at Danielle as her eyes filled with tears.

"Is everything okay with the baby?" Danielle bit her bottom lip.

The doctor smiled. "Everything looks perfect."

Relief swept over Levi like sun rays on a wintry day.

"Do you want to know what it is, a boy or a girl?"

Danielle looked up at Levi, and he nodded.

Levi couldn't breathe. Any second, he would know if they were going to have a girl or a boy. He wasn't sure Danielle was breathing either.

"Congratulations, Mr. and Mrs. Detweiler." The doctor smiled. "You are having a boy."

Danielle looked up at him as she squeezed his hand. "We're having a son, Levi."

It was everything Levi could do not to cry. It was the strangest feeling. He knew in his heart that he hadn't created this baby.

God had.

And He had chosen Levi to be the father.

*"Be a father to this child, Levi. He will do great things in the future."*

Levi heard the voice loud and clear, and if he'd ever doubted that the Lord's hand was resting on Him, Danielle, and the baby . . . he didn't anymore.

"Have you picked out a name?" The doctor smiled as she packed up the ultrasound machine and cleaned off Danielle's belly.

Danielle looked up at Levi. "Maybe."

The doctor smiled. "I'll be eager to hear it when you've decided. Danielle, just check with the receptionist on your way out to make your next appointment."

Danielle nodded, then looked back at Levi as the doctor closed the door behind her. "I'd like to name him Joshua, if that's okay with you?"

Levi swallowed hard. He doubted that Danielle knew the

biblical meaning behind the name, that Joshua succeeded Moses as leader of the Israelites, leading the people to the Promised Land. Danielle probably didn't know that Joshua was the Hebrew word for Jesus.

"I think that is a great name." He shifted his weight, reaching for her hand. "What made you choose it?"

She sat up and pulled her shirt down. Then she shrugged. "I don't know." She let go of his hand and slid off the table. She pulled on her shoes, then picked up her purse from the chair. Reaching for the door, she stopped and faced him. "Actually . . ." She pushed her hair behind her ear. "I woke up the other morning with that name in my head."

Danielle smiled before walking out the door and down the hall. Levi stood there for a few moments before he followed her. God had given her the name. Just as surely as he'd just spoken to Levi.

About an hour later, they pulled into the driveway, and Levi shook his head as he looked around the yard at all the work that needed to be done. He was glad they'd repaired the porch steps, which had been a priority since Danielle was pregnant, but there were still cracked windowpanes and a fence surrounding the front yard that was about to topple over. And that was just the outside. He recalled the pristine way his family kept their property and comforted himself, knowing it would take time to have their own place looking like that.

But when he followed Danielle into the living room, he couldn't help but eye the paper plate on the floor next to one of the rocking chairs, two half-empty glasses, and an *Englisch* magazine with a pretty woman on the cover. As they made their way to the kitchen, Levi scrunched his nose. Something smelled unpleasant.

"What's that smell?" He gazed upon the stack of unwashed dishes that had been there for several days.

Danielle put her purse on the counter as she turned to face him. "What smell?"

"Something smells bad."

She walked to the refrigerator and pulled out a bottle of water. "I don't smell anything."

Levi cringed. He was thankful that his mother hadn't seen the way they were living. "Want me to help you clean up the kitchen?" He was used to being at work all day, coming home to eat, bathe, and read his Bible, then before he knew it . . . time for bed. Today he was off work to go with Danielle to the doctor, and for the first time, made himself take a good look around. Didn't his new *fraa* know how to clean house? Even though she worked most afternoons, she still had the mornings to do a little cleanup.

Danielle walked into the living room, slid the paper plate on the floor over with her foot, and sat down. "No, that's okay. I'll get it done tomorrow."

*Really?* Levi sat down in the other rocker and reached for his Bible on the makeshift table next to him. A cardboard box.

"Why do you still read the Bible every day when you don't have to anymore? I mean, since you're not Amish." She cocked her head to one side.

Levi marked his place with his finger. "I just like to. I think about what I've read, talk to God, and pray about things on my mind."

"Like what?"

Levi closed the book. Danielle rarely wanted to talk about

anything to do with God, even though he knew she felt God's presence sometimes, just like she had at the little church where they'd been married. Or maybe even that morning, when she'd decided on their son's name. "Uh, well . . . today I'm thanking the Lord that the baby looks healthy and that everything went well at the doctor."

Danielle kicked the rocker into motion with her foot. "Hmm . . ." She laid a hand across her stomach.

Levi missed the family devotion time with his parents and Betsy. "Do you want to . . . uh, pray with me?"

She shook her head. "No. But you go ahead." She leaned her head back against the rocker but turned her head to face him. "Is that bad?"

He shrugged. "No. It's not *bad*." He opened the Bible again but couldn't focus. Holding his spot, he said, "Do you pray? I mean . . . ever?" He held his breath. *Please, God, let her say yes.*

"Sometimes."

Relief washed over him.

"You know how I feel about all the God stuff." She paused, biting her bottom lip. "But sometimes I feel . . ." She shrugged. "I dunno. Like maybe there is Someone out there far, far away that I just can't reach. Maybe I don't try hard enough. Or maybe I'm not worthy."

This was the most he'd gotten out of Danielle about God since he'd known her, and it thrilled him to be having this discussion. "None of us are worthy, Danielle. Only Christ's sacrifice made us forever-worthy."

"Then why do it, the praying, the talking to Him?"

Levi closed the book and twisted his body in the chair to face her. "Because when you feel the Holy Spirit, or when God answers a prayer, it's an amazing feeling, and you know you're a part of something so much bigger than just yourself."

Danielle stared at him with a blank look for a few moments. "Do you see how you're acting?"

"What?"

"You're so excited talking about God." She frowned. "And I just don't get it. I don't feel it, Levi. And I don't know if I ever will." She shook her head. "But I will never, ever do anything to interfere with your, uh . . . relationship . . . with God."

Levi hung his head for a moment, but quickly looked back into her beautiful green eyes, noticing the small scar on her cheek. He tried to understand how her past had affected the present and possibly their future. He'd always been taught that God had a plan. Levi wondered if he'd been in Danielle's shoes, if he would have questioned God's plan too. But her being tolerant of his relationship with God just wasn't enough. He wanted her to know God; anything less was cheating herself out of the most beautiful part of life.

"Will you do me a favor?" Levi reached for her hand and intertwined their fingers.

She smiled. "I'll do anything for you."

"Pray with me, then."

He felt her try and edge away, but he kept a firm hold, pretending like he didn't notice.

"Oh, okay." She bit her lip again for a second. "But you'll have to do all the talking."

Levi smiled. "No problem." He bowed his head, unsure if she was doing the same. He closed his eyes, and before he spoke aloud, he prayed that the Lord would touch Danielle somehow, that He would give Levi the right words to get through to her.

"My dear Lord in heaven, today I thank You for Your many blessings . . . for Danielle, and for our baby Joshua, a true miracle and gift. I pray, Lord, that You will guide our hands to be *gut* parents and that we will raise our *kinner* according to . . ." Levi had almost said the *Ordnung* when he remembered that their children wouldn't be raised Amish. "To be *gut* Christians. I pray that You will bless our food, the work of our hands, and that we will be generous and kind to all those we meet. I ask You to bless this new home of ours and all who come here. And, Lord, I pray that You will bless my marriage to Danielle. Please keep Your hand on us and help us to stay on the path You've chosen for us. Amen."

Within a matter of seconds, Danielle had jumped from her rocking chair and into Levi's lap. She buried her head against his chest.

"Ladybug?" He tried to ease her away, but she kept her face against his shirt, now damp with her tears. "Danielle, what is it? Why are you crying?" He ran a hand the length of her hair. "Tell me."

She kept her head buried in his chest as she mumbled, "I don't know."

"Did I say something in my prayer that upset you?" He tried again to get her to sit up and look at him, but she clung to his shirt and kept her face buried.

She shook her head. "No, Levi. You didn't upset me. I just feel . . . emotional."

Levi pulled her closer. "That's a *gut* thing." Levi smiled, stroking her hair. "Sometimes, I think when God is reaching out to us, it can be a little overwhelming."

She eased away, and Levi began to kiss away her tears.

"I'm sorry I'm crying." She swiped at her eyes. "I must seem dumb."

Levi smiled before he kissed her on the mouth. "No. It's not dumb at all."

"I just . . ." She shrugged. "I don't know how to explain it, so can we not talk about it anymore?"

"Okay."

She buried her face in his chest again. Levi knew that his new wife might not realize it yet, but the hand of the Lord was on her. It always had been. But maybe this was the first time that she felt Him near.

*What an amazing feeling.*

Levi pulled her closer. *Thank You, Lord. Thank You, thank You . . .*

AN HOUR LATER, Danielle was at her little church, sitting in the front row. She'd told Levi that she was going to the store for milk, and that was true. But now here she was. Unsure why. Again.

She took a deep breath, crossed her legs, and stared at the front of the church. As she kicked her foot into action, her thoughts were awhirl. When Levi had prayed for them, she'd felt hopeful, but scared at the same time. What if she allowed God into her heart and He let her down again? Was the payoff worth the risk?

And what was in the back of her mind, something that seemed buried in the memories of life with her mother? It was like a seed that had sprouted and was climbing through thick soil, stretching for daylight, but never quite making it to the surface. Sometimes, like today with Levi, it felt like the topsoil was beginning to loosen and crack, but the light still seemed out of reach.

*God, was I a bad child?*

It was the only thing that came to mind.

She could barely remember when her father was alive, even though she was eleven when he died. Why was that? She knew she'd felt loved when he was around, which was far too seldom. He'd worked a lot. But why couldn't she remember much else?

*I'm going to go now. I'll probably come back.*

She stood up and walked out of the church.


LEVI ANSWERED THE door, excited to see Emily, and even more excited that she was carrying a large bag. "I hope that's food." He rubbed his hands together before he pulled her into a hug.

"*Ya.* It is. *Mamm* said you looked thin at worship service."

Levi eased away from Emily and closed the door behind her, giving it a hard kick. "She barely spoke to me or Danielle."

"It will take her some time, Levi. She'll come around." Emily handed him the bag. "Is Danielle here?"

"*Nee.* She went to town to get milk. She'll be back soon. Doesn't take long when you have a car." He offered a weak smile, a little embarrassed by the luxury. Then he remembered the way the kitchen looked. He scooped up the paper plates and glasses on the floor in the living room. "Here, sit. I'll put this in the kitchen and be right back."

Levi hurried to the kitchen, put the bag on the counter,

and stuffed the plates in the garbage. When he turned around, Emily was standing in the doorway.

"Sorry about the mess." Levi glanced around the kitchen.

"*Ach*, it's okay." Emily smiled. "I stopped by unannounced."

Levi shook his head. "It's not okay, but I don't know what to do about it." He walked to where his sister was standing and whispered . . . even though no one else was around. "I don't think Danielle knows how to clean house."

Emily grimaced. "Really?"

Levi waved a hand toward the sink full of dishes. "Or this just doesn't bother her. I don't know. And I don't want to hurt her feelings, but . . ."

Emily untied her black bonnet and pulled it off her head, then straightened her white prayer covering. "Maybe she wasn't taught how to clean properly."

"I don't know." Levi shook his head. "Martha kept a neat house, but I think she had to stay on Danielle about cleaning up after herself. Danielle's mentioned that."

"Maybe she's just tired. I hear that pregnant women are tired a lot." His sister got a faraway look in her eyes. Levi knew how much Emily and David wanted a baby, and it just hadn't happened yet.

"So, what's in the bag?" Levi tapped the brown paper bag, then took a peek inside, inhaling deeply. "Bread. I'm so thankful."

"And some chicken and rice casserole and a pecan pie." Emily frowned. "Does it hurt Danielle's feelings when I bring food?"

Levi laughed. "*Nee*. I think she's as grateful as I am." He faced his sister. "If you ever have time, maybe you can teach her some of *Mamm's* recipes? She's been trying to make bread, but it never comes out. We eat lots of food out of boxes and from the freezer. And what I wouldn't do to have some meatloaf . . ."

"I'll be happy to." Emily nodded at the lantern Levi kept on the kitchen counter. "How is Danielle handling not having electricity?"

"Doesn't really seem to bother her. She charges her cell phone in Martha's car when she comes to visit or at their house when she goes there. And I told her I liked her hair with the natural wave, so she doesn't straighten it with that iron anymore when she's at Martha's." He pulled the bread out of the bag as he talked. "But I did tell her I'd put in some solar panels when I can afford it."

Emily grinned. "Well, since you're in the business, I'm sure *Daed* will give you a *gut* deal."

Levi leaned against the counter. "I guess I'm enjoying living the way I used to live for as long as I can."

Emily touched Levi on the arm. "I know all of this is new and strange for you, Levi. But I continue to pray for you every day. I think what you're doing is honorable. And you will be a *gut* father."

"It's a boy." Levi smiled. "We went to the *Englisch* doctor today, and they told us we're having a boy. We're naming him Joshua." He knew pride was a sin, but the feeling was abundant just the same.

Emily wrapped him in her arms for a quick hug. "*Ach*, that's wonderful, Levi. Joshua will be a lucky little boy to have you in his life." She stepped back. "Now, I need to go. Enjoy the food, and tell Danielle that I will be happy to show her how to make bread and some of your favorite recipes. If you're sure she'd welcome that idea."

"*Danki*, Emily." He followed her out of the kitchen and through the living room to the front door.

"No problem. I don't have anything else to do." She sighed.

"God will bless you with *kinner* soon. I know it."

Levi watched Emily walk to her buggy, and he thought about everything she'd been through. The rape back in Middlefield, her enduring the trial. It had been a horrible time for all of them. Emily still had a small scar above her eyebrow from the incident, about the same size as the scar on Danielle's cheek. But God had lovingly healed Emily and sent David into her life. They were a wonderful couple, and Levi was going to remember to say an extra prayer for his sister, that the Lord would bless them with children soon.

For the first time, he thought about the similarities between Emily and Danielle. In so many ways, they weren't anything alike, at least not to someone who didn't know them. But they'd both suffered abuse. Levi tried to picture Danielle being abused over and over again. The thought caused his jaw to tighten as his hands clenched into fists at his sides.

Levi hoped he never laid eyes on Danielle's mother. His new wife hardly ever mentioned her, and he hoped Danielle was healing, but Levi wasn't sure he could keep in accordance with the *Ordnung* around the woman.

Once again, he remembered. *I'm not Amish.*

And that thought weighed heavily on him. He wondered if he'd ever stop feeling that way. He'd preached to everyone about how he could take his faith with him wherever he went, and he had, but his heart hurt, knowing that he was leaving behind the tradition of his people. A way of life he loved.

Danielle walked in the door, her eyes wet with tears. He'd been so lost in thought, he hadn't heard the car pull up.

"What is it?" he asked, pulling her into his arms. "What's wrong?"

She clung to him. "I stopped by Martha and Arnold's on the way home. I got a letter from my mother."

# Sixteen

LEVI HELD HIS WIFE FOR A WHILE LONGER AS SHE cried. When she finally eased away, she sniffled and pushed the envelope in his direction.

Levi took it. "Is she sorry about everything, asking for forgiveness?" Levi knew that forgiveness wouldn't come easy for Danielle.

"Just read it." She swiped at her eyes, sniffling again.

Levi pulled the letter out and read it.

Danielle,

I've met someone. He's a wonderful man, like your father was. His name is Louis, and we're getting married on August 12. I know that's only a month away, but neither of us want to wait. I've told him all about you, and I can't wait for you to meet him. He's changed me, Danielle. We go to church every Sunday. Louis has been such a positive influence in my life, and the Lord blessed me with this second chance.

I know we had to walk separate paths for a while, but

isn't it time we come back together again? This is an exciting time in my life, and I'd really like for you to be a part of it. Hope to hear from you soon.

Love,

Mom

Levi had never met Vivian, but this wasn't what he expected. If she had truly changed, wouldn't she be seeking forgiveness for the way she'd treated Danielle over the years? It didn't seem like Vivian was even aware of the damage she had caused, physically or emotionally. But when Levi's eyes met his wife's, he knew that if Danielle really desired healing, she was going to have to forgive her mother, even if her mother wasn't ready to ask for it.

Danielle's bottom lip trembled. "I *hate* her."

"You don't mean that."

"Yes, I do." She spit the words out, gritting her teeth. Then she started to cry again. "Did you read that?" She pointed toward the note in his hands. "Do you see, now, how she is? How self-serving . . . The whole world revolves around her! And where do the rest of us land? We're nothing but garbage in the road."

"Maybe this was a first step for her." He cupped his wife's cheek. "Maybe she's working her way toward asking for your forgiveness."

Danielle stepped back and away from him. "I would think that'd be her *first* goal if she wants to have a relationship with me." She waved a hand in the air. "It doesn't matter anyway. I don't forgive her. I don't want her in my life. And I'm definitely not writing her back."

Levi's feet were rooted to the wood floor, unsure what to do. He watched her walk around the corner, heading toward their bedroom. Slowly, he followed her, praying the entire time.

VERA WAS JUST finishing a dress for Betsy when she heard a knock at the door. "Betsy, run and get that. I'll be there in a minute." She bit the thread with her teeth and put the dress down on her sewing table. By the time she reached the living room, Betsy had the door open.

"I've told you over and over that you don't have to knock." Vera pulled Emily into a hug, quickly stepping back. "Now tell me. How is your *bruder*?"

"He's *gut*, *Mamm*. I took him some more food."

Vera put a hand to her chest. "*Ach, gut*. That girl isn't feeding him."

Emily sat down on the couch. "Apparently Danielle doesn't really know how to cook. Levi said that they eat things out of boxes or out of the freezer."

Vera gasped, shaking her head. "Our poor boy." She sat down next to Emily and put her head in her hands.

"He seems happy, though, *Mamm*. I think he really loves Danielle."

Vera slowly raised her head and folded her hands in her lap. "I don't know how he can be happy living in that run-down house and eating food from boxes."

"*Mamm* . . ." Emily laid a hand on Vera's. "We need to gather a group together and go help them get the inside of that *haus* in order. Maybe that'd inspire her to learn how to cook? I know Jacob, Arnold, and some others have helped

Levi with the outside, but . . . they need a lot of help with the inside."

"I'm not an evil person, Emily. Of course we'll help them." Vera raised her chin and pressed her lips together.

"Then why haven't you been over there?"

"I will. Soon."

Emily stood up from the couch. "I hope you will. I sense that Levi feels a bit lost, making his way. I'm sure he would enjoy a visit from you." She walked toward the door. "I can't stay. I just dropped by because you wanted to know about Levi. I've got a stack of sewing and mending I need to get to."

"I'm sure he *does* feel lost," Vera mumbled as she rose and followed Emily to the door. "He's stepped so far off of God's path that he's knee-deep in—"

"*Mamm.*" Emily spun around. "It's not for you to decide God's plan for Levi's life. Levi said he felt called to marry Danielle and raise this child. You need to accept him at his word."

Vera put her hands on her hips, looked at the floor, and shook her head. She knew in her mind that Emily was right, but the steps to get her heart in line weren't coming easily. Every time she felt she was getting closer, she found herself wishing it was all a nightmare from which she'd wake soon. But it wasn't. It was her son's new life. And she didn't want to lose him entirely. Emily was right . . . "I will pay them a visit soon."

"When?"

"This week. Or next, at the latest."

Vera watched her daughter drive away in her buggy, thanking God that both Emily and Jacob had chosen *gut* Amish spouses and that they were living their lives the way God intended by following the *Ordnung*. She was praying extra hard that young Betsy would follow in their footsteps.

Because if two of her children left the Order, she just might have a heart attack.

A WEEK LATER, Danielle sat down to write her mother a letter. No matter how many letters she wrote, Danielle didn't think she'd ever heal. She stared out the window, watching as the leaves on the tree rustled in the wind. It wasn't the physical abuse . . . even the memory of her mother's harsh slaps across the face and fists against her back now seemed like a grainy documentary. For Danielle, it was the lack of love. Her mother's ability to walk away from her and never return, never call. Even in the face of Martha's wrath and threats, didn't a mother who loved a child do *something* to reach out?

And yet she'd had the audacity to sign the letter *Love, Mom*.

Danielle started to write four times, then wadded up the paper and aimed for the trash can across the room, missing all four times. Standing up, she went to another window and raised a tattered shade all the way up so she'd have more light at the kitchen table. Surprisingly, the lack of electricity hadn't bothered her all that much. Except she did miss a microwave for reheating food. And television.

Taking a deep breath, she started again.

Dear Mom,

I'm married. I'm happy. I'm pregnant. Don't write me anymore.

As a tear spilled down her cheek, she scrunched up this latest version and tossed it where the others rested, on the floor by the trash can. Then, for a few moments, she closed her eyes and pretended that things were different between her and her mother. She imagined her mom cuddling Joshua, loving him, and telling Danielle how proud of her she was. But the daydream faded quickly. She didn't want Vivian Kent anywhere near her baby. No one, *no one*, would ever be allowed to hurt him. Not if Danielle could help it.

Levi had been at work for nearly four hours, and this was Danielle's only mission for the day, to write her mother a letter. But the words just weren't coming. As she'd expected, the restaurant had cut her hours—and Sue's—so no work today. They had planned to have lunch and go shopping, but Sue had canceled to have lunch with a new guy she was seeing. Danielle didn't fault her for that, but between the new man in Sue's life and their reduced work hours, they were seeing less and less of each other.

There was a knock at the door, and Danielle rose, happy for the interruption. "Martha!" she said with a smile as she eyed a bag of groceries. "Whatcha got there?" She pushed the door wide.

"Food." Martha kissed her on the cheek.

"We have enough food, you know. We're not starving." She reached out to accept the bag of groceries that Martha handed her, following her through the house.

Martha moved through the living room, her eyebrows narrowing into a frown. Then, without invitation, she shuffled across the wooden floor into the kitchen. Danielle followed, stopping at the kitchen threshold. She cringed, knowing what was coming.

"Danielle, this place is a pigsty." Martha slammed her hands to her hips. "I know this is how you kept your room at home, but you are a wife now, and soon to be a mother. I stayed quiet, up front, with you being a newlywed and all. But now . . . Girl, it's seriously time to get your act together."

Danielle took a few steps forward. "What? It's not that bad."

Martha squinted her eyes, crinkling her nose. "You're kidding me, right? This place is a wreck."

"Well, it's not your place, so don't worry about it." Danielle shifted her weight, folding her arms across her chest.

"Look here, missy. There is a baby coming into this world, and babies need a clean place to live."

"Levi doesn't seem to mind."

"Hogwash! Vera's house is immaculate, and I guarantee that boy doesn't like living like this. You're just still on your honeymoon, and he doesn't want to hurt your feelings."

Danielle pondered that for a few moments. Levi *had* asked her a week ago if she wanted him to help her clean the dishes . . .

Martha walked around the kitchen, taking a closer inspection. "What do you do all day?" She raised an eyebrow.

"Sometimes I work in the afternoons, and I have these crazy nap-attacks, with the baby and all . . . and they've cut my hours, so I'm off again today. But I stay busy. Married life . . . Well, you know. You take care of your husband." Danielle frowned, thinking over her daily routine. She'd read her magazines yesterday morning and painted her toenails. Sometimes she fell asleep on the couch listening to her iPod, if she'd remembered to charge it. Plus, she'd learned how to download movies onto her iPhone. She hadn't mentioned that to Levi just yet. "You'll be happy to hear that I make our bed every day."

Martha snorted. "Well, that takes a grand total of three minutes."

"Did you stop by just to criticize me, or is there some other reason for your visit?"

Martha pulled out a chair at the kitchen table and sat down. "I wanted to know what the letter from your mother said." She nodded to the wadded-up pieces of paper by the garbage can. "And if you were writing her back."

Danielle didn't sit down. She nodded to the letter on the table next to her pad and pen. "Go ahead and read it."

Martha picked up the letter, and Danielle bit her nail while she read it. Martha shook her head as she put it down. "Honey, I'm sorry. I'm sure you were hoping for some sort of apology or something."

"Nope. I don't need anything from her. I don't care what she does."

Martha cupped her chin in her hands, resting her elbows on the table. "Then why are you writing her back? And struggling with it?"

"I'm not." Danielle scooped up all the failed attempts and stuffed them in the garbage. "I thought about it. But there's just no good way to tell your own mother that you hate her."

"You don't hate her, Danielle."

"Yes, I do."

Martha stared at Danielle in that all-knowing way that made Danielle want to yell at her, whether or not she was right. Danielle braced herself for a lecture about love, forgiveness, and, of course . . . God. But instead, Martha just slowly stood up and walked to Danielle. She gave her a hug and kissed her on the cheek again.

"You want me to stay? Help you clean up a little?"

"Nah. I'll get to it. Eventually," she added with a smirk.

"I sure hope so. You know that Arnold and I are here for you, right?" She smiled. "And we're going to be the best grandparents on the planet. Everyone knows that." She started toward the front door, Danielle on her heels. Martha turned around. "Vera ever come by here?"

Danielle shook her head. "No."

"She will. Give her time."

Danielle grunted. "I'm tired of everyone saying that. I wish that she'd come around for Levi's sake, but I don't need her judging me. I'm just the bad *Englisch* girl that stole her baby boy away from the Amish world."

"You know, Danielle . . . if you'd see yourself differently, then others would too." She pointed a red fingernail at Danielle. "Just food for thought, missy." Then with a tender smile, she turned to leave.

"Martha!" Danielle said, covering her own smile with her hand.

Martha reached the bottom porch step and turned around. "What?"

"Did you know that you have two large streaks of mud running down the back of your blouse?"

Martha stiffened. "Good grief! Do I really?"

Danielle laughed, which felt good.

"That dog of Arnold's! He almost tackled me to the ground this morning. Guess his paws were muddy." She shook her head.

"But Arnold loves that beast, so I tolerate the occasional tackling. He's gonna cause me to break a hip or something." She turned back around and headed to her car.

Danielle had seen Martha with Dude enough to question who loved "the beast" more . . . Martha or Arnold.

Danielle knew she was lucky to have them both in her life. People willing to accept her child as their "grandchild."

*Thank You, Lord, for Martha and Arnold.*

Well, wasn't that odd. The prayer seemed to come out of nowhere, and Danielle wasn't sure what to make of it. At Levi's insistence, they'd been praying together at night. Maybe some of it had rubbed off on Danielle.

But whatever. She was thankful for Martha and Arnold.

She glanced around the house and decided maybe Martha was right.

*At least cleaning the house will keep my mind off my mother . . .*


THROUGH MID-AUGUST, THE fields filled with wildflowers, and it was as if the sun never took a rest, shining brightly from early morning and staying with them until almost nine o'clock at night.

Levi's father and brother—and sometimes Arnold—had done a lot of repairs on the house. They'd replaced cracked windows, repaired the fence, and even put a new coat of paint on the outside of the house. Martha and Emily had come by a few times and helped Danielle with the cleaning. And thanks to Emily, Danielle had mastered the art of making homemade bread, much to her husband's delight, and learned to make meatloaf, his ultimate favorite.

Ironically, she and Levi lived almost exactly like the Amish did, and she'd learned to live without the luxuries she had before. But her life seemed pretty full. Things were wonderful between her and her new husband. The only thing that seemed to bother them both was their relationships with their mothers. Or *lack* of relationship. Danielle rarely talked about the void she felt in her life, but Levi mentioned his mother in passing quite often, and Danielle knew he missed her. So today she was going to make an effort to bring Levi and his mother closer.

She knocked on the Detweilers' door on a sunny Monday afternoon, carrying a pecan pie that Emily had showed her how to make. Danielle and Levi saw Vera every other Sunday since they still attended Amish worship, but the conversations were strained, and Danielle knew it was as much her fault as Vera's. Danielle had thought about what Martha said—that if Danielle thought more highly of herself, others would too. So today she stood tall as she waited for Vera to answer the door.

"Danielle." Vera swiped her forearm across a sweaty forehead. "What are you doing here?"

"I brought you a pie." She pushed the glass dish a few inches in front of her, hoping Vera would open the door.

"Today is Monday. Wash day." Vera made the comment in a chipper voice, seemingly glad that she wasn't going to have to invite Danielle in.

"Oh yeah. I forgot." She forced a smile. "Well, please, take the pie anyway. I made one for me and Levi too." She waited until Vera slowly opened the screen door. Taking the pie, Vera nodded.

"*Danki*, Danielle."

"You're welcome." She swallowed hard, then turned to go. Knowing it was important to Levi, she'd made her best effort. She was already in the yard when Vera called out to her. She turned around.

"I need a break. Why don't you come in and we'll have a piece of this pie and some *kaffi*."

Danielle waddled back up the steps. That's how she felt these days. At five months pregnant, she'd really ballooned up. Levi said she was glowing and beautiful, but she was pretty sure that in addition to the baby, she was just fat. And suddenly she was nervous about being alone with Vera. The woman was civil when they saw each other at church or some other gathering, but nothing changed the facts. Vera blamed Danielle for dragging Levi away from his people.

Vera held the door open, and Danielle walked into the living room. All the windows were open and a cool breeze blew through the room. She couldn't remember the last time she'd been inside the Detweilers' house, but it sure smelled good today. Like freshly baked bread. Danielle wondered if her pie would be acceptable.

"Have a seat, and I'll go cut us a piece of pie. Tea or coffee?" Vera wasn't smiling, but she wasn't frowning either.

"Tea, please." Danielle glanced around the room, and the feel of family wrapped around her. She was taking in her surroundings when Betsy came bouncing down the stairs. The nine-year-old let out a small gasp when she entered the living room.

"Danielle!" She ran to her side and plopped down on the couch. "You never come to our *haus*." Betsy put a finger to her lips for a moment. "And we never go to your *haus*."

Danielle swallowed hard. "I brought a pie."

"What kind of pie?"

"Pecan."

Betsy was quiet.

"Do you like pecan pie?" Danielle shifted her weight and hoped that things might be less tense with Betsy in the room. Although, one could never be sure what might come out of her mouth.

"*Ya*, I like pecan pie." Betsy eyed Danielle's stomach. Danielle had broken down and bought some maternity clothes a few weeks ago, and today she had on blue jeans with a stretch waist and a breezy yellow blouse. "You're going to have a baby."

"Yes. His name is Joshua, and he'll be here in four months." Danielle smiled at the thought. "He's kicking. Want to feel?" She picked up Betsy's hand and placed it on her stomach. Betsy's face lit up.

"Oooh. I feel him." Her hand was still on Danielle's stomach when Vera returned with two pieces of pie.

"Betsy, Danielle might not want you doing that." Vera's eyebrows drew together as she set Danielle's piece on the table beside her. Betsy pulled back her hand.

"It's okay. I asked her if she wanted to feel the baby kicking."

Vera smiled. Barely. "Betsy, do you want pie?"

"*Nee*," the girl said. "I'm still full from lunch."

Vera walked back to the kitchen and returned with two glasses of tea.

"Thank you." Danielle took a bite of the pie, savoring the sweet crunch of the pecans in the juice, knowing she'd knocked it out of the park.

Vera sat down in a rocking chair across from where Danielle and Betsy were sitting on the couch.

Betsy stared at Danielle, and Danielle wondered what was coming. But Betsy was quiet.

They were all quiet. Danielle was wishing she hadn't come. "I forgot today was wash day." Danielle smiled.

"How do you wash clothes? Emily tells me you have no power there." Vera kept her eyes on Danielle even as she took a bite of pie.

"I usually go to Martha's and use her washer and dryer."

"Of course."

Betsy still had her eyes on Danielle's stomach, and Danielle shifted her weight uneasily, wishing Betsy would focus on something else. Vera had never mentioned Danielle's pregnancy, but these days, there was no missing it. Levi had told his father that they were having a boy and naming him Joshua, so Danielle assumed that Vera knew it too.

Betsy scooted a little closer to Danielle. "Will I be able to hold the baby when he gets here?"

Danielle avoided Vera's eyes. "Sure." She smiled at Betsy.

"Do you think he'll weigh over nine pounds? Because then you might have to have a cesarean section."

"Betsy. Don't say such things." Vera shook her head.

"*Ach*, it's true, *Mamm*. Sometimes babies are breach, or they're too big, and they have to be cut right out of the mother's stomach." Betsy's eyes rounded as she spoke.

"*Ya*, I know, Betsy. But . . ." Vera glanced at Danielle. "Sorry. Betsy always has something on her mind."

Danielle smiled, even though Vera's cheeks were turning redder and redder. "It's okay." She turned to Betsy. "I'm hoping that I'll be able to have the baby the natural way. The doctor said everything looks good so far."

Betsy moved on to another subject, pointing to Danielle's flat silver sandals. "I like those."

"Thanks. Levi took me shopping last week for my birthday."

Betsy gasped. "Did you have cake?" She glanced back and forth between Danielle and Vera. "You have to have cake on your birthday."

"Yes, I did. We went to Martha and Arnold's to celebrate." She glanced at Vera, whose head was down.

"How old are you?" Betsy scooted even closer and put a hand on Danielle's leg.

"I'm nineteen now."

"Plenty old enough to have *kinner*, I'd say." Betsy gave a taut nod of her head, and Danielle watched Vera slowly close her eyes, then open them again.

Danielle placed her empty plate on the coffee table, wondering if she should carry it to the kitchen.

"Did you come in a car?" Betsy's sweet face stared up at her.

"Yes, I did."

"I won't ever get to have a car because we're Amish." Betsy frowned.

"I—I know." Danielle knew what Vera must be thinking—how Levi probably said the same thing before he was shackled and hauled off by the pregnant *Englisch* girl. Again, she was reminded about what Martha said. "*Think better about yourself and others will too.*"

"Will baby Joshua sleep in his own bed? He has to have his own bed, you know." Betsy rolled her eyes. "Otherwise my brother could roll over and squash him to death!"

"Betsy . . ." Vera sighed. "Don't you have something to do?"

"*Nee*. Nothing." She grinned, and Danielle couldn't help but smile too.

"No, we don't have a crib or anything like that yet. But we're saving our money, hoping to soon." Danielle stood up. "Vera, I'll let you get back to your washing. I just wanted to bring the pie and stop in to say hello."

Vera placed her half-eaten piece on the table beside the rocking chair. "*Danki* for the pie." She walked Danielle to the door.

"Okay, bye then." Danielle gave a quick wave.

Betsy wound around Vera until she was standing on the porch. "Bye, Danielle! Come back soon to see us! *Mamm* said she didn't understand why you don't ever come over!"

Danielle locked eyes with Vera and stifled a smile. "Well, you and your mom are certainly welcome to come to our house anytime." Danielle thought about how excited Levi would be if his family came to supper. "As a matter of fact, would you like to come for supper on Saturday?"

Vera opened her mouth to speak, probably to decline, but Betsy started jumping up and down. "*Ya! Ya!*"

"I—I suppose so," Vera finally answered. "What time?"

"Five o'clock."

"*Gut.* See you then."

"See you then," Danielle repeated with a smile. But as she turned away and climbed into her car, she thought, *What did I just do?*

# Seventeen

DANIELLE WALKED INTO MARTHA'S BEDROOM AND leaned over the bed. "I can't believe this happened." She eyed Martha's broken foot protruding from beneath the quilt at the end of the bed.

"I can. I'm lucky that dog didn't kill me." Martha rolled her eyes at Dude, who merely yawned from the floor and happily resumed sleeping. "Pull up a chair. I'm glad to see you. Katie Ann has been coming over and fussing over me like I'm an old woman. Arnold too. Both of them . . . fuss, fuss, fuss." Martha shook her head, but Danielle knew that there probably wasn't anything that Martha liked better than to be fussed over.

"How long do you have to stay off your foot?" Danielle scooted a chair close to Martha's bed and eased into it.

"Until it doesn't hurt anymore. And that could take forever."

Danielle straightened, then repositioned herself when she felt Joshua kicking. "Arnold said you fell down the porch steps."

"Yep. I was heading to market, and I guess Dude didn't

216

want me to go. He rushed me like an offensive tackle, and down I went."

Danielle covered her mouth with one hand.

Martha rolled her eyes. "Go ahead and laugh. I'm sure it was quite the sight."

"Well, I'm sorry you're hurting and laid up."

Martha waved her hand. "Tell me about you. Morning sickness gone?"

"Yep. Feeling really good these days." She put a hand on her stomach. "He's a feisty little guy, always kicking."

"That's good. So I hear."

"Guess what?" Danielle leaned closer, grinning. "Levi's whole family is coming to our house for supper Saturday night. Levi is so excited. I'm making your chicken lasagna. I've watched you do it a hundred times, so I'm going to try. Emily has been teaching me to cook some things, but I want to make something different."

"Vera is coming too?"

"Yes. So I want everything to go just perfectly." Danielle sighed. "I want her to like me."

"Honey, someday Vera will come to know what a fantastic, wonderful person you are. It's the concept of you taking her baby boy away that gets in the way for her."

"I know. She didn't even like us being friends, it freaked her out so much. And now . . . But maybe if she could see that we are happy, and that Levi is happy . . ." She paused, smiling. "Have I mentioned how happy we are?"

"Four hundred thousand times." Martha laughed, patting her hand. "And I'm happy for you. Just don't get your hopes up about Vera. She'll come around, but it will take her awhile."

"That's what everyone says—Levi and Emily too. But we've been married two months." Danielle sighed. "Well, either way, I'm looking forward to them coming. Levi will love it."

There was a knock at the door, and Katie Ann walked in.

Martha frowned. "Where's my baby? I thought you were bringing Jonas to see me today?"

"He was napping, and Ida Mae was at the *haus* with the twins, so she offered to stay while I came to check on you." Katie Ann pulled a container out of a small bag. "I brought you more creamed celery."

"You are forgiven." Martha licked her lips. "Nothing like creamed celery to heal all that ails a person."

"Hi, Danielle." Katie Ann smiled, and Danielle was glad the woman lived so close and felt compelled to take care of Martha. Danielle would do anything for Martha, but Katie Ann had a nurturing way about her that Danielle didn't think she herself had. Maybe that came with being a mother.

The three women chatted for a while, and Danielle half listened as she thought about Saturday night. She was going to make sure it was a great night for Levi.

LEVI WATCHED HIS beautiful wife scurrying around the kitchen on Saturday night, and he'd never been more proud. "Why haven't you made this before?" he asked, leaning over the stove and taking a peek under the tinfoil. The chicken lasagna looked delicious.

Danielle playfully slapped his hand. "Stay out of that now." She secured the foil again. "I had to get Martha to write the recipe down. She's made it so many times that she just knows it in her head and couldn't find the actual recipe." Danielle laughed. "Funny that it's the only thing she knows how to make. But . . ." She pointed to the written version on the counter by the sink. "I'm not sure if she meant teaspoons or tablespoons here, so I hope I did it right."

Levi wrapped his arms around her full belly. "It will be great." He was so thankful that Emily had been coming around and teaching Danielle how to cook. They had homemade bread on a regular basis now, and Danielle had mastered some of Levi's favorites, like his mother's chicken and rice casserole and meatloaf.

Danielle eased away from him, then paced the kitchen. Levi was as nervous as she was. His mother would be watching her like a hawk, and Levi wanted his mother to see that they were happy and living a good life. Danielle still prayed with him every night, and they attended Amish worship. It wasn't the same, but it was familiar, and it made Levi feel like he hadn't given up everything.

In the evenings, he laid his head near Danielle's stomach and talked to Joshua. He felt a strong bond with the child that he hadn't expected. Danielle wanted him to be in the room at the hospital when the baby was born, but he'd nearly passed out more than once when he'd witnessed a calf being born. Not wanting to admit that fact, he told her he would.

"They're here!" Danielle jumped, then frowned as she glanced around the kitchen. The house was cleaner than Levi had ever seen it, and he knew he had Martha to thank for that. She might have hurt Danielle's feelings a little, but whatever fire Martha lit underneath Danielle had sparked a cleaning frenzy that seemed to have changed her ways forever.

Levi kissed her. "I'll get the door. Don't worry about anything."

"DON'T LOOK SO uptight," Elam whispered to Vera as they waited for someone to answer the door.

"I'm not uptight." Vera snapped her head in his direction. "I'm happy to be seeing *mei sohn*."

"Less than four months until baby time!" Betsy squealed from beside Vera.

"Hush now." Vera latched on to Betsy's hand and, as always, worried what else Betsy might say this night.

Levi answered the door, and Vera rushed into his arms.

"*Mamm*, I just saw you last week." Levi laughed and kissed her on the cheek.

Vera stepped back and eyed him up and down. "I think you've lost weight since then."

"No, *Mamm*. I haven't." He stepped aside and ushered them in. "Ignore the walls. We can't paint them while Danielle is pregnant." He paused. "Someone said we could, using low-odor paint, but I don't want to take any chances."

Vera fought the urge to cringe every time the baby was mentioned. She loved children, but thoughts of Danielle and the child she carried just brought up unpleasant associations. *That doesn't make me bad.*

Danielle came into the room and greeted everyone, but Vera hardly noticed what she said. Vera's eyes were on her son and the way he watched Danielle, with a twinkle in his eye. Vera could practically feel the love radiating from him. Within the first minute of their visit, Vera realized that she was no longer the number one woman in Levi's life. She remembered when the realization hit her with Jacob, when he'd married Beth Ann. But marrying Beth Ann had been a wise move for Jacob.

Danielle was still talking, and Vera still wasn't listening. She watched her son, and without intending to, she felt a smile spread across her face. *He is happy.*

She decided to try and relax into the evening, even if just a little.

"Emily hasn't been by in a while," Danielle said as she served everyone chicken lasagna following the blessing. "Is she all right?"

Vera couldn't contain the smile that stretched across her face.

"*Mamm* . . . what is it?" Levi asked, his fork hovering in front of his mouth.

Vera shook her head. "*Ach,* I really can't say." Even though there was nothing she wanted to do *more* than to tell Emily's news.

"*Mamm,* you have to tell us now." Levi took the bite, chewed, and waited. Then it hit him. "Emily's pregnant, isn't she?"

"Yeessssss!" Betsy bounced up and down in her chair. "She is, isn't she?"

Vera covered her red face with her napkin for a moment. "I can't say."

"Too late!" Levi pointed his fork at her. "She is!"

Vera sighed. "Well, *ya.* Since you guessed, I guess I can't deny it."

"That's wonderful." Danielle sat down after serving everyone. "Levi said they've been hoping for a family. When is her baby due?" Danielle passed a basket of bread to her left.

"April." Vera took a slice of bread and passed it on. "Our first grandchild." She made the comment without even thinking, but when the table went silent, not even the clink of a fork, Vera looked up to see Levi's eyes burning into her skin. "I mean—except for—except for Danielle's baby." Vera could feel the heat rising from her neck and filling her cheeks. *I am the most insensitive person alive.*

"It's not Danielle's baby, *Mamm.* It's *our* baby." Levi looked at her with such disgust that Vera wished she could leave. She looked at Elam for help, but he had his head tucked, chewing on a bite of chicken lasagna.

"I know that, Levi. I just wasn't thinking." And that was the truth. She turned to Danielle, who wouldn't meet her eyes. "Danielle, this is really *gut* chicken lasagna. It tastes just like Martha's. You did an excellent job."

Danielle barely looked at her, but she smiled politely. "Thank you."

"She worked all day cleaning and cooking, wanting it to be a special night." Levi's tone was bordering on fury.

"And everything is lovely." Vera was losing her appetite, but forced another bite down so as to not further offend Danielle. *How could I be so* dumm?

"Thank you," Danielle said, her eyes still on her plate.

"I always thought that Beth Ann would be the first of the *kinner* to be with child." Vera spoke slowly, carefully. "But now it looks like you and Levi will be first, then Emily and David." She smiled at Levi, but he also wouldn't meet her eyes for more than a second.

Elam cleared his throat. "Levi, I've been thinking . . . I've got some extra solar panels in the shed at home, extra ones that I ordered when there was a sale. You should take a couple of the larger ones and get your new *fraa* some power going in here." Elam smiled. "I'd be doing that myself since Bishop Esh allows it, if your mom wasn't so against any type of progression."

"I think that's a *gut* idea," Vera added. "Especially with a baby coming, and Danielle isn't used to tending an infant, especially without power." Vera thought she was being positive, reassuring, but one look from Levi said otherwise. *I give up.*

Elam raised his plate. "Danielle, I'm going to need another large scoop of this lasagna." He passed his plate, which made their daughter-in-law smile.

"Did you make dessert, Danielle?" Betsy sat taller. "I ate all my supper."

"I did." Danielle smiled at Betsy too. "Emily said that your brother likes carrot cake, so I made your mother's recipe." Then Danielle gave Vera a thin-lipped smile, nothing like the one she'd given Elam and Betsy. Vera took another bite of lasagna and kept her head down. That was a family recipe, not for sharing. Didn't Emily know that? *But I guess Danielle is family now.* She took a deep breath, resolved to keep her mouth shut through the rest of the meal.

After the main meal, Danielle served everyone a piece of carrot cake, and Vera had to admit, it was as good as hers. She ate every bite and commented several times about how good it was. But clearly, the damage was done.

"Excuse me a moment, please." Danielle politely got up and left the kitchen.

"I'm sorry, Levi," Vera whispered. "I just wasn't thinking, and this is all new for me. I'm so sorry."

"*Mamm* . . ." Levi lowered his head, stroking his beard.

Vera wasn't sure why he'd grown the beard since he didn't have to. He looked up at her. "That baby is as much mine as if . . ." He glanced at Betsy, then back at his mother. "You know what I mean."

"I'm not a *dummkopp.*" Betsy scowled, talking with a mouthful of cake.

"*Nee*, you're not, my little one." Elam stood from the table. "Come out on the porch with your old *daed* and let's get some fresh air. Levi, care to join us?"

Levi shook his head. "*Danki, Daed.* I'll wait for Danielle and help her clean the kitchen."

"Levi, you can go with your father. Cleaning is women's work. I'll help Danielle." Vera stood up and began gathering plates.

"I help her every night. Because I want to." Her son began putting the butter and jars of chowchow in the refrigerator.

They were both putting dishes in the sink when Vera heard Danielle faintly call Levi's name from the middle of the living room. He twisted his head. "What is it, Ladybug?"

Vera began running hot water in the sink, eager to avoid her son seeing her surprise over his pet name. Then Levi dropped a plate in the sink so hard it broke and ran across the room. Vera spun around, the water still running.

Levi ran to Danielle and wrapped an arm around her waist. The girl could barely stand up, and her face was the color of the white clapboard walls. Vera instinctively moved toward them. By the time she reached Danielle and Levi, she saw blood running down Danielle's leg, her skirt staining a crimson red.

"*Mamm*, help. *Mamm!* What do we do?" Levi's voice cracked as he spoke, and maybe for the first time since everything had happened, Vera took note that there was a real live little person coming into their lives, and that life was now at stake. She ran the other direction, out toward the porch.

It had been a long time since their *rumschpringe*, but she remembered the tan automobile Elam drove for a few months.

"Elam! Do you remember how to drive a car? We have to get Danielle to a hospital right now!"

# Eighteen

LEVI FINALLY CAME OUT OF THE EMERGENCY ROOM where Danielle was.

"She and the baby are going to be okay, but she's going to have to be on bed rest for the rest of her pregnancy."

Vera took a deep breath. "Thank the Lord. Should I call Martha?"

"No. I asked her, but it's late, and Danielle said no. Plus, Martha is laid up with a broken foot."

"That's right," Vera said. She touched Levi's arm. "*Sohn*, what can I do? I'll do anything I can to help."

"Danielle's going to need some help with everything since she needs to stay off her feet. I was thinking about asking Emily . . . and maybe Katie Ann and Lillian if they can help, and—"

"No! I will help Danielle. Emily is suffering from terrible morning sickness, Katie Ann has been helping Martha and has little Jonas. And Lillian has her two little ones. I'm sure that Betsy and I can take care of things at your house." She rubbed his arms, her eyes pleading with him. "Please, Levi.

I'd like to. It will give me a chance to get to know Danielle better."

Levi shook his head. "I'm not sure I like that idea, *Mamm*. Danielle is sensitive, and you . . ." He shrugged, but then almost smiled. "You're just *you*, *Mamm*. A big heart. And a big mouth sometimes."

"Levi! You can't talk to me that." Vera put her hands on her hips. "No one can take better care of that girl than I can. You know that."

Levi stroked his beard. "You'd be *gut* to her, no?"

Vera's heart sank. "I can't believe you'd even have to ask me that."

Levi leaned down and kissed her on the cheek. "I know you, *Mamm*. And when you get to know Danielle the way I do, you'll love her too."

Vera didn't know about that, but she was going to do what she could to get back in her son's good graces. And she was thankful that the baby was going to be all right, a child that Levi considered his own. *Lord, help me.* Vera just didn't know if she could ever consider Danielle's child as real family. But even if she couldn't . . . she was still very thankful. She'd prayed all the way to the hospital that Danielle wouldn't lose the baby.

But she would have done that for anyone.

DANIELLE LISTENED TO Levi's prayers of thanks as he leaned over her hospital bed, and she thought back to when she first saw the blood in the bathroom. The first thing that she'd done was to ask God to help her. What did that mean?

She recalled her thoughts when she was in the chapel. What if she allowed God into her heart and He let her down again? Was the payoff worth the risk?

Touching her stomach, she realized that there was no risk too great to endure for her baby, which made her wonder if God had saved Joshua. She caught the end of Levi's prayer when he squeezed her hand.

"Can I go home now?"

"*Ya*. The doctor said you're going to have to take some medicines because you're having some early contractions. And you have to mostly stay off your feet."

"Okay." Danielle was wondering how she was going to take care of things when Levi spoke up.

"*Mamm* will be coming over to cook, clean, and take care of you. Her and Betsy."

Danielle's jaw dropped as she raised her head from the pillow. It had been hard enough to endure one evening with Vera.

"It'll be fine, and *Mamm* wants to do it. It's a chance for you two to get to know each other better." Levi kissed her on the forehead. "And that would make me happy."

"Levi . . ." She bit her bottom lip. "Your mom is never going to accept me. Or like me. Her being around all the time is just going to make us both miserable."

He pushed back a strand of hair that had fallen across her face. "She wants to do it, Danielle. You might be surprised."

She thought about her options for a moment. Martha was in bed with a broken foot. She touched her stomach, knowing the most important thing in her world was Joshua. *It's gonna be a long few months.* "Okay," she finally said, forcing a smile.

Two days later, Vera showed up at Levi's house at eight in the morning, carting cleaning supplies and food. She'd doubted Danielle kept much of either on hand, and at least while she was taking care of things, she could make sure that her son had decent meals and the house was clean. She pushed the door open. "Danielle, don't get up. I'm here."

Danielle met her in the doorway. "Vera, I feel bad that you have to—"

"You should be in bed." Vera didn't want Danielle losing that baby, on her shift or any other. It might not feel like her grandchild, but that life inside of Danielle was struggling. "Don't worry about a thing. I've brought plenty to keep me busy."

"Where's Betsy?"

"I dropped her with Lillian to play with the girls. She'll probably be with me tomorrow." Vera set down her tote filled with cleansers and scrub brushes, then moved toward the kitchen. She stowed the groceries in the refrigerator and cabinet, turning to find Danielle standing in the doorway. "Are you hungry? I can make you something now, but you should do what the doctor said and keep off your feet."

"I don't eat breakfast. And I feel weird having you do all this."

Vera frowned. "You must eat a healthy breakfast. It's *gut* for the *boppli*." She waved her off. "Shoo, now. You go lie down, and I will bring you something to eat."

Danielle shuffled across the living room in a long pink robe. She was moving slowly, clearly unhappy about Vera being there, but just as clearly trying to hide it.

Ten minutes later, she took Danielle a bowl of oatmeal, fresh fruit, and a piece of toast with rhubarb jam. She carried it in on a tray and walked in to see Danielle sitting up in the bed, a dark expression on her face.

Vera set the tray on the table by the bed. "Do you feel bad?"

Danielle's eyes filled with tears. "I don't feel the baby moving."

Vera swallowed hard. *Please, Lord, keep this baby safe.* She pulled up a chair next to the bed and sat down. "Maybe he's just . . . sleeping." She held her breath for a few moments as Danielle swiped at her eyes.

Instinctively, Vera lowered her head.

"Are you praying?"

Vera raised her eyes to Danielle's. "*Ya*, I am."

"Will you pray out loud?"

"Of course." Vera lowered her head again. "Dear heavenly Father, please keep baby Joshua strong so that he will be healthy when he comes into our world. Please put Your—"

Danielle gasped. "He kicked."

Vera looked up, and the girl was smiling. *Thank You, Lord.* "*Ach, gut.* Wonderful, indeed." She flinched slightly as Danielle grabbed her hand and placed it atop the pink robe on her belly.

"Feel him?" Danielle sniffled. "Do you feel him?"

It had been a long time since Vera had felt the miracle of a new life in the womb. Feeling another woman's stomach wasn't normally something she would do, but Danielle was grasping her hand so tightly, she had little choice. And feeling the movement sent a warm feeling through Vera. "*Ya*. I feel him," she said with a smile. "A strong kick."

Vera eased her hand away. "See. He was just sleeping." She picked up the tray and offered it to Danielle. "Now let's feed the little fellow so he'll stay strong."

Danielle took the tray, and Vera turned to leave. "I'm just going to clean things up a bit this morning."

"Vera."

She turned around at the doorway. "*Ya?* Do you need something else?"

Danielle shook her head. "No. I just wanted to say thank you."

"You're wel—"

"Not just for the food." Danielle smiled. "But for calling him Joshua."

Vera smiled, then left the room. As she walked through the living room, she noticed the Bible on a square box by one of the rocking chairs. *Thank goodness for the Bible, but these kids need some furniture.* She scanned her mind and remembered that she had some extra furniture stored in her basement at home. She'd have a look tonight.

The rest of the morning, she swept the wooden floors, cleaned the windows, scrubbed the bathroom, and occasionally sat down to chat with Danielle. It was idle chitchat, but gradually, Danielle seemed to welcome it. And Vera realized she did too.

DANIELLE WAITED UNTIL after Vera left before she called Martha.

"Well, how'd it go with Vera?"

"It went okay. It was kinda awkward sometimes, but I could tell she was trying." Danielle laid her hand across her stomach when Joshua moved.

"Vera's a good person. She really is. But she tries to control things, and your little family just wasn't in her plans. She'll come around. I'm glad you're giving her a chance."

"Well, I didn't have much choice. I don't want to do anything that would cause Joshua to come early. The doctor said I need to carry him at least until the end of October, preferably longer." She paused. "And Levi seems to think it would be good for me and his mom to get to know each other better."

"Levi is right."

Danielle shifted her weight when the baby scrunched to her left side, the side he seemed to prefer. "How are you feeling?"

"Terrible. Just terrible. And I'm not taking the pain meds that the doctor gave me because they make me feel all loopy. So I just have to lie here and suffer."

Danielle tried not to grin. "Can you get up and walk around on your crutches?"

"No. Absolutely not. Much too painful."

"I'm sorry. I wish I was there to take care of you."

"And I wish I was there to take care of you. What a mess we are!" Martha snorted. "But I'll be around as soon as I can. Arnold and Katie Ann will make me bonkers with all their fussing."

"Hey, my cell phone is almost dead, but I'll send it with Levi tomorrow and see if he can find a place to charge it."

"You know, they have solar chargers for phones. Maybe see if Levi can get you one."

"Hmm . . . Good idea. I'll mention it to him." She paused, wondering why she hadn't thought of that. "Anyway, I hope you feel better."

"I won't. But you take care of yourself and our little one. And give ol' Vera a chance. The woman has a huge heart, but like I said . . . she's often misdirected in her actions."

After they hung up, Danielle looked at the clock on the nightstand. It was only two o'clock. Vera said she would be back around four to heat something up for supper. It sure seemed like a lot of work for Vera, but Danielle was thankful. She folded her arms across her stomach and yawned. The most important thing in her world right now was for Joshua to arrive safely. So maybe a nap was in order . . .

LEVI WALKED INTO the house just as his mother was packing up to leave. For the first time, the house smelled lemony fresh, like home, mixed with the aroma of something heavenly simmering on the stove.

"Smells *gut* in here." Levi dropped his hat on the rack and moved toward the stove. Even though he wasn't Amish anymore, he'd taken to wearing his hat again. He felt like something was missing without it. "*Daed* said to tell you that he was stopping by Katie Ann's on the way home to drop off some pieces of cedar that Eli needs for a chest he's working on. We picked up the wood on the way home for him."

*Mamm* was carting her cleaning supplies in a carryall on her hip as she nodded. "There's baked chicken in the oven, and mashed potatoes and green beans simmering. I left you two loaves of homemade bread and some whoopee pies."

Levi hugged his mother. "You're the best. *Danki* for everything you're doing."

*Mamm's* cheeks flushed. "It wasn't much. Tell Danielle I'll see her tomorrow morning."

Levi knew his mother had worked hard, but he was anxious to see his wife. "I'll tell her. Good night."

"Good night, Levi."

He closed the door behind her—now swinging easily shut after a good sanding—and hurried to the bedroom.

"I feel bad lying in bed while your mom is doing everything." Danielle eased up against her pillow and tucked her hair behind both ears as Levi entered. "And it feels weird."

Levi sat down on the edge of the bed, kissed her, and placed a hand on her stomach. "Well, that's what you have to do for now. For Joshua."

"I know. And I will." She leaned forward and kissed him again. "How was your day, dear?" She giggled. "That's how everyone talks on those old TV reruns, so I thought I'd give it a try."

Levi hadn't ever watched much television, so he didn't really get it, but he smiled because seeing her smile made him happy. "*Mei* day was *gut.*"

"You still sound Amish." She reached up and gently scratched his short beard.

"You don't like the beard, do you?" He closed his eyes for a moment, knowing he'd shave it off if she wanted him to. He'd just always figured that he would grow one after he got married.

"I love the beard. And I love you." She grinned. "You look like a grown-up with it."

"I *am* a grown-up." Levi waited until she eased her hand away before he kissed her, remembering that she was only nineteen. Sometimes their four-year difference in age seemed huge. "And I'll probably always sound a little Amish." *And be a little Amish.*

"Your mom prayed with me today. I couldn't feel the baby kick, and I got really scared."

Levi swallowed hard. "Was everything okay?"

"Yep. Everything is fine." She touched her stomach, then looked up at him with tender eyes. "You know, on the way to the hospital, I prayed. Do you think God saved Joshua, kept our baby from coming early?"

"I think God can do anything, and the power of prayer is an amazing thing." Levi cupped her cheek.

"You know how I feel . . . about God." She paused. "I'm so scared He will let me down. But even if God doesn't like me all that much, I think it's worth the prayers for Joshua. I think Joshua deserves that."

"Sweet Ladybug." Levi shook his head, grasping her hand. "God doesn't just like you. He *loves* you. And once you open your heart up to Him, you'll never be the same."

"I know you say that, Levi. And I'm really trying."

"I'm going to take a shower, then I'll bring us both a tray of food in here, and we can eat together in bed. How's that?"

"Perfect."

Levi pulled off his work boots and headed for the bathroom. Once he was in the shower, he let the warm water run down his back, and he fought the urge to cry. He was a grown man, an adult, as Danielle pointed out. Yet everything weighed on his shoulders—worry about the baby, about Danielle . . . and the realization that he'd been called to minister to his wife. It wasn't something his people did, and he was in new territory.

*What if I fail, God? What if she never comes around to really know You?*

He thought back to how all this started . . . the dreams . . . the pull to marry Danielle.

Levi loved her. And the baby. But was he really the right man for this job?

VERA WAS EXHAUSTED when she pulled into her driveway. She was used to hard work, so it wasn't a physical drain, more of an emotional depletion. The entire situation was stressful, and even though she wanted to try and get to know her daughter-in-law, it was going to take its toll. And when Danielle had said the baby wasn't moving, Vera's heart had stopped for a couple of seconds.

As she gathered up her cleaning supplies, she heard horse hooves coming up the driveway, so she waited. Surprised to see Anna Marie—Matthew's mother—she moved toward the woman's buggy, knowing whatever she had to say, it was far too late. The damage was done, and they were all just going to have to make the best of it.

Anna Marie stepped out of the buggy. "Hello, Vera. I can't stay long or I won't get back to Alamosa by dark. But do you have a few minutes to talk?"

Vera motioned for Anna Marie to follow. "Of course."

A few minutes later, both women were sitting at the kitchen table drinking a cup of coffee. Vera glanced at the clock on the wall, knowing Lillian would be by any minute to drop Betsy off. The last thing Vera needed was for Betsy to burst through the door asking a lot of questions.

"I just wanted you to know that I've had several phone calls with Matthew." Anna Marie took a sip from her coffee cup. "Both his *daed* and I have talked to him, and we're trying very *hatt* to get him to come home and to do right by the child."

Vera swallowed hard. If Matthew came back now, it would complicate things for her son, who now thought of Joshua as his own child. "I don't see the point now. Danielle and Levi are married. When I didn't hear from you, I assumed that Matthew was out of the picture for *gut*."

"We are trying to make him see things clearly, that his son will be born soon, and that he needs to come home. He needs to be a part of the *boppli's* life."

Vera moved uneasily in her chair. How many times had she heard Levi refer to Joshua as his own son? "I suppose you can't force him."

"*Nee*, but we are praying."

"The baby will be named Joshua." Vera offered up a weak smile as her stomach churned.

Anna Marie brought a hand to her mouth for a moment. "A boy." She blinked her eyes a few times. "A son named Joshua." She smiled. "I will pass this news along to Matthew. Maybe it will make it seem real to him. Sometimes I think I am getting through to him. Other times he seems to be in his own world . . . searching for something his father and I don't understand."

Vera took a long sip of her coffee, then slowly put her cup on the table. "I will send word when the child is born."

"*Danki*." Anna Marie paused. "I'm sorry things didn't work out like either of us hoped and prayed."

Vera thought about how happy Levi was, and how he looked forward to the safe arrival of "his" baby. "We can't ever know God's plan."

Anna Marie took a deep breath. "When Matthew comes back, we will need to set up custody and visitation like so many of the *Englisch* do." She shook her head, and Vera frowned.

"*If* he comes back, don't you mean?"

"*Ya*, I suppose that is what I mean."

They were quiet for a few moments, and Vera found herself hoping that Matthew wouldn't come back. For Levi's sake.

Vera walked Anna Marie out, promising again to let her know when the baby arrived. She watched as Anna Marie's buggy turned the corner and wondered how their lives had gotten so complicated. But one thing she knew for sure—if Matthew came back to Canaan, things would get even more problematic.

# Nineteen

For the next couple of weeks, Danielle and Vera coexisted for a couple of hours in the morning and again in the afternoon. Most days, Betsy hung out with Danielle while her mother cooked and cleaned, but that morning Betsy elected to go to Lillian's to play with the girls. It was quiet, except for the sound of Vera running the sweeper across the floor in the living room.

When Danielle had told the restaurant manager that she couldn't work for a few months, they had both agreed to part ways. Levi had already said he wanted her to stay at home with Joshua after he was born.

Danielle plugged in her earbuds for her iPhone and checked her e-mail, something she hadn't done in a long time. Levi had been good about charging her phone every few days so she could play games and check a few favorite websites, but she'd never really been much of an e-mailer. Today, she had thirty-six e-mails when she opened the tab. Scanning through them, they were mostly junk. But the one from Vivian Kent Shephard caused her heart to skip a beat.

She'd never written her mother back, and the day had passed since her mother's planned marriage. She stared at the e-mail for a while before she clicked on it.

> Hi Danielle,
>
> I hope you received my letter, but since I haven't been able to reach you by phone, I'm trying your old e-mail account, with high hopes I'll hear from you. Louis and I are married, and like I said in my letter, the Lord has blessed me with a second chance. I loved your father so much, and I didn't think I'd ever find another man to live the rest of my life with.

Tears streamed down Danielle's face, anger burning in her heart. *The Lord? Seriously, Mother?* Danielle was struggling to get God to like her and to establish some sort of relationship with Him for Levi's sake. And Joshua's. But would God actually bestow happiness on someone like Vivian? Or was it all just lies? She pressed her palms to her eyes for a moment, then went on.

> I hope that things are going well with you. Please let me hear from you.
>
> Love,
> Mom

Danielle stared at the letter. Once again, not an ounce of regret, and no desire for forgiveness. While she was unsure whether or not she would forgive her mother, even if she asked, it would have been nice if Danielle had been a factor in her mother's new future.

"What's wrong? Are you in pain?" Vera rushed into the room carrying a feather duster.

Danielle squeezed her eyes closed, not wanting to get into this with Vera. Sniffling, she looked up at her. "No. I'm not in pain." *Such a lie.* Pain gripped her from head to toe.

Vera walked right up to the bed, her eyebrows drawn, her lips pinched together. "Then what is it? Why are you crying?"

Danielle swallowed the lump in her throat. "It's a letter from my mother." Another tear slipped down her cheek. "Or the woman who calls herself my mother, I guess I should say."

Vera pulled the chair up close and sat down. "This upset isn't *gut* for the *boppli*. Do you want to talk about it?"

Danielle shook her head, but then words spewed forth without thought. "I hate her! I hate my mother!" She buried her head in her hands. When she looked back up, Vera's eyes were softer and kinder than usual, but the woman didn't say anything. "She beat me. Did you know that? And now . . ." She started sobbing so hard she could barely talk. "She wants to talk to me about God, about her second chances and her new husband. I hate her."

Vera was quiet, and Danielle regretted her outburst, but Vera was only with her because of Levi, and right now, she didn't care if Vera liked her or not. Her own mother didn't like her.

Danielle cried for another minute or so. Vera just sat there. "I'm sorry," Danielle finally said. "I'm sorry that you are seeing me like this. But I guess in my mind, I just . . . I just keep waiting for my mother to say she's sorry. And she never does. How can God bless someone like her? She doesn't even *know* Him!"

VERA WAITED ANOTHER minute until Danielle gathered herself, unsure exactly how to proceed. Vera loved her children as much as life itself, and she'd do anything to keep them safe and protected. She knew about Danielle's history from Martha, even though Levi had never said anything to her about it. In the beginning, she'd wondered if Danielle had been an unruly child who pushed her mother to the edge, but even if that had been the case, that was no reason to raise a hand to a youngster outside of just a spanking. Vera knew she needed to choose her words carefully.

"Maybe your mother has come to know the Lord since you last spoke with her." Vera cringed as she watched Danielle's face take on a contorted expression.

"So that's how God works?" She grunted, rubbing her belly. "Do whatever evil things you want, then all you have to do is say you're sorry, and all is well? So now my mother is forgiven, loved by God, and living a happy life. Good for her!" She started to sob again.

Vera took a deep breath. Her people believed in Jesus as their Lord and Savior, but they also believed that a person should live according to the *Ordnung*, a life of dedication to the Lord, hard work, and worship. But Vera knew that a personal relationship with God didn't come easily for everyone, no matter what their religious upbringing was. Vera was proof of that. Even though she knew that the Lord was as much a part of her as the air she breathed, truly knowing Him was a discovery she'd made late in life. Yet she'd never admitted it to another living soul. But as she watched Danielle suffering, she felt the Lord calling her to share her story with Danielle. *I'm not sure I can.*

She ignored the pull at her heart to open up to Danielle, and instead said, "Forgiveness doesn't come easily, Danielle. And sometimes saying you're sorry doesn't either. I'm sure your mother regrets how she hurt you. Maybe she just doesn't know how to say it." Vera folded her lands in her lap, resolved that her secret would remain her own.

Danielle stared straight ahead at the peeling white wall, avoiding Vera's eyes. "She doesn't love me. But I'm going to make up for her lack of love for me, and I'm going to love Joshua with my heart and soul. I will never hurt him. Ever."

Vera eased her posture, leaning back against the chair. "*Ya*, you will hurt him. Maybe not the same way your mother hurt you, but you'll hurt him, even if it's not intentional. We love them," she said with a shrug, "and yet inevitably hurt them."

Danielle studied her and then looked away, fiddling with the edge of the blanket as she recalled saying almost that exact same thing to Levi once. "My mom and I . . . parted badly. We haven't talked in a long time. But now she claims to have this wonderful second chance with her new husband *and* a relationship with God? How does that work, Vera?" She threw her hands up. "Because I just don't get it."

Vera tried to organize her thoughts. It was not the Amish way to minister to others, and Vera wasn't sure what to do. Again, her own secret tugged at her heart, and again, she pushed it aside. "We are all the Lord's children, and—"

"Yes. I've heard all that before. Repeatedly, from Martha. And from Levi. And I've been praying with Levi. I've been praying for Joshua. But I don't hear anything back. Nothing. God has never been there for me, and this letter from my mother . . . it's a slap in the face from both my mother *and* God."

Vera felt a huge sense of relief that Levi and Danielle had been praying together; it gave her hope that they would raise the child in a Christian home, even if they weren't Amish. But Vera knew that it was her job as a good Amish woman to stay true to her own faith. One could never be sure if an outsider was truly faithful; the Amish could only trust other Amish in their commitment to the Lord. Vera knew the *Englisch* could commit to a life of servitude to the Lord . . . but you just never knew for sure.

That said, Danielle was as far detached from God as any person she'd ever known. The girl was solely responsible for pulling her son away from his faith.

So, why had Vera's own past come calling now?

"What if your mother never says she's sorry?" Vera leaned forward, tempted to put her hand on Danielle's. "You must try to forgive her anyway. Otherwise it will be hard to have the kind of relationship with God that you want."

Vera thought about Danielle's circumstances. She could see why the child would think God was never there for her, however misdirected. *She just doesn't understand.*

"I just don't get it." Danielle swiped at her eyes, shaking her head.

Vera held her breath, knowing that there was no way that Danielle could comprehend the sting that Vera felt at hearing those very words, and Vera knew that it was no coincidence. God was speaking to Vera directly. He might as well have said aloud, "Vera, you know what you have to do. Send her to Me."

Vera laid her head in her hands for a moment and prayed, *Lord, help me do as You've asked.* She looked up at Danielle and locked eyes with her. "I haven't always had the faith, Danielle."

The girl didn't say anything, and her expression didn't change much. Vera knew Danielle didn't realize what a big step this was for Vera. She took a deep breath and went on. "I was baptized into the faith, married Levi's father, and I'd had two children before I had a real relationship with God." Vera swallowed hard, pulling her eyes from Danielle's. "And I've never told a living soul about it." She finally looked back to Danielle, who was expressionless, listening and waiting for her to go on.

"Of course, I went to worship every other Sunday. I studied the *Ordnung*, and my life was filled with devotions, Bible study, and fellowship with others in our community." Vera hung her head for a moment. "But I never *knew* Him." She looked up at Danielle. She covered her mouth with her hand as tears threatened to spill and shame wrapped around her. She knew in her heart that shame was the work of the enemy, yet having to tell this story out loud brought forth a wave of it just the same. "It's not about good deeds, Bible study, devotions, church . . ." She held up one finger. "Don't get me wrong. These things are *gut* and very important. But there is something more. So much more. When you allow God into your heart in a way that . . ." Vera's words trailed off as she struggled to find the right phrasing. How could she possibly make Danielle understand this?

"Go on," Danielle said softly, her eyes steadfast on Vera.

"There's a feeling you get, an all-knowing sense of peace that comes with knowing the Lord. I'm not sure I know how to explain it. I just remember when the peace settled over me, it was different from anything that I'd ever known. It's a love so strong that you never have to be afraid, never have to worry, and never have to fear." She swallowed back tears as she realized that she had been doing all of those things, knowing that she'd been blocking the voice of God in her effort to control things with Levi and Danielle. "His love endures forever, Danielle. Talk to the Lord like you would your best friend and open your heart to Him with total trust. Place your future—and your past—in His hands. Life will never go the way you plan. But putting your total trust in God is the answer."

Vera took a deep breath as Danielle leaned forward, her expression still blank and unreadable. It was impossible to tell what she was thinking.

"When?" Danielle squinted one eye.

Vera blinked. "When, what?"

"When did the peace settle over you? When did it happen?"

Vera pulled her eyes from Danielle's, wishing she could offer up some partial version of the truth, but Vera knew exactly when she'd truly opened her heart and gotten to know God in an intimate way. She stared at Danielle, unable to believe that she was about to tell this young girl her deepest secret.

She sighed. "When I forgave my mother." She swallowed past a thick knot in her throat.

Danielle just sat there. Vera wanted to yell at her to say something, anything, for Danielle to know that she was revealing a part of her past she'd long since buried in an effort to help.

"Did she hit you?" Danielle said steadily.

"No! Of course not." Vera leaned back, squinting. "My mother would never do that."

Danielle lowered her head, and Vera regretted her sharp comeback, but it was true—her mother would have never laid a hand on any of her children.

"Then what was it? What did you have to forgive her for?"

Vera wished she'd never brought it up, that she'd found another way to reach her . . . "I'd rather not say," Vera finally said. "But the point is that forgiveness is essential to healing, and . . ."

Danielle shrugged. "Okay."

But it wasn't okay. Vera had lost Danielle's attention, and somehow the importance of this confession was reduced to a shrug, and that wasn't acceptable. Vera had come this far; she supposed she couldn't expect Danielle to just accept her on her word without all the details.

"I—I—" Vera sighed. She'd never said it aloud before. She'd never even told Elam. "I walked in on my mother with another man. One day while my father was working the fields. He was another Amish man in our community." She looked at Danielle and could tell she had the girl's full attention. "I was eleven years old."

"What did you do?" Danielle pushed back her covers and folded her legs beneath her.

"I ran out of the room, and it was never spoken of. Until today."

"You didn't ask your mother about it?"

Vera was lost in the memory for a few moments, the look on her mother's face, the man she knew as Roy Hostetler with his lips pressed against her mother's in her parents' bedroom. "No. But from then on, everything I'd been taught, and would be taught for the next ten years, sounded like hollow words to me. I went through the motions, said my prayers, and . . . and had to face Roy in worship every other Sunday until we moved here several years ago." She stood up and paced the room for a moment, then turned to Danielle. "I don't know why I'm telling you all this. I just thought it might help. I had to forgive my mother even though she didn't seem to require it from me. Maybe she had made her peace with God on her own." She smoothed the wrinkles from her black apron, wishing Danielle's expression would give a hint as to whether Vera was getting through to her.

"Why did it take you ten years before you got close to God again?"

Then Vera gave her the most honest, regrettable answer she had, the hardest part of the story. "I don't know."

Danielle was quiet, her head cocked to one side.

"But one day I couldn't stand the emptiness I felt, despite all that I'd been blessed with. I had a loving husband and my boys. But something was amiss. I'd always prayed and done all the things I mentioned to you before, but something still wasn't right in my heart." Vera sat down again. "So I set out to figure out what it was. I couldn't talk to any of our people because . . . well, I'd been brought up Amish, and I didn't think anyone would understand why I didn't trust the Lord and why I constantly questioned His will. It just isn't our way."

Danielle was quiet.

"One day I walked out into a full field of wildflowers back in Middlefield. A neighbor was caring for Jacob and Levi that day. I sat down in the field." Vera paused as she blinked back tears at the recollection. "And I remember I just felt so *alone*. And I didn't want to feel that way anymore. I poured out everything I had inside of me, the built-up resentments, the fears, the worries ... and I gave it all to God. I opened my heart and let Him in, and I cried for a long, long time." Vera realized she was crying now. She looked up at Danielle, who still appeared emotionless, and Vera felt ridiculous. Apparently today wasn't nearly so much about Danielle as it was about herself. She straightened, sniffled, and looked away from Danielle for a moment, then turned back to her.

"He is the only way. That's what I'm saying. If you're feeling alone or longing for peace, *He* is the way." She turned to leave, feeling a flush rising up her neck and filling her cheeks. "You must be weary of my yammering on. I'll leave you be now and finish cleaning."

"Vera?"

Stopping in the doorway, Vera slowly turned around and raised an eyebrow, wishing she could just go home and think. "*Ya?*" Danielle rose and walked toward her. "*Ach*, back to bed now. You shouldn't be up." But the girl kept coming until she stood right in front of her. Vera waited.

"Is that all I have to do?" Danielle bit her bottom lip and blinked a few times. "Just forgive my mother and open my heart to God, trust Him, and give Him my worries and fears?"

Vera smiled. "It's a lot, my child. But, *ya* ... We can do all things through Christ who strengthens us. Talk to God like a friend. He will be there for you."

Danielle stepped closer and threw her arms around Vera's neck, and Vera didn't move for a moment. The girl trembled, weeping. Then slowly she wrapped her arms around Danielle and cried with her. They stood there for several long minutes, and Vera silently thanked God for giving her courage and strength. She would pray that Danielle would turn to Him, but today was also a huge reminder for Vera about who was in control. She herself was far from perfect, and living as Christ asked was a daily battle. *But it's so worth it . . .*

"Thank you," Danielle whispered, sniffling.

Vera eased her away and smiled. "*Nee*, thank you, child."

# Twenty

A FEW DAYS LATER, DANIELLE PICKED UP HER CELL to call Martha. It was around two o'clock, in between Vera's morning and late-afternoon visits. She talked to Martha every day, but it had taken this long for her conversation with Vera to soak in enough to feel comfortable mentioning it to Martha. She hadn't done what Vera suggested yet—forgive her mother and give it all to God—but she was thinking about it.

Martha answered, sounding groggy and grumpy.

"Hi. It's me. How are you feeling? How's the foot today?" Danielle shuffled across the floor and closed the partially opened window. Earlier the room had felt stuffy, so she'd welcomed the cool breeze drifting through the bedroom amidst the rays of sun that beamed down on the wooden floors. But as predicted, the temperature was steadily dropping today.

"It still hurts. I'm not sure when I'm ever going to be able to walk on it again." Martha sighed. "But if there is anything good about this terrible situation, it's all the creamed celery Katie Ann has been bringing me. How are you feeling?"

Danielle settled into the rocking chair that Vera had brought over for their bedroom. Earlier in the week, she'd shown up with a coffee table and two end tables for the living room. "I feel good. Fat, but good. I just don't feel like I need to stay in the bed all the time."

"You do exactly what the doctor said. It's only September, and you need to keep that baby inside until at least the end of October, preferably all the way until Christmas. Do you hear me?"

"Yes, ma'am." Danielle smiled. "Hey, I've been meaning to tell you that Vera and I are getting along really well."

"I told you. Vera is a good person. Stubborn sometimes. And controlling. But she has a heart of gold, I tell ya."

"Yeah, I think you might be right. We had a really long conversation a few days ago. About God." Danielle recalled Vera's tears. And her own.

"Well, I hope someone can get through that thick skull of yours. The world shines a whole lot brighter with God in your heart."

Danielle smiled over her gruff words. "I've been praying, you know. Vera explained it to me in a way that makes sense. I think. I don't know. Maybe not. But she opened up to me, and . . . anyway . . . we're a lot closer now. And I can tell that it makes Levi happy too."

"Honey, that's great. I miss you so much. I'd come over there, but this foot is just killing me." Martha paused, groaning. "And I hate being in this bed having everyone wait on me."

*Sure you do.* Danielle smiled. She'd had a broken bone before and knew that Martha was probably well on the road to healing. "Well, Vera is actually doing a very good job taking care of me. She makes sure I have three balanced meals every day, the house is clean, and . . . the last couple days, we've talked a lot. I feel more like a daughter to her now."

Martha was silent.

"Martha? You still there?"

"Uh, yes. Just listening to Dude snore here on the floor next to the bed. Big lug of a dog stays in my room all the time. He's supposed to be Arnold's dog. Anyway, dear, I better go. Take care of yourself and our baby."

"I will."

MARTHA SHOT UP in the bed, swung her legs over the side, and yelled, "Arnold!"

A few minutes later, her husband rushed into the room. "What is it, my love? Are you in pain?"

"I'd like to take a bath and put some makeup on. And do my hair. I look a wreck, and I don't know how you're putting up with me like this." She pushed herself from the bed, balancing on one foot.

"Careful, dear." Arnold reached for her, but she eased his hand away.

"Just hand me those crutches and please help me to the bathroom. I'm going to bathe and make myself presentable." Arnold eased the crutches under each of her arms. She glanced at the wheelchair Arnold had rented and frowned. "I'm not getting in that thing anymore. It makes me feel like an old woman."

Arnold stood in front of her, his hands extended like he might have to catch her. "Have you ever walked on crutches? Do you know how?"

"How hard can it be?" She let her weight fall onto the crutches, pinching her underarm on the left side. *Argh*. She resituated them and tried again until she was finally able to take a step toward the doorway.

"Snookums, you don't have to get all dolled up just for me. I'm happy to give you a sponge bath here in the bed. You know that." His eyes twinkled, but Martha just looked at him and shook her head.

"I'm not getting dolled up for you." She eased past him. "I'm getting myself ready so I can go see Danielle. You know, I love that Vera, but she's up to her old tricks again. This time she's trying to steal my daughter." She twisted to face Arnold. "Why haven't you been going over there to keep an eye on things?"

Arnold's mouth dropped open. "Because you said you needed me here. Because you have been in awful pain." He rubbed his chin, frowning. "I don't think you should be going anywhere. You don't seem . . . yourself."

Martha carted herself out of the bedroom door and down the hall in less than a minute, yelling over her shoulder, "Vera has her own daughters! I'm not letting her steal mine."

An hour later, Martha pulled into Danielle and Levi's driveway, and sure enough, Vera's horse and buggy were hitched up out front. Martha lifted her left leg and swung her cast outside the car, then caught her breath before she maneuvered the crutches across the seat in front of her. It took effort, but she was finally on her feet, the crutches under her arms. Arnold had tried to insist on driving, but there was nothing wrong with her right foot, and in this part of the world, that was the only foot she needed to operate a car. She carried herself across the yard but stopped at the porch steps. *Good grief.*

They looked like a mountain in front of her. She hadn't factored those into her plan. Arnold had helped her down the steps at home.

She was eyeing the first step and wondering how she would hold the handrail and both crutches when Vera came out on the porch.

"Martha, what in the world are you doing?" She put her hands on her hips. "Did you drive yourself here?"

"Back off, Vera. I'm coming up." She stepped up and onto the first step with her right foot, but that was about it. Vera was quickly at her side, and Martha decided if she was going to see Danielle, she'd better let the woman help her into the house.

"Back off? Why do you sound so angry?" Vera grunted, her hand around Martha's waist, as the two women struggled up the steps.

"Oh, never you mind. I'm here to see Danielle." She marched on her crutches past Vera and into the living room while Vera held the screen open. Right away, Martha noticed the differences. A few new pieces of furniture, and the place smelled clean.

"Are we a wee bit cranky today?" Vera lifted one eyebrow, those hands back on her hips again.

Martha stopped in the middle of the living room and lifted a crutch toward Vera's chest. "You have your own daughters. Quit trying to steal mine." She kept the crutch there for a moment as Vera stepped back, hand to her chest.

"Are you crazy? What are you talking about? And quit pointing that thing at me."

"Danielle told me all about how the two of you have gotten

so close." She gave the crutch a little push. "But Danielle and I are *closer.*"

Vera took a step backward. "Put that crutch down before you fall. And you're being ridiculous." She paused, smiling. "She said we've gotten close?"

"Yeah, yeah. But I think I'm plenty well enough to take care of her now, so you can pack up and go home." Martha cringed as she almost stumbled and barely caught her balance.

"*Ya.* I see that."

Vera's catty smile was enough to make Martha want to smack her. "Danielle, I'm here now, honey!" She hobbled across the living room and into the bedroom. "There you are. I'm here to take care of you."

Danielle put down a magazine next to her on the bed. "What are you doing here? What about your foot?" Danielle slid her feet over the side of the bed, got up, and walked to Martha. It felt good to have Danielle's arms around her neck. "I've missed you, but you didn't have to get out. I told you Vera is taking good care of me."

"Not anymore." She kissed Danielle on the cheek. "I've dismissed her."

Martha turned around when she heard Vera grunt in the entryway.

"*Dismissed* me?" Vera's hands were back on her hips.

"Yes. You heard me." She plastered a wide smile across her face. "Thank you for taking care of Danielle until I was well enough to do it myself. But I'll be here daily now."

"Really?" Vera let out a haughty little laugh. "And how will you do all the cooking and cleaning in your condition?" She tapped a finger to her chin. "Do you even cook?"

Martha eased away from Danielle, taking deep breaths. "Yes, Vera. You know I cook. I believe Danielle made you my famous chicken lasagna. And I'll hire someone to clean this place."

Vera rolled her eyes. "I'm sure the children will get tired of chicken lasagna every night, and . . . well, it wonders me why you would hire someone to clean when I am perfectly able to tend to this *haus*. And Levi is *mei sohn*, and Danielle is . . ."

DANIELLE WONDERED HOW Vera might have finished the sentence, but she'd just tapered off and took a deep breath. Danielle was glad to see Martha, but she couldn't help but think about all the great meals Vera had been cooking, and poor Martha could barely keep her balance on the crutches. Danielle wondered who would be taking care of whom.

"Martha, everything is fine here, really." Danielle flinched as Martha nearly stumbled as she turned to look at her. "You should let Arnold take care of you, and Vera has been great, and . . ." She paused as Martha blinked a few times, then grunted. "It's not that I don't need you, because you know I do." She glanced over Martha's shoulder. Vera was smiling, and Danielle stifled a giggle. Then she just burst out laughing.

"What's so funny?" Martha puckered her lips, and Vera moved farther into the room until she was standing next to Martha, a confused expression replacing the smile.

Danielle bent at the waist and laughed harder. When she stood back up, she swiped at her eyes. "This is just kind of funny. My own mother couldn't stand me and only wanted me around to serve *her*, but you two . . ." She laughed through her tears.

Martha and Vera turned to each other, frowned, then looked back at Danielle.

"Honey . . ." Martha shifted her weight, leaning onto the left crutch. "Are you okay?"

"Yeah. I'm fine. I just . . ." She shrugged. "I think I'm a lucky person to have you both in my life."

Vera edged forward, her face flushed. "I will stop coming if you want me to, if you feel like Martha can take care of you."

"Oh good grief." Martha made her way to the rocking chair in the bedroom and settled into it, rolling her eyes. "Don't sound so pitiful, Vera."

Vera spun around. "I am not being pitiful. You're just cranky." She turned back to face Danielle. "It's up to you, Danielle."

Danielle glanced back and forth between the two women, and she couldn't stop smiling amidst the tears filling her eyes. *Thank You, Lord*, she found herself praying. *For two moms, when I felt I had none.* She settled her hands across her belly, then she looked out the window. "Look." She nodded outside. "It's snowing."

She walked to the window and stared into a dusty mist of white swirls as clouds slowly eased across the horizon, leaving an orange glow in the distance. A few moments later, she heard the click of Martha's crutches coming across the wooden floor behind her, along with a set of footsteps. As Vera and Martha joined her at the window on either side, they stared at the crystalline flakes dancing downward.

"I love the first snow of the season," Vera whispered. "It's early this year."

Danielle thought about the two women standing next

to her, different in so many ways, but with several things in common. They both had a strong faith, and they both wanted to take care of her. To teach her about another way of life that included a peacefulness that they both seemed to know. Danielle wanted to feel peace, and it seemed that faith was the way to that goal. She latched on to Martha's hand and squeezed. Hesitantly, she reached for Vera's too, and she smiled when Vera squeezed her hand first.

And as the snow deepened into a heavy blanket of white, Danielle knew what she was going to do.

IT WAS LATE in the evening when she heard Levi snoring next to her. Their bedroom was toasty warm from the propane heater, but Danielle couldn't sleep. She picked up the flashlight next to the bed, shone it on the floor in front of her, and made her way to the living room. After adding another small log to the fire, she went to the kitchen and lit the propane lamp they kept on the kitchen table. She carried it to the window. Peeking out, she could see that the snow had stopped, just a sheen of white outside.

She put the lamp in the middle of the table, then walked to a kitchen drawer and took out a pad of paper and pen. Putting them on the table, she pulled out a chair and sat down. She stared at the paper and pen and wondered if this was a dumb idea. After trying to intimately communicate with God earlier, she couldn't seem to get her thoughts together. But then she'd remembered keeping a diary, once upon a time. Writing things down seemed to help. It was sort of like a letter to herself, helping her get her thoughts in order.

But this was a different kind of letter. And she wanted to get it right. She picked up the pen and tapped it lightly against the table, thinking about everything that had happened since Martha had taken her in.

She'd started dating Matthew and gotten pregnant. Matthew had deserted her and Joshua. Levi had married her. And the biggest surprise of all—Vera seemed to now genuinely care about her and the baby. With Vera and Martha sharing her care, Danielle felt better cared for than at any other point in her life. Loved.

As Danielle thought about her life, the word *blessed* just kept coming to her mind. She thought about where she'd come from. A broken home, an abusive mother. To love. From Martha, Arnold, Levi. And now all of Levi's family was slowly coming around. As she rubbed her stomach, Joshua gave a hard kick, and a tear rolled down her cheek.

She didn't miss Matthew at all, but she couldn't help but think how sad it was that he wouldn't know his child. Or would he? Would he come back someday? And if so, how would Levi feel about that? They'd talked about it once, and Levi had said that Matthew had a right to see his son. She supposed they'd figure it out if it happened.

Something was missing, though, and Vera's story had run through Danielle's mind over and over again. She picked up the pen and listened for a moment as the winds howled against the clapboard house. Taking a deep breath, she began.

Dear God,

Hi. I'm Danielle. I know You probably know me, but I don't really know You.

She put the pen down. *This is so dumb.* She leaned back and slouched into the chair.

Joshua kicked again, and she smiled. This new life was worth all the risks her heart had to take, even if it meant God didn't hear her. She wanted to talk to Him anyway.

I'm not sure I'm worthy to ask for Your help and for You to bless me, Joshua, and Levi, but if You would consider doing that, I will promise to talk to You every day and try to get to know You better. I'll also promise to try to live a good life.

She paused, her eyes filling with tears.

God, I want to be a great mother. Can You please help me with that?

And I want to thank You for Joshua, Levi, Martha, Vera, and all of my family and friends.

She stopped writing again and sniffled. Her hand started shaking.

I forgive Matthew for leaving us, and I hope You help him be happy.

And, God, I don't know how to forgive my mother, but I'm going to try.

Please be with me, Lord. I need You. I know I do. Please help me . . .

I give it all to You.

Love,
Danielle

She lowered her head and cried softly. Then she stood up, picked up the letter, and eased across the kitchen floor. She slipped on Levi's large work boots by the front door and pulled on his heavy black coat. She carried the lantern out the door and made her way down the porch steps and across the snow in the front yard.

Shivering from head to toe, she knew she needed to get out of the night air and back to bed, for Joshua's sake. She read the letter one more time, then lifted her eyes to the sky. The air was bitterly cold as she lifted the letter high above her head, as if offering it to God. Before she could consciously decide to let it go, a swirl of wind scooped it from her hand; she watched it spin above her head, higher and higher, silently praying that her words would make it all the way to heaven, to God. And that He would hear her.

She walked back to the house, careful not to slip or do anything that could harm the life she carried inside of her.

When she opened the door, her eyes rounded and she gasped.

"What are you doing out there?" Levi rubbed his eyes as he walked toward her. "What's wrong? Are you okay?" He gently grabbed her shoulders. "What's wrong?"

Danielle stared into his loving, kind eyes. "I—I just—" Tears started again, but something besides sadness made the tears flow down her cheeks, a feeling she didn't think she'd ever had before. "I think I just gave it all to God."

"What?" Levi rubbed his eyes with one hand and squinted at her like he hadn't heard her right. "You did what?"

"I gave it all to God." She leaned up and kissed him. "My past. My future."

He helped her out of his coat and his boots. "Are you sure you're okay?"

She smiled. "I'm better than okay. So much better, Levi. I can feel God's love."

# Twenty-One

SARAH EASED HER BUGGY PAST THE CHILDREN walking with their parents toward a nearby subdivision to ask for candy, something the *Englisch* did the last day of every October. Sarah's family and the other Amish in the district didn't participate in Halloween, and most of the area *Englisch* knew not to come to their homes asking for treats. Sarah recalled several children knocking on their door a few years ago dressed as a ghost, a devil, and some sort of fancy princess. Her father had tried to ignore the knock, but eventually her mother answered the door and gave them each a few coins, which seemed to please the children. When she'd been young, she'd wished she could participate and gather candy with the *Englisch* children.

Once she'd safely passed the children and their parents, she flicked the reins and picked up the pace, thankful it wasn't snowing this afternoon. The temperature was hovering around thirty, but the sun shined brightly. She was bundled up in her heavy winter coat and wearing her warmest black tights under a blue dress. She clicked her tongue, and the horse picked up speed, probably as anxious as she to get home before dark.

A few minutes later, she passed by the Sangre de Cristo Chapel and knew it to be the *Englisch* church where Levi and Danielle had married. Her heart still ached at the thought of losing Levi to Danielle, and while she'd examined her heart for any remorse in her attempt to sway him, she never discovered any measure of guilt. She'd seen Levi at worship service, and he was always polite, but distant. She knew from others that Danielle was on bed rest and unable to attend their worship. On the surface, Vera was polite as well, but pretty cold when they had any time together. It left Sarah feeling betrayed. She'd heard that Levi's mother spent a lot of time at Levi and Danielle's—so apparently she'd made her peace with the girl, leaving Sarah to look like the villain.

The old woman, Martha—she didn't even try to be polite, huffing at Sarah when she saw her for the first time last week at worship service, hobbling in on crutches. Sarah didn't think the grumpy woman belonged among their people anyway. It all seemed so unfair to Sarah. She'd lived her entire life according to the *Ordnung*. Despite her prayers, bitterness crept over her every time she thought about it all or saw one of them. It was unnerving to see Levi attending Amish worship, yet living as an *Englischer* with his pregnant wife. He was trying to have it both ways, and God would surely punish him for that. A part of Sarah hoped so.

She slowed the buggy when she passed a man walking on the shoulder of the road. She wasn't one to pick up a stranger, but this man looked Amish. He wore a black felt hat common to their people, and a long black coat, his hands stuffed deep into the pockets, his head tucked. *Awfully cold to be walking this time of day*. Unless you were one of the children and their parents weathering the cold for treats.

She eased the buggy to a stop and twisted to see him walking faster toward her. Her stomach lurched when she saw his face, flushed a rosy red from the wind. He wasn't clean-shaven like an unmarried man, nor did he have the traditional beard of a husband. He looked like he just hadn't shaved recently, with scraggly whiskers, and as she passed him, Sarah glanced over her shoulder to see if he had bobbed bangs on his forehead. It didn't look like it. She turned around, prepared to move along, when he yelled at her.

"Wait! Please wait!"

Her heart was beating faster as she glanced back again. He was smiling and running toward her. "Please! Wait!"

Sarah paused, unsure what to do. His voice sounded desperate, and she knew it would be dark soon, the temperatures dipping into the teens. What if he was a visiting relative of one of their own and Sarah left him on the side of the road? Her heart still beating fast in her chest, she swallowed hard and waited.

"*Wie bischt! Danki* for stopping." The young man was about her age, and when he smiled, his green eyes glowed.

Relief flooded over her as she heard his use of their dialect, even through chattering teeth. And she couldn't help but return a smile when she looked at his handsome face. "Where can I carry you?"

He climbed into the buggy and quickly began warming his hands on the portable heater blowing in the seat in between them. "*Ach*, I'm not sure."

Sarah's heart thumped inside her chest as she once again questioned if she should have stopped for this stranger. "Uh . . ." She thought for a moment. "Do you live near here?"

"Not too far, in Alamosa. But I know that's too far for you to travel by buggy this late at night. Do you know anyone near here, a driver I could hire to get me there?"

"There's a man named Wayne who lives up the road a bit. He might be able to take you to Alamosa. I can give you a ride to his *haus*."

"*Danki, danki*. That would be *gut*."

Sarah was again relieved to hear the familiar dialect. "Where are you coming from?"

"I've been a long way from home, hitching rides to get back. But my latest ride was only going as far as Canaan, so if you hadn't come along, I might have frozen to death."

Sarah stopped breathing for a moment, again wondering about this fellow. None of their people—that she knew of—would hitch a ride anywhere. But then he smiled again, putting her heart at ease a little. "I'm glad to be of help." She moved the reins into her left hand and extended her right. "I'm Sarah Troyer." Sarah trembled as they shook hands.

"Nice to meet you, Sarah. I'm Matthew. Matthew Lapp."

He was frightfully handsome—the handsomest Amish man she'd ever met. A shiver of excitement ran down her back and she wondered if he had a girl waiting in Alamosa for him. But even as she thought about it, his name kept echoing in her mind. *Matthew, Matthew Lapp, from Alamosa. Matthew Lapp!*

Sarah felt a slow smile grow across her face. After all this time, God had seen fit to punish Levi and Danielle for their poor choices.

LEVI LAY IN bed with Danielle, his ear against her stomach as Joshua squirmed beneath him. The doctor had said that Danielle was most likely going to deliver early. She was slightly dilated, and even though Levi didn't quite know what that meant, he did understand that the baby would be coming sooner than they'd hoped. More than ever, the doctor had stressed that Danielle needed to stay in bed and take it easy.

This morning they were enjoying a lazy Sunday morning since it wasn't a worship day. For once, neither Vera nor Martha was at the house, and it felt nice to be alone.

"I'm so tired of being in this bed." Danielle shifted slightly beneath him.

"I know. But you heard the doctor. You need to keep Joshua inside at least another four weeks if you can."

"I'm so fat." Danielle turned her head against the pillow.

"You're beautiful." He lifted up, kissed her, then rolled over onto his side, but he kept his hand on her belly. He couldn't wait until Joshua was born. Levi didn't think the baby could be any more his own if he'd actually fathered him. Levi knew that he'd been right to heed the voice of the Lord, to follow the calling to marry Danielle. They were so in love, so happy. And Joshua would complete their family . . . at least until they were settled enough to enjoy having even more *kinner*.

Levi's father, his cousin Eli, Jacob, David, and lots of other members of the Amish community had visited and helped Levi do more repairs to the house. They'd ended up using some low-odor paint after all, and Danielle and Levi had spent two nights with Emily and David while the house aired out. Jacob had also helped Levi put in new counters in the kitchen and a new sink in the bathroom since the old one leaked around the base. And Danielle had found the Lord that snowy night . . . Life seemed so perfect, and Levi thanked God repeatedly for His grace and love.

*I'm a blessed man. Thank You, Lord.*

THE LAST THING Vera expected on her quiet Sunday was for Sarah to show up on her doorstep. Betsy was at Vera's side when she answered the door, and Elam was reading a farming magazine.

"*Wie bischt*, Vera?" Sarah smiled as she handed Vera a Tupperware container. "These are from *Mamm*. She made a huge batch of raisin puff cookies for the bake sale yesterday, and there are lots left. She asked me to drop some off for you."

"How nice of your *mudder*. *Danki*." Vera accepted the cookies, hoping she didn't have to invite Sarah in. Maybe it was Vera's own guilt that made it difficult to be around the girl. After all, she'd encouraged Sarah to talk Levi out of the marriage. Now, when she thought about how happy Levi and Danielle were, she was reminded of the un-Christian way she'd behaved. And nothing was a bigger reminder to her than Sarah.

Sarah folded her hands in front of her black jacket and her teeth chattered.

Vera eased Betsy back with her free hand. "*Kumm* in, warm yourself by the fire."

"*Danki*." Sarah removed her coat and bonnet and hung them on the rack by the door as Vera forced a smile.

"It's too cold to be driving around today, Sarah." Elam pulled off his reading glasses and set the magazine on the coffee table in front of him.

"It's not so bad. Lots of sunshine, and not much of a breeze." Sarah sat down in one of the rocking chairs across the room as Betsy sat down in the other one. Vera held her breath, hoping Betsy behaved, but her daughter just stared at Sarah. Vera couldn't help but sense that there was some other reason for Sarah's visit. She hoped Sarah didn't want to quiz her about Levi and Danielle. Her son's own excitement about the imminent arrival fueled Vera's, and she knew Levi was going to be a wonderful father. It was still far from the perfect situation since they weren't all Amish, but it almost felt like they were sometimes, since they attended worship and lived in a house without electricity and most modern conveniences.

"Can I get you some hot cocoa?" Vera wiped at some flour on her black apron. She'd just finished two loaves of bread before Sarah arrived.

"*Danki*. That would be *gut*."

"Me too, please, *Mamm*!" Betsy kicked the rocker in motion, still staring at Sarah. Vera hesitated to leave Betsy with Sarah, but Elam gave Vera a nod, silently telling her he'd keep an eye on their precocious young daughter.

Vera was pouring cocoa into two mugs when she heard footsteps coming into the kitchen. She turned to see Sarah walk to the kitchen table and pull out a chair. Vera set her cup down in front of her.

"I'll be right back." Vera delivered Betsy's cocoa, then went back into the kitchen, taking a seat across the table from Sarah, wondering what was on the young woman's mind. Clearly, she wanted to discuss something in private.

Sarah sipped from her cocoa, and Vera felt herself tensing, wondering if perhaps the girl had come to apologize.

"Is there something you have to say, Sarah?"

"Not really." Sarah cocked her head to one side. "I mostly came to see how you were doing."

Vera frowned a little in confusion. "I'm doing *gut*. Very *gut*. Why?"

Sarah reached over and put her hand on Vera's, and Vera fought the urge to pull away. "I was just concerned when I heard that Matthew Lapp was back in town. I wasn't sure if he was going to cause problems for Levi and Danielle." Sarah shrugged, keeping her eyes on Vera.

Vera swallowed hard as she eased her hand from beneath Sarah's. "He—he's back?"

"*Ya*. I saw him yesterday. He's back in Alamosa with his parents."

"To stay?" Vera avoided Sarah's eyes as she thought about what this might mean for Levi and Danielle. Levi talked about "their" baby all the time, and Levi often referred to Vera as the baby's grandmother, something she'd gotten used to. Would all of that change if Matthew was back and going to be an active part of their lives? That would make Anna Marie the grandmother, not Vera . . .

"I don't know." Sarah shook her head. "I gave him a ride yesterday to Wayne's *haus*, and then Wayne carted him to his folks' in Alamosa. I didn't mention anything, since he didn't. But you'd told me that he knew about the *boppli* before he left. I assume that's why he's returned."

Vera was lost in her thoughts, protective instincts kicking in for Levi. Her son had built a crib, prepared the baby's room, been at the doctor's visits, and planned to be the father to the child. Could Matthew just swoop back into their lives and stake claim to Joshua? Of course he could. Vera's heart ached. Logically, she knew that Matthew should be a part of Joshua's life, but they'd all gotten used to him *not* being around.

"*Danki* for telling me." Vera eyed Sarah and wanted to smack the smug grin from her face. Once again, Sarah was stirring up trouble. They would have found out eventually anyway, but did the girl have to revel in it?

"It wonders me what will happen now." Sarah shook her head before taking another sip of her cocoa.

"Nothing will change," Vera insisted. "A child can't have too much love." She heard herself say the words, but found herself wishing that Matthew hadn't returned. For Levi's sake.

Sarah stood up, a self-satisfied expression still on her face. "I'm sure it won't. *Danki*, Vera, for the cocoa. I best be delivering the rest of the cookies before it gets too late."

Vera followed Sarah to the door, and as Sarah bundled in her coat and bonnet, she told Betsy and Elam good-bye, then turned to Vera and gave her a hug. "I'm sorry to give you such news."

*No, you're not.* Vera eased away and only nodded before she closed the door behind Sarah.

Vera was attached to a baby who wasn't even born, a child who wasn't biologically her grandchild. Why had she opened her heart like that? She thought about Anna Marie's visit, when she'd used the words *custody* and *visitation*. She watched from the window as Sarah led her horse down the driveway, but turned around when Betsy spoke.

"I don't like her."

"Betsy. Don't say things like that." She went to the couch and sat beside Elam, who was reading his magazine again.

"You don't like her either." Betsy put her cocoa down on the table beside the rocker and pushed with her slippers against the floor.

Elam raised his eyes above his gold-rimmed glasses. "Betsy, you heard your mother. We don't talk like that about others."

Vera was quiet. She was wondering if she should break this news to Levi and Danielle. Or maybe they already knew? She hadn't had time to completely gather her thoughts when she heard another buggy pulling in. *What now?*

She was relieved to see it was Emily, although a bit surprised.

Vera pulled her into a hug after she shed her winter coat, relieved for the distraction. "What brings you here this evening? Where's David?"

Her daughter walked to Elam, kissed him on the cheek, then also kissed Betsy before she sat down in one of the rockers. "He's at Lillian and Samuel's, talking to them."

Vera's heart sank. Had Emily lost the baby? *It must be important.* "What's wrong?"

"*Ach, Mamm.* Everything is fine with the *boppli.*" Emily folded her hands across her stomach. She wasn't even showing yet, but relief fell over Vera.

She put a hand to her chest and allowed herself to breathe. "Thank You, Lord." She paused. "But you came to talk to us about something, *ya?*"

Emily nodded as she crossed her legs. "I wanted to let you know that David and I are going to be traveling to Lancaster County soon."

Vera frowned. "Why? And when? Thanksgiving will be here soon."

"We're going to go in a couple of weeks, so we won't be here for Thanksgiving, *Mamm*."

Elam closed the magazine again, pulling off his glasses. "*Dochder*, is there a problem?"

Lillian, Samuel, David, Anna, and Elizabeth had all moved to Canaan from Lancaster County after Lillian's grandfather had left them a large chunk of land in the valley.

Emily sighed. "*Ya*, I guess you could say there is a problem. Remember hearing about David's *Onkel* Noah? He's Samuel's brother, the one who gave David a kidney."

"*Ya, ya.*" Vera sat down next to Elam, leaning forward. "What about, him?"

"Well . . ." Emily shook her head. "There is a new bishop in town. David said that Bishop Ebersol had been the bishop for David's entire life, but he died this past winter. Remember how upset David, Lillian, and Samuel were because they weren't able to travel to the funeral?"

Vera nodded as she recalled the bad weather in Colorado during that week.

"Anyway, the new bishop is very strict, and he's changing everything in the district. Things that have always been allowed are no longer acceptable, and everyone's upset."

Vera scratched her forehead. "But why are you and David traveling there now? I don't understand."

"David's *Onkel* Noah runs a clinic in Paradise, and all the Amish have gone to him for years. David says he is a kind, wonderful man. But the new bishop has now banned anyone from going to Noah's clinic since he isn't Amish."

"That doesn't make sense. We all use *Englisch* doctors. And I wouldn't think it would be any different there." The Amish always tried to utilize an herbal doctor before turning to traditional *Englisch* medicine, but for many years they'd been going to *Englisch* doctors when that failed.

"Noah was shunned years ago. The new bishop said that everyone must practice the ban, even though it hasn't been practiced against Noah for a long time."

Elam spoke up. "What difference can David make with a visit?"

Emily shrugged. "We're not sure. But David loves his *Onkel* Noah very much, and he wants to try to help somehow. To talk to the bishop, maybe make him understand how Noah saved his life, and how he's saved the lives of many of the Amish there."

Vera shook her head. "You're pregnant and shouldn't be traveling."

"*Mamm*, I'm early into my pregnancy, and the doctor says I'm fine. We'll be staying with David's 'Auntie' Rebecca and her family. It's a chance for me to meet a lot of David's family."

"Why do you have to go before the holidays? And you know your *bruder's* baby . . ." Vera paused, pressing her lips together as she recalled Sarah's visit. "The baby is coming in a few weeks."

"I know, and I'll hate to miss that, but David is anxious to go see if he can help Noah." She stopped rocking and crossed her legs again.

Vera wasn't sure how David could make a difference, but her son-in-law was a *gut* man with a huge heart. "I understand. How long will you be gone?"

"We don't know."

"You have to tend to your own health above all else, and

that of the *boppli*." Elam pushed himself to the edge of the couch, and Vera was glad to hear him speak her thoughts.

"I know, *Daed*. It comforts me, given that Noah is a doctor. Plus, I don't think there will be any problems. I'm not even having morning sickness anymore."

Vera understood her daughter's need to support her husband, as it should be, but her thoughts wandered from Emily's babe to Danielle's, and then to the news at hand.

Was it her responsibility to warn them that Matthew was back?

## Twenty-Two

WHEN DANIELLE OPENED THE FRONT DOOR, MATTHEW'S amber-green eyes were just like she remembered, his smile was still adorable, and even with scraggly facial hair, he was as handsome as ever—but Danielle didn't feel one thing for him.

Matthew stared at her stomach. "Hi, Danielle." He paused. "How much longer?"

"Seven weeks." Cold air blew through the open door, but she wasn't about to let him into Levi's home. Her home. And soon to be Joshua's home. She blinked, trying to decipher if she was dreaming. "Why are you here?"

"*Mamm* told me that you married Levi. I always thought you were only friends." He stuffed his hands in the pockets of a black jacket.

"We were friends," she said, staring at him. "But things change."

"I'll say." Matthew grunted, a slight grin on his face. "Kinda fast, don'tcha think?"

Tears burned the corners of Danielle's eyes and she

straightened. "Matthew, what do you want?"

"I came back to visit *Mamm* and *Daed*." He shrugged, then focused his eyes on her belly again. "And to see . . . you know . . ."

Danielle laid a hand across her stomach as Joshua kicked more than ever before. "No, I don't know. Why don't you explain it to me?"

"Well, I'm going to be a father, so I thought I ought to be around for it." He grinned as if life hadn't gone on in his absence, as if he hadn't totally deserted her and shirked all responsibility. Anger wrapped around her at his nonchalant attitude, even though the hurt she'd once felt had been replaced by Levi's love, tenfold. Her heart hurt for Levi. With Matthew back in the picture, how was Levi going to feel?

"I don't have anything to say to you, Matthew."

The smirky grin faded. "I'm sorry for the way I left, Danielle. I really am. It was all just more than I could handle, but I've had time to sort out my thoughts. I should be here to raise my son."

"Levi and I will be raising Joshua." Danielle pressed her lips firmly together, resisting the urge to just slam the door. *How could he possibly think—*

"I guess we'll have to share him. I have rights, Danielle. Levi can't just step in and replace me."

Danielle leaned forward. "Replace you? You've never been here, Matthew. He stepped in after you ran away." She shook her head, tears building. "I don't want to talk to you about this."

"I'm sorry, Danielle. I really am. For everything. I'm so, so sorry that you got pregnant."

Danielle felt the life inside of her moving around, and

his words cut deep. She wasn't sorry about anything. She'd learned that everything was God's plan, and Joshua was part of that plan, so she didn't feel shame over her pregnancy. She'd grown to love Joshua before he was even born, and she knew Levi had also.

"I have to go." She closed the door in his face and leaned her forehead against it as tears poured down her face. She tried to stifle her crying, waiting for the creak of the porch floorboards as Matthew turned and walked away. She didn't weep for him, the biological father of her child. She wept for Levi, Joshua's true father—and what he would have to endure now that Matthew had returned.

She hadn't been back in the bed for thirty minutes when she heard the front door open, and a few moments later, Vera walked in. "What's wrong?"

Danielle swiped at her tears, dreading this conversation almost as much as the one to come with Levi. "Matthew . . . the baby's . . . real father was here." She held up her index finger. "No. He's not Joshua's *real* father. Levi is." She gave in to the tears again, and Vera came and sat down on the bed, waiting silently. "But he was here. And apparently, he wants to be in the baby's life."

"I heard he was in town." Vera sighed, then reached for Danielle's hand and squeezed. "We will work it out. I'm sure his mother will want to be a grandmother to the baby, and—"

"You don't want to be his grandma anymore? Just because Matthew came back, now you don't want to be Joshua's grandmother?" Danielle knew she was whining and crying like a child, but right now, she couldn't help it. Was Vera ready to bail? So soon?

VERA'S HEART WAS heavy, knowing that in some ways she would have to step aside to make room for Matthew's family. "Of course I'm going to be a *mammi* to the *boppli*. It's just that—"

"His name is *Joshua*. Remember?"

Vera bit her tongue, knowing Danielle was hurting. "*Ya*, Joshua. I know that."

"I don't want Matthew in our lives. This baby is Levi's, and biology doesn't matter."

Vera had come to agree, but she knew that things were going to change. "The Lord has other plans." She cringed, waiting for Danielle's reaction.

"I know," Danielle said calmly. "I just don't want to tell Levi."

"Levi has a strong faith. He will realize that this is the Lord's plan, and somehow, everyone will make it work."

"I hope so."

Vera stood up, deciding that she would give the stove a good scrubbing, something to keep her mind occupied.

DANIELLE WAS SITTING on the edge of the couch, her hands folded in her lap, when Levi walked in the door after work.

"Why aren't you in bed?" He walked to her, kissed her on the forehead, then sat down beside her. "Are you okay?"

She shook her head and avoided his eyes.

Levi gently lifted her chin until she looked at him. "What is it, Ladybug? What's wrong?"

Danielle swallowed hard, and again she pulled her eyes

from Levi's, not wanting to see the pain in his expression when she told him about her visitor. But she had to tell him, so she took a deep breath, then blew it out slowly. "Matthew was here today."

"What did he want?" Levi's nostrils flared as his face turned red. "Tell me, Danielle. Is he here to stay?"

"Yes."

Levi stood up, put his hands on his hips, then paced, his eyes on the floor.

"Say something." She swiped at her eyes as she wondered if maybe she'd put too much faith in God. They'd been so happy. Standing up, she walked to him and touched his arm. For the first time ever, he pulled away.

"Just give me a minute," he said, not looking at her as he held up a hand. When he finally did meet her eyes, he blinked, as if trying to decide on his words. "Does he want to be in Joshua's life?"

Danielle nodded. "I'm sorry. He's your baby, Levi. You know that, right? We will raise him together." She started to cry, but Levi didn't move to offer any comfort. Was this going to change everything? Danielle wished more than anything in the world that Levi was Joshua's biological father. But she wouldn't ever believe that Joshua was a mistake. Somewhere in all of this, there had to be joy, happiness, and peace for all of them. *Please, God. Help us.*

"I need some air." Levi was still in his coat when he moved toward the door. Danielle was on his heels.

"Levi, I love you. Please don't leave," she cried as she reached for his arm, but he didn't turn around. She watched him cross the yard as the sun began to set behind the San Juan

Mountains, and within a few minutes, he was walking down the road . . . growing smaller and smaller in the distance.

LEVI HADN'T THOUGHT about Joshua being anyone's son but his own for months, and he felt like he'd been kicked in the gut. In the back of his mind, he'd known this was a possibility, but he'd pushed it so far back that he'd all but convinced himself that he was Joshua's father.

He walked down the road as the wind stung his cheeks. He'd left Danielle crying in the doorway, and he felt like a louse. But right now, he needed to deal with his own hurt before he could comfort her, as wrong as it was. As a man and a husband, he should put his wife's needs ahead of his own, but anger strangled him. How could Matthew just mosey in after all this time and expect to be a part of Joshua's life?

Levi walked faster, his heart pounding from exhaustion and pain. He knew he was behaving poorly, but it didn't stop him from wanting someone, anyone to understand the hurt he was feeling.

He thought about all the times he'd lain next to Danielle's rounded belly and talked to Joshua so the boy would know Levi's voice. And Levi knew he shouldn't be detailing in his mind everything that he'd done to prepare their lives for the baby's arrival; he'd been happy to do it all. But now he felt cheated, unappreciated.

And selfish.

*Lord, help me to understand Your plan. I did what You asked me to. Why did You guide me to fall in love with Danielle, to marry her, and to love a baby who isn't even born yet? If they're not to be mine, in total? Why?*

Would Matthew and Danielle share a bond that Levi and Danielle could never feel? Would it make her wonder if she married the wrong man? Made a mistake? Would she turn away from him, the man who had given her everything he had?

He allowed himself to experience all his selfish thoughts, and as his eyes filled with tears, he thought about the way he'd left his wife, crying in the living room. *What kind of man am I?*

He turned around and walked back to the house. He was still angry, confused about his own emotions, and questioning the Lord's will.

But three things he knew for sure.

He loved Danielle with all his heart. He loved Joshua. And he loved God.

And there wasn't anything anyone could do to block that love.

## *Twenty-Three*

DANIELLE CRIED IN LEVI'S ARMS, ALTHOUGH HE kept asking her repeatedly to stop, telling her it wasn't good for her and her baby.

"Joshua is *our* baby," Danielle pleaded, silently begging him to agree.

"*Ya*. He is. Please don't cry." He pulled her into his lap on the couch. "I'm so sorry for the way I acted. I just . . . well, I want him to be mine, and sometimes . . . like now, I'm reminded that there is someone else in the picture, someone who has a right to be in Joshua's life . . . but I . . ." He laid a hand on her stomach. "I already love him."

Danielle cupped his cheeks in her hands. "And he loves you. He'll know your voice, and you'll be his father."

"Along with Matthew." Levi grabbed one of her hands and kissed it. "And that's okay. I'll just have to get used to it. Matthew's been gone, and I guess I've just put him out of my mind. I know that he needs to be a part of Joshua's life. As it should be."

"Oh, Levi, I love you so much." She kissed him, running

a hand through his hair as she thought about the past several months. "I can't imagine loving you any more than I do right now."

"I love you too."

Danielle could hear the worry in his voice, whether he realized it or not, and she wanted to tell him something that she'd been thinking about, something that might brighten his day. But she knew it wasn't the right time.

At Levi's insistence, he helped her back to bed, then brought in two bowls of soup and some butter bread that Vera had brought over earlier. After they ate, Levi took the dishes to the kitchen, took a bath, and climbed into bed next to her. He laid his head against her belly and talked to Joshua. "My son, you are a gift from God. There can never be too much love for you."

Danielle leaned back and closed her eyes, feeling Joshua moving around, responding to Levi's voice. She knew that they were going to both have to adjust their thinking to make room for Matthew. But for this moment, she just wanted to lie quietly with her husband and listen to him talk to Joshua.


MARTHA WALKED UP the steps at Danielle and Levi's house, glad to be free of her cast and toting a batch of chicken lasagna. She let herself in, put the casserole dish in the refrigerator, then made her way to the fireplace. As she heaved another log in the fire, orange sparks shimmied up, and she pulled off her gloves and warmed her hands. They'd had barely an inch of snow during the night, but the temperature wasn't even going to reach twenty degrees today. Glancing at the firewood next to the hearth, she was glad to see that Levi had left a plentiful stack.

"I'm here!" She unbuttoned her coat and hung it on the rack by the door, then she glanced around. It looked just like any of the Amish homes in the area, and she couldn't believe that Danielle hadn't thrown a fit months ago and pushed Levi for electricity. But over and over, Danielle had behaved exactly the opposite of how Martha expected.

Instead of flat-ironing her long blond hair, she'd taken to pulling it into a loose side braid, and Levi charged her cell phone every other day or so when he was in town with his father on a job. Danielle's car hadn't been driven in months, since the doctor put her on bed rest, and when Martha had questioned her about the heat, Danielle had said that her favorite part of the day was cozying up with Levi by the fire at night. And they had propane heaters in the rest of the house.

Television. That was the one thing Martha knew she wouldn't be able to do without, and she'd suspected it would have been a tough thing for Danielle to give up, but Danielle said she kept up with the news and her favorite shows on her cell phone. Martha shook her head, knowing that most of the Amish folks she knew had cell phones and probably did the same thing.

She moved toward Danielle's closed bedroom door and gave a gentle knock. "You decent?"

Martha's heart ached for her and Levi, and Martha wondered how Levi had taken the news of Matthew's return. She loved her Amish friends, but they were sticklers about certain things and not others. You couldn't have electricity in the house or you might face a shunning. But knock up an *Englisch* girl and you could still be baptized into the faith? Martha felt like they needed to reprioritize some things.

She pushed the door open, but Danielle wasn't there. She edged out and down the hallway toward the bathroom. "Honey, you okay? You in there?" She tapped on the door, and it slowly opened.

Danielle was standing in the bathroom, white as the snow outside, still in her floor-length white nightgown Vera had bought her awhile back, and she was holding her bulging belly, a strained look on her face. "Something is happening."

Martha's heart flipped in her chest. "Like what? What do you mean?"

"I don't know." Danielle flinched as she bent slightly. "Like cramping."

"Good grief! Do you think you're in labor?" Martha didn't mean to shout it, but Danielle shot her a stricken look. Martha wasn't sure, but cramping sounded like a trip to the hospital was in order, regardless. "Maybe it's not labor. But let's get you dressed and take a trip to town. Where's your little red suitcase I told you to have packed?"

"In the bedroom." Danielle didn't move, but Martha scurried around the corner faster than she'd moved in a while.

SARAH HAD JUST bagged two loaves of bread for an *Englisch* customer when she looked up and saw Matthew walking in the door of Abbey's Bakery. After giving him a ride the other night—and figuring out who he was—the last thing she wanted to do was to get involved with him. She almost felt sorry for Levi and Danielle that he'd come around. Almost.

"*Wie bischt*, Matthew? What can I get you?" She smoothed the wrinkles from her white apron and forced a smile.

"You look mighty pretty today, Sarah." He smiled, and Sarah had to struggle not to let his flattery affect her as she felt her cheeks warm.

"*Danki.*" She took a quick glance around, glad the other ladies were in the back. "What brings you here to Canaan? I'm sure they have bakeries in Alamosa."

Grinning, he tipped back the rim of his black felt hat. "The prettiest girls are here in Canaan."

Sarah rolled her eyes as she fingered the string of her *kapp*. "Are you Amish or not? I'm confused." She wondered if he was wearing the traditional clothing beneath his long black coat.

"I think part of me will always be Amish." He smiled again.

"Are you planning to be baptized into the faith?" Sarah wasn't sure why she was asking. He certainly wasn't a courting possibility for her. "I mean . . . now that you're going to be a father, raising a child who is being reared in the *Englisch* world." She raised a brow.

Matthew's smile faded, but only briefly, before he flashed another teasing grin. "Are you judging me, Sarah Troyer?"

"Hardly. Only God can do that." She straightened a pile of receipts on the counter, avoiding his incredible green eyes. *Maybe under different circumstances . . .*

"So I heard what you did to try to break up Danielle and Levi."

Sarah looked up, swallowing hard. "What are you talking about?"

"The kisses, then telling Danielle."

Sarah held her breath as heat filled her cheeks. "You don't

even live here. How could you possibly know what you're talk-ing about?"

Matthew laughed. "Alamosa isn't all that far, and we have mutual friends." He scratched his chin. "Wow. You must have really wanted to break them up."

Sarah wanted to run to the back before tears spilled, but she steeled herself. "Do you have a reason for being here? Other than to spread idle gossip?"

"Don't get upset." He leaned his elbows down on the coun-ter and leaned closer to her. "I thought it was a great attempt. Brave for an Amish girl."

Sarah had been dealing with what she'd done in her own way, but if the entire community knew, what must they think of her? "What do you want, Matthew?"

"I'm going to need two loaves of banana nut bread and some of those raisin puffs." He pointed inside the glass cabi-net that separated them. "*Mei mamm's* oven is on the fritz, and it'll please her to come home from her quilting party to some treats."

Sarah reached inside the glass counter for the cookies. "I'll be back with the bread."

A few moments later, she had everything bagged up and totaled. "Twelve dollars and twenty-two cents."

Matthew reached into the pocket of his coat and handed her a twenty-dollar bill.

Sarah made change and handed it to him. "*Danki.*"

"I bet everyone tells you how beautiful you are."

As his dimples rounded, Sarah thought what a shame it was that such a handsome man was unavailable, at least to her anyway. "Are you flirting with me?"

"Is that what you think I'm doing?" He grinned as he accepted the bag of baked goods from her.

"I would hope not, under the circumstances." She lifted her chin. "It would be inappropriate." She shrugged. "It wouldn't matter one way or the other, though. I wouldn't go out with you even if things were different."

He leaned down on the counter, putting him close enough to make Sarah take a step backward. "Oh, I think you would." He winked before he turned to leave, but spun around as he neared the exit, tipping his hat. "Have a wonderful day, Sarah Troyer."

Sarah gritted her teeth as she watched him walk toward the door. Why was she allowing this man to have this kind of effect on her?

He was almost to the door when Sarah heard a ringing. Matthew stopped as he reached in the pocket of his coat and brought the cell phone to his ear.

"Now? She's having the baby now?"

He didn't turn around as he kept the phone to his ear and walked out the door.

Sarah just shook her head. *What a waste.* Danielle had snagged two of the hottest guys around, messed up both their lives, and left them both unsuitable for courtship.

*A terrible shame.*

LEVI'S STOMACH ACHED as Arnold drove him to the hospital in Monte Vista. Everyone else was already there. His father hadn't told anyone that they had to go back to a job from earlier in the week to make some adjustments to the solar panels, so by the time Arnold had found Levi and his father, Martha had been gone with Danielle for almost two hours. And his mother, Emily, Lillian, Samuel, David, Katie Ann, and Eli were already at the hospital. *Mamm* had told Levi that Emily called Matthew on his cell phone. Danielle had reluctantly given her the number.

Levi resented that Emily had tracked Matthew down, even though Levi knew in his heart that it was the right thing to do. But Levi wanted to be the one at the hospital with Danielle. He wondered if Matthew had gone into her room to see her. Twice, Levi had tried to call Danielle's cell phone using Arnold's phone, and both times, there was no answer.

"At least it's not snowing," Arnold said as he puttered down the highway. Levi had only driven a few times, but he was sure he could get them to the hospital faster than Arnold. His stomach churned as he worried over Danielle and the baby.

After what seemed like forever, Arnold pulled into the parking lot. "Just go. I'll park the car and find you shortly."

Levi jumped out of the car, ran to the large double doors, and paused briefly as they opened automatically. He already knew that Danielle was on the third floor in room 302. As he exited the elevator, he saw most of his family gathered in a small waiting room. Martha was the only one he didn't see. Matthew wasn't out there either, and he instantly wondered if he was in the room with Danielle.

"Is everything okay?" He walked straight to his mother. "Is Danielle okay? The baby?"

His mother grabbed his shoulders. "The baby is going to come early, *sohn*. He is going to be tiny. Danielle is in labor. Martha is in there with her." *Mamm* nodded to her right. "Down that hall; room 302 is on the left."

Levi turned to go but then looked back at his mother.

"Only Martha is in there," she said, reading the question in his eyes.

Levi ran in that direction, and when he reached the door, he caught his breath, then eased it open. Danielle's face was strained, but when she saw him, she held out a hand.

"Ladybug, I'm here." He leaned over the rail of her bed. "Are you in pain?" *What a dumb question.* He could tell by her expression that she was. "What can I do?" He glanced at Martha, who was standing on the other side of the bed.

"She's hurting pretty good. And the baby is coming fast."

"He's going to be very small, Levi." Danielle squeezed her eyes shut as she groaned for a moment. Levi waited, his heart thumping. "Maybe only four or five pounds."

"What does that mean? Will he be okay?" Levi directed the question at Martha.

"God is in this room," Martha said firmly. "And everything is going to be just fine. It's just going to take our Joshua a little time to grow after he gets here. The doctor said he might have to stay in the hospital a few weeks."

Levi tried not to flinch as Danielle squeezed his hand so tight he thought she might break it. Then a nurse walked in, a young woman with blond hair tucked into a bun on her head. She was wearing blue pants and a blue shirt with a pink and yellow flower pattern.

"Let's see how far along you are." The nurse eased Danielle's knees up and pushed back the white blanket. Levi felt the color rushing from his face.

"Here ya go, big guy." Martha cupped his elbow and turned him toward the door. "Why don't we stand outside?"

Levi's knees felt weak beneath him, but he eased away. "No, I'm staying."

He walked to Danielle's side and gripped her hand, keeping his eyes on hers. "I'm here. And I'm not leaving you."

"It won't be long," the smiling nurse said as she put the sheet back down and stood up. "The doctor is down the hall delivering another baby, Danielle, but he'll be in to see you soon. Call me if you need something in the meantime." She turned to Levi. "And I'm assuming you are the father?"

Levi didn't move, but Danielle quickly spoke up. "Yes. He is the father." She smiled at him, right before she flinched again.

The nurse patted him on the arm. "Okay, Dad. Hang in there. And she can have some of those ice chips if she wants them. I'll be back shortly to check on you."

After the nurse left, Martha said, "I'm going to leave you two alone. I'll go fill the others in and let them know that it won't be long."



VERA PACED THE small waiting room as they all waited for the newest, tiny little life to come into their world. She was glad Levi had arrived in time to be with Danielle, but Vera knew something no one else knew. The baby's biological father was downstairs in the lobby, along with his mother. Vera had seen Anna Marie when her group walked in, and she could only assume that the young man with her was Matthew. They were sitting off by themselves in a far corner, deep in conversation. Vera had thought about approaching them, but she wasn't sure what to say. She'd been nervous for the past hour, assuming Anna Marie and Matthew would eventually make their way to the small waiting room on the third floor where the rest of them were.

She went and sat down by Emily, patted her on the leg, then spoke to the entire group. "I'm glad you're all here to support Levi and Danielle."

"We're all glad to be here, *Mamm*." Emily smiled, glancing around the room. "We're very happy for them."

Vera thought about her role in all of this; how she'd grown to love Danielle, anticipated the baby coming, and almost come to terms with the fact that Levi was not living a life according to the *Ordnung*. The saving grace was that Danielle had accepted the Lord and she and Levi were good Christians. But was Vera's heart safe?

Downstairs was the baby's real grandmother.

"Where are the *kinner*?" She turned to face Lillian. Vera had left Betsy at Beth Ann's, and her daughter-in-law had said that they would all come by later today.

"Ida Mae has them."

They were all quiet for a while, and Vera couldn't seem to sit still. "Does everyone know you're leaving?" she asked Emily.

"*Ya*." Emily looked around the room as some of the family nodded. Their family was the only one in the small waiting room. "We're going to try to leave next week."

"I hate that you'll miss Thanksgiving," Lillian said, frowning for a moment, then her face brightened. "But you'll love Samuel's family. His sister Rebecca is great. You'll like staying there."

"I'm excited to meet everyone, but sad about the circumstances." Emily looked up at her husband. "I'm hoping David can help to change the bishop's mind about his *Onkel* Noah."

Vera leaned back against the chair and put a hand on Emily's knee. "Sure you don't want to wait until after Thanksgiving? Do you know when you'll be back?"

"We're not sure." Emily smiled. "Way before the baby is due, *Mamm.*"

"*Ach*, I should hope so. That's months away." Vera lifted her eyebrows. "Maybe you'll be back before Christmas?"

Emily looked at David, then back at her mother. "I think we will probably stay through Christmas, *Mamm.* But we'll see."

That seemed like a long time to Vera, and the way Emily kept looking at David . . . it made Vera nervous. Emily had told her several times how David had never wanted to leave Lancaster County, and Vera couldn't help but worry if David was considering a move back. That seemed a stretch since his mother, father, and young sisters lived in Canaan, but the worry had found its way into Vera's heart just the same.

Martha stood up from where she was sitting next to Eli. "I'm going to go check on Danielle."

Vera wanted to go too, but again . . . she found her role in all of this unclear. She'd been the one to tend to Danielle all this time, felt the baby move, and even gone with Danielle to her last doctor's appointment, along with Martha. Both women had gotten to hear the baby's heartbeat. There was a bond that Vera hadn't expected, yet with Anna Marie downstairs, that threatened Vera's place. She wished they weren't here and Vera could go on pretending that this new life would be exclusive to her family.

## Twenty-Four

LEVI HELD HIS BREATH AS DANIELLE SCREAMED. The room was filled with people—the on-call doctor, a gray-haired man with black-rimmed glasses, the same blond nurse, as well as two others. One of the women had pushed in an incubator, and the doctor had already warned them that they would be taking Joshua by helicopter to the nearest neonatal intensive care unit if there were any problems.

Levi felt woozy as he stepped back from Danielle. She didn't even seem to know if he was there or not, and every minute or so, she howled like a wild animal. Levi just wished someone would tell him what to do. He couldn't stand to see her in such pain, but he was scared to leave her. "Should I go?" he asked the nearest nurse.

"No, honey," the older woman said, patting him on the arm. "Go ahead and move around here. You should be able to see the head soon."

Levi wished he was outside the room, like his father had been. "*Nee, nee.* That's okay." He took a step backward, away from Danielle, but she screamed . . . calling his name this time.

"I'm here," he said as he stepped up again. He reached for her hand. "I'm here."

"Don't go! Don't leave me!"

"I'm not. I'll stay right here." He tried to keep his hand steady as he reached for hers.

The blond nurse said, "Go ahead and push with the next contraction, Danielle." She nodded to Levi. "Sure you don't want to come watch?"

Levi shook his head, glancing down at the yellow gown they'd had him throw over his clothes, and wondered where he'd left his hat. And he wondered if Matthew was here. How small would Joshua be? Would he be healthy? Was Danielle going to survive this? He'd never heard anyone scream the way she was now.

Then the nurses gathered at the end of the bed, flanking the doctor, and Danielle gritted her teeth, bearing down through the next contraction, and her screams turned to moans in between.

"Here he comes," the doctor said. "You're doing a great job, Danielle. Once more, and you should have your baby in your arms." He stared at the monitor, watching her contraction build. "Get ready . . ."

Levi stroked her cheek and watched as her face grew red from the effort of pushing. When her head fell back against the pillow, he glanced toward the doctor again, just in time to see him cut the umbilical cord and hand Joshua to one of the nurses.

He was so tiny.

But there was no crying, and the doctor and nurses moved in a flurry to a table where they laid Joshua down, keeping their backs to him and Danielle.

"Is he okay? Why isn't he crying?" Danielle cried, her questions coming in tired gasps. "Tell me. Is he okay?"

Then Levi's world stopped spinning for a moment as this new life let go with a wail and everyone breathed a sigh of relief.

"There we go." The doctor's words rang through the room. "That's what I like to hear. Let me just give his lungs a quick listen." The nurses parted, and Levi and Danielle could see him bend over the tiny, red, squalling babe and listen to his chest with a stethoscope. Then, smiling, he handed the baby to a nurse, and she brought him over and laid him in Danielle's arms. Levi looked down at the tiny little person he'd talked to for months. Joshua was swaddled in a blue blanket, his face red, his eyes barely open . . . until he heard Danielle's voice. When mother and son met eyes, Levi swallowed back the lump in his throat. *Oh, Lord, what a miracle.*

Danielle kept her eyes on the small bundle for another minute before she looked up at Levi. "Our Joshua." She smiled in a way that Levi would remember for the rest of his life. "Isn't he beautiful?"

Levi couldn't take his eyes from the baby. "He's the most beautiful thing I've ever seen."

Then Joshua looked toward him, and a tear slid down Levi's cheek.

"We have to take him now. He's very small, only a little over four pounds." The doctor had already excused himself to go down the hall to check on another patient, and the nurse reached for Joshua. "We'll keep a close eye on him, but overall he looks to be doing quite well."

Danielle reluctantly handed him over to the nurse, and awhile later, the room was clear. Levi knew that Martha would arrive soon, and he wanted to enjoy this moment with his wife.

"He's perfect." Levi leaned down and kissed her.

"He is, isn't he?" Danielle pushed back her hair, still sweaty from all her hard work. "Can you believe how small he is?"

"He'll grow fast." Levi kissed her again. There'd been so much going on that he'd postponed his worry about Matthew, but now that things were calming down, he was sure that the man must be lurking around somewhere.

His son had just been born.

AN HOUR LATER, Vera stared through the large glass window into a room that held three premature babies, each in their own incubator. Two of the babies had tiny tubes in their mouths, and Vera was sure one of them could have fit in the palm of her hand. She was glad that Joshua was the largest of the three and that he didn't require any tubes in his mouth.

"The doctor said he's doing *gut*."

Vera turned to see Levi standing next to her, looking as proud as any father would be, and it warmed her heart. She still hadn't seen Matthew or his mother again, and that left her a bit uneasy, as if they might pounce at any moment.

"He's a beautiful child." Vera gazed upon the bundle with her son.

"*Ya*." Levi paused, and Vera glanced his way. "It was something. I mean, being there and watching him be born."

She touched her son's arm when his voice cracked. "A true miracle."

Levi took a deep breath. "Where is everyone?"

"They all left and said they would be back to visit tomorrow. Except for Martha. She went downstairs to get something to eat with Arnold." She turned to Levi. "I bet you haven't eaten today. You should get something too."

Levi shook his head. "No, I'm going back to Danielle. I don't want to leave her, and—"

"I will go to be with Danielle. I'm sure she's going to eat her dinner when they bring it in." Vera smiled. "After all that hard work, she's probably starving." She waved a hand at him. "Scoot. Go eat. I'll stay with her."

"*Danki, Mamm.*" Levi smiled, then walked down the hall and toward the exit. He was crossing through the main lobby when he heard a woman's voice.

"Please, Matthew. Please."

Levi eased to a halt and slowly turned around. A woman dressed in an Amish prayer covering and long blue dress had a coat and bonnet in her hands, and she was facing a man about Levi's age. The fellow was wearing blue jeans, tennis shoes, a black coat, and a black hat. He looked half-Amish, half-*Englisch*. Levi walked toward them. He slowed as he got closer, listening.

"Please don't do this. He is your child. Go see him. You will change your mind."

Levi didn't move as the woman went on. She was crying. "How can you do this?"

"*Mamm*, you shouldn't have dragged me here."

"But you said you wanted to be in the *boppli's* life. When you came back, you said you would be a father. Matthew, you said all those things, and—"

"I know, *Mamm*." Matthew hung his head for a moment before he looked back up at his mother. "I know what I said.

And I was trying to make you happy, and I thought I could do this. But this was never part of my plan."

"But it's God's plan for you. He is your child, Matthew." The woman brought her hands to her face, weeping. When she looked back up, she said, "I wish your father was here." She shook her head, still crying. "He'd surely talk some sense into you."

Levi edged closer, and Matthew eyed him.

"Matthew? Matthew Lapp?" Levi's heart was pounding out of his chest.

"*Ya?*"

"I'm Levi Detweiler." It took everything in Levi's power to extend his hand to Matthew, but in his heart, he knew he had to.

Matthew slowly reached out, and the handshake was brief.

"I will excuse myself." Mrs. Lapp covered her mouth with one hand and hurried away.

"Do you want to see the *boppli*?" Levi struggled to keep his voice steady.

Matthew hung his head. "*Nee.*" He looked up. "I'm not worthy."

Levi didn't say anything for a moment as he silently asked God to keep bitterness from his heart and to guide his words. "None of us are worthy."

Matthew stared at Levi for a moment. "I reckon you think I'm selfish, leaving Danielle and the *boppli*?"

Levi didn't like hearing him say Danielle's name, and he didn't care if the man left and never came back, but something deep within him begged him to recognize Matthew's own hurt. "I'm not one to judge you. Only God can do that."

"I'm sure He has." Matthew shoved his hands in his pockets and looked at the white speckled tile beneath their feet.

"Danielle named him Joshua."

Matthew's eyes softened, as if he recognized the significance of the name. "I don't like that I'm the kind of man who would do this. I came back to the valley to claim *mei sohn*, to make you step aside and let me be a father to him. But now that I'm here, and the *boppli* is here . . ." Matthew shrugged.

Levi swallowed hard but waited for him to go on.

"You will raise him as your own?" Matthew lifted his chin, and he focused worried eyes on Levi.

"I will."

Matthew glanced at his mother, across the waiting room. The woman sat on a couch, her head buried in her hands. Then he looked back at Levi. "Give Joshua your last name. Give him a *gut* home and a *gut* life."

Before Levi could answer, Matthew turned on his heel and quickly went through the automatic doors that led to the parking lot. His mother rose and quickly followed him, calling his name.

Levi went back to the elevator. He'd lost his appetite, and he wanted to be with his wife.

And to have another look at his son.

IT WAS LATER in the afternoon when Vera told Danielle and Levi good-bye. Martha and Arnold were back in the cafeteria, and Vera told them she'd meet them there. Vera was sure that no one ate as often as those two. The hospital had said that Levi could stay in the reclining chair in Danielle's room.

"I will have Wayne bring me for a visit tomorrow." She kissed Levi on the forehead, then leaned down and kissed Danielle on the cheek. She was in the doorway when she paused, remembering. "Have you chosen a middle name for Joshua?"

Levi shook his head, but Danielle spoke up. "I'd like to name him Joshua Abraham." Danielle smiled, and Levi's face lit up.

Vera put a hand to her chest, smiling, remembering the day she'd given Levi the name Levi Abraham. "How *gut*. How very, very *gut*." She blew them a kiss and left.

On her way to the lobby, she thanked God for the blessing of Joshua. He was tiny, but healthy, and she couldn't ever remember seeing Levi glow the way he did when he gazed upon or spoke of the child. Her son had already told her about the visit with Matthew, and Vera knew that she should feel relief in her heart, but there was a sadness she couldn't quite identify.

She crossed the lobby and was almost out the door when she noticed Anna Marie sitting in a chair in the corner. The woman was just staring across the room.

"Anna Marie?" Vera approached slowly.

Anna Marie looked up at Vera with tired, swollen eyes. "I know I need to go home, but I just . . ." She smiled a bit. "I can't seem to bring myself to call the driver."

"Where is Matthew?" Vera sat down beside her.

"He is gone." She looked up at Vera. "And I have no more tears." But a tear trailed down her cheek anyway.

Vera wasn't sure what to say. She knew how devastated she would be if Levi had fled the community. She'd learned to live with the fact that Levi wasn't Amish, but her heart would have broken in two if he'd given up his birthright and gone to live far away. "I know you are going to miss him terribly."

"*Ya.*" She stood up and gazed into Vera's eyes. "I know this isn't the way you wanted things, but I will trust and pray that you will be a *gut mammi* to the *boppli.*"

Guilt wrapped around Vera as she thought back to her visit with Anna Marie, and how desperate she was to have Levi removed from this situation. Then there would have been no Joshua in her life. "I will," she said softly.

Anna Marie rushed toward the door.

"Wait!" Vera called out to her, the way the Lord had just called to Vera.

Anna Marie turned around, and Vera walked to her. "Come on." She looped her arm in Anna Marie's.

"What?"

Vera smiled and said firmly, "Let's go see our grandchild." She pulled Anna Marie along, and a few moments later, as they stood outside the window of the nursery, Anna Marie cried as she gazed upon her grandchild for the first time.

"He is beautiful, no?" Anna Marie dabbed at her eyes.

"*Ya*, he is." Vera reached for Anna Marie's hand and squeezed. "And he will be very much loved with *all* of us in his life."

Anna Marie cried harder, and Vera couldn't believe that she'd been so wrapped up in her own worries that she'd never considered Anna Marie. She'd been so afraid of being pushed from her son's life, and then this baby's, and all the while, Anna Marie was feeling the same way.

DANIELLE WAS SURE that the hardest thing she'd ever done in her life was leaving Joshua in the hospital to go home. She and Levi drove to the hospital every day, and each time they left, Danielle cried, and Levi struggled to be strong for all of them. Thanksgiving had been particularly rough, especially since Emily and David left for Lancaster County a few days before the holiday, and Joshua was still in the hospital.

But three days ago, Joshua was able to come home, and now that they were getting settled, it was time to tackle an issue heavy on her heart. She'd thought about her mother a lot since Joshua arrived, and sometimes the void seemed too huge to ever span. When painful memories pushed to the front of her mind, she reminded herself that she'd turned her worries over to God. But she knew that if she was going to truly find peace, she was going to have to forgive her mother.

Levi was working. Joshua was sleeping. This was a good time to take the first step toward that goal.

Dear Mom,

It sounds like you have turned your life around and are happy. I'm glad for that. Things have changed for me too. I am married—to Levi Detweiler, and we have a son, Joshua, who is almost a month old. He is a blessing, and I adore him in a way that I didn't know was possible. I know all this probably comes as a shock, but I needed time, Mom, to be able to turn my life around. I did that by finding a relationship with God, and it sounds like you found your way to Him as well.

I'm not ready to see you. I don't know when I'll be

ready. But I wanted you to know that I am married, that I have a son, and . . . that I forgive you. Maybe you don't care one way or the other. I don't know. But if there is remorse in your heart, then I hope that you will forgive yourself also. There is nothing we can do about what's happened in the past. As I look at Joshua, and know that I would gladly give my life for him, it's hard for me to understand how you could hit your child. Over and over again. Every time I try to weigh it out in my mind, I think that the pain you felt must have just overwhelmed you, and you took it out on me. Maybe it was because you missed Dad so much, or something else.

Anyway, I'm very happy. And I want you to be happy also. I have enclosed a picture of Joshua. Please don't come visit me. But if you'd like to call me, I'll answer. Or if you'd rather write me a letter, that would be good too.

Love,

Danielle

She read the letter two more times, then put it in an envelope to mail. As she put a stamp on it, she thought about everything she'd been through with her mother and where she was in her life today. Despite the abuse, if things had gone any other way, she wouldn't be exactly where she was today. *God had a plan all along.*

LATER THAT EVENING, she watched as Levi rocked Joshua. Vera had already mentioned how heartwarming it was to see Levi with Joshua. Amish men rarely had much to do with young babies, and Vera had been doubly surprised when she'd walked in and found Levi changing a diaper.

Danielle waited until her husband carried Joshua to bed before she motioned for him to follow her into the living room. She turned up both propane lamps and patted the couch next to her. "Come sit by me. I have something to tell you."

"What's on your mind, Ladybug?" He wrapped his arm around her shoulders and kissed her tenderly, then whispered, "Because I'm hungry."

Danielle giggled. "You're always hungry." She eased away, deciding to tell him on a full stomach. "Wait here. I'll feed you first. I made some potato soup today."

"Really?"

"Yep. Your mom's recipe."

Levi rubbed his belly, and Danielle went to the kitchen.

As she dished them both a bowl of soup, she thought about her mother—again—and wondered if she would hear from her. It made her think about others "missing" from their lives. Matthew had left town shortly after Joshua was born, and to her knowledge, never laid eyes on his son. But Anna Marie had come to visit them in Canaan twice. Vera had told her that a baby could never have too much love, and if Vera was accepting of Anna Marie, then Danielle was going to try to be equally as compassionate. Both times Anna Marie had said that her husband was working. Danielle wondered if there was more to it than that. No one had seen Sarah in weeks, and Sarah's parents were evasive to those who asked. "She's gone to visit relatives," was all they'd say. Danielle wasn't going to miss her.

After they ate, Danielle curled up on the couch and waited for Levi to join her.

"You've been so *gut* about not pushing me to get solar panels or electricity," Levi said as he snuggled up beside her. "And now that things have settled down, I'm going to fix things up for you." He chuckled. "You've almost been living like an Amish person."

Danielle couldn't stop the smile from spreading across her face. "Actually . . ." She bit her bottom lip, still grinning. "That's what I want to talk to you about."

Levi twisted to face her. "What?"

She grabbed his hand and squeezed. "I've talked to Bishop Esh, and he can baptize us both two weeks from now. He said that I've been attending worship service and that he knows I will continue to learn about the *Ordnung* as your wife."

"What?" Levi blinked his eyes a few times. "Danielle, what are you saying?"

She cupped his face in her hands. "I'm telling you that I know everything you gave up for me—and for Joshua. It was the most unselfish thing in the world, and I wish that I could say I was telling you that I want to be Amish as a way to show you how selfless I can be . . . but the truth is, I want to be Amish all the way, and to raise Joshua that way. For me as well as you. Your mom has been teaching me the *Ordnung*, even though I don't think she realized it. I still have a lot to learn, but I know that you'll teach me too."

"Danielle . . ." Levi kissed her on the mouth, several times. "Are you sure this is what you want?"

"I'm positive. God has blessed me far more than I could

have imagined. I know Him now, Levi. And I think Joshua could get to know Him whether or not he was raised Christian or Amish, but I want this for all of us." She waved a hand down at her knee-length green dress. "You haven't even noticed, have you?"

"I—I thought you were just wearing those dresses because they were more comfortable, you know, after the baby was born."

Danielle laughed. "They *are* more comfortable."

Levi grinned. "This makes me very happy. How long have you been planning this?"

"I've been thinking about it since before Joshua was born."

"Does *mei mamm* know?"

"No. I thought we'd tell her together."

Levi pulled her close and kissed her on the top of the head. "*Ach.* She is going to be very happy. What does Martha think about it?"

"She said that if I'm going to be Amish that I have to learn how to make creamed celery the way she likes it."

They both laughed, snuggling on the couch.

After a while, Danielle said, "You know, your mother told me something, and I never forgot it." She paused, recalling Vera's words. "She said, 'His love endures forever.' She told me to talk to the Lord like I would a friend and to open my heart to Him. She said life will never go the way you plan. But putting your total trust in God is the answer."

Levi's eyes settled on her. "His love does endure forever. And so will my love for you. Forever."

"Mine too."

She settled into Levi's arms as the light from the lanterns flickered and danced on the ceiling, and she thought about all they'd been through in such a short period of time.

Now they had a lifetime to look forward to. Together. With their son. And God.

# Discussion Questions

1. Do you believe that God communicates with us through our dreams? Has this ever happened to you or someone you know?
2. Levi meets three people in his dream. One of them is his father, and he doesn't recognize the other two. Is the dream image of Levi's earthly father representative of his heavenly Father? If so, who were other two people that Levi met on the path?
3. Danielle and Levi are best friends when they get married. What if Danielle and Levi's relationship had never progressed past that of friendship? How important is romance in our lives, regarding our lifetime mate?
4. Danielle still loves her mother despite her abusive ways, even though she says several times that she hates her. Have you ever been in a situation when you thought "why me, Lord?" only to find out way down the road that these bad experiences ultimately brought you to a much better place?
5. Vera feels that her world is falling apart when Levi marries Danielle. What are some examples of God working through Vera for the good of all? And what does Vera learn about herself through the process?
6. Do you think that Danielle ever really loved Matthew? Or did she just think she did, longing to fill a void in her life? What if she hadn't gotten pregnant? Would she have ended up leaving with Matthew? Or would Matthew have treated her exactly the same—pregnant or not—when he finally left

his people for a life in the outside world?

7. Like so many married couples, Levi and Danielle must adjust to each other's ways. What are some instances when they both compromise?

8. Vera snubs Sarah after Sarah kissed Levi and told Danielle about it. Was Vera justified in doing this?

9. Even though the Amish usually don't minister to the *Englisch*, Levi finds himself doing just that with Danielle. Have you ever felt called to minister to someone who seems an unlikely candidate for change, causing you to question why God would ask you to do so? What was the result?

10. Forgiveness abounds in the book. Forgiveness of self and forgiveness of others. What are some instances when the characters ultimately forgive, and how does it benefit that person—and those they are forgiving? Or does it?

11. The Bible does not condone premarital sex, but Danielle sleeps with Matthew. Is she already on God's path, even though she has gone against what we are taught? Or, as only God can do, does He constantly adjust our paths based on the choices we make in an effort to bring us to Him?

12. Emily and David are heading back to Lancaster County, Pennsylvania, for a visit. What do you think will happen? There is a new bishop in Lancaster County who is stirring things up in the community. Emily is pregnant. David never wanted to leave Lancaster County in the first place. Are their roots in Canaan strong enough to keep David from wanting to move back to his hometown of Paradise?

# *Acknowledgments*

THANKS BE TO GOD FOR ALL THE LIFE EXPERIENCES I have had up to this point. Although, during the dark times, it was often hard to see the light, and I was guilty of questioning His will. But I now know that those experiences were preparing me for a life of servitude to Him through stories of His grace and redemption.

As always, if this book changes one life or brings one person closer to God, then I have done my job for Him. Although, writing these books also ministers to my own soul, and with each story that God lays upon my heart, I know that He does this not just for readers—but for my own growth, healing, and understanding of the role He plays in my life.

Our lives are as perfect as the peace we feel in our hearts. God's love will take you from the dark places, and when His light shines within you, others will see it and want it. Peace comes from sharing that light with others.

To my husband, Patrick, and my family and friends— this journey wouldn't be the same without you all traveling along with me. With each new book, my sense of family is nourished, bonds of friendship are strengthened, and I cherish even more my relationship with my husband. Thank you all. I'd especially like to thank two dear friends: Barbie Beiler for all her help over the past five years. And to Janet Murphy, my fabulous assistant—you're the best!

Many thanks go to my publishing team at Thomas Nelson and my agent, Mary Sue Seymour.

# *Amish Recipes*

## Pickled Okra

| | | | |
|---|---|---|---|
| 3 | lbs. small tender okra pods | 1 | pint white vinegar |
| 1 | small hot pepper, per jar | 1 | quart water |
| 1 | clove garlic, per jar | 1/4 | tsp. pickling spice |

Sterilize canning jars and lids. Pack okra pods into hot, sterilized jars just tight enough to have them stand upright. Put 1 hot pepper and 1 garlic glove in each jar. Combine vinegar, water, and pickling spice in a saucepan and bring to a boil. Pour boiling vinegar solution over okra, leaving 1/2 inch headroom. Seal with sterilized lids. Process in hot boiling water for 5 minutes.

## Vera's Stew

| | | | |
|---|---|---|---|
| 2 | lbs. stew meat | 1/4 | tsp. paprika |
| 3/4 | cup chopped onion | 1/4 | tsp. ground thyme |
| 2 | cups beef bullion | 1/2 | tsp. garlic powder |
| 2 | cups water | 1/4 | tsp. pepper |
| 1 | can cream of mushroom soup | 1/4 | tsp. salt |
| 1/2 | cup burgundy cooking wine | 7 | small potatoes |
| | | | Small jar mushrooms, including juice |

Brown stew meat with onion. Add rest of ingredients and simmer on low until potatoes are done.

## Lemon Pie

| | | | |
|---|---|---|---|
| 1 | 8-inch pie shell, cooled | 1 | tsp. grated lemon rind or |
| 1 1/3 | cup (15 oz.) Eagle Brand Sweetened Condensed Milk | 1/4 | tsp. lemon extract |
| 1/2 | cup lemon juice | 2 | egg yolks |

Put condensed milk, lemon juice, lemon rind or extract, and egg yolks into mixing bowl; stir until mixture thickens. Pour filling into cooled pie shell.

*Meringue*

| | | | |
|---|---|---|---|
| 1/4 | tsp. cream of tartar, if desired | 2 | egg whites |
| | | 4 | T. sugar |

Add cream of tartar to egg whites and beat until almost stiff enough to hold a peak. Then add sugar gradually, beating until stiff and glossy but not dry. Pile lightly on pie filling and seal to pie crust all around. Bake at 325 degrees until top is lightly browned, about 15 minutes. Cool.

# About the Author

BETH WISEMAN IS THE AWARD-WINNING and bestselling author of the Daughters of the Promise, Land of Canaan, and Amish Secrets series. While she is best known for her Amish novels, Beth has also written contemporary novels including *Need You Now*, *The House that Love Built*, and *The Promise*.

You can read the first chapter of all of Beth's books at WWW.BETHWISEMAN.COM.

What would cause the Amish to move to Colorado, leaving family and friends behind?

## The Land of Canaan Series

Also available in e-book formats

THOMAS NELSON
Since 1798

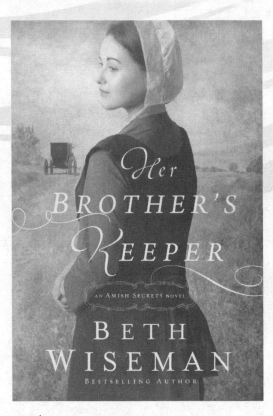